JARROD BLACK

Hospital Pass

An Unashamed Football Novel

JARROD BLACK

Hospital Pass

An Unashamed Football Novel

Texi Smith

P☁ PCORN
PRESS

First published in 2019 by Popcorn Press, a division of Fair Play Publishing

PO Box 4101, Balgowlah Heights NSW 2093 Australia

www.popcornpress.com.au

ISBN: 978-0-6484073-2-4

ISBN: 978-0-6484073-0-0(ePub)

Design and typesetting by Retta Laraway, Looksee Design.

All inquiries should be made to the Publisher via sales@fairplaypublishing.com.au

A catalogue record for this book is available from the National Library of Australia

Disclaimer

$1 from the sale of each edition of Jarrod Black - Hospital Pass will be given by Fair Play Publishing to the National Breast Cancer Foundation www.nbcf.org.au

To my wife Dominique,
a true fighter and the inspiration for this story.

Contents

Part One **Carnival** 1

Part Two **Clinic** 20

Part Three **Hammer Blow** 54

Part Four **Scan** 67

Part Five **Tense** 111

Part Six **Ready** 136

Part Seven **Operate** 148

Part Eight **Coping** 187

Part Nine **Poised** 199

Part Ten **Emotional** 227

Part Eleven **Final Score** 240

Acknowledgements 253

Part One
Carnival

The bus pulled in to the car park at the Arena, still wet after having recently been washed at the depot. The players stirred in the reception area, some getting up out of their seats, others lifting themselves off the bannister of the wheelchair ramp in anticipation of boarding. A four hour trip awaited them for this Tuesday night fixture in the East Midlands, taking on one of the oldest clubs in the league in Notts County, and the mood was calm and professional. The players knew what they had to do to maintain the promotion challenge to League One at the first attempt.

The season had gone almost as expected; the excitement of reaching the Football League was matched by some entertaining games in the opening rounds where Darlington had gone toe-to-toe with some of the heavyweights of the division and had immediately established themselves as promotion candidates. A late October reality check, a run of three defeats against three of the five bottom teams, dropped them down the table before the ship was steadied. They had since gradually climbed back up into a promotion spot where they had been since December. Now, with eight games to go until the conclusion of the season in early May, the focus was on maintaining that spot in the top three – two other teams breathing down their neck though with games in hand – and promotion was not entirely in their own hands.

The appearance of Gary Hollister down the stairs, after locking up his office, got the rest of the players to their feet and Jarrod caught his eye as he strode past him from reception and out to check with the admin staff and coaches who were loading the coach with equipment and bags. Gary had proven to be a master tactician this season, proving that he could react to situations and turn a game around with some key substitutions and tactic changes, and he had even taken Jarrod off when the situation arose and got the desired reaction from his players. There was mutual respect between manager and captain, and the little fist-pump that Gary gave him as he walked past affirmed that Gary was expecting a battle today and a battling performance.

Jarrod's phone gave a shake and a ting to alert that a text message had arrived, and he fumbled in his pocket. His phone had lodged itself around the seam of the pocket, making it difficult to pull out. It was his wife Marianne.

BURSITIS. EVER HAD THAT ONE?

Marianne had been at the doctors after a comedy-sized lump had appeared on her left elbow. It was as though she had a new knee but in the wrong place. It was soft and spongy. Thinking back, she pinpointed the cause to a moment on the golf course when she was guiding a small group of youngsters on the first tee and one of them, a left-hander, got too close with their swing and clipped her right arm on the funny bone causing her to yelp and jump. They had all laughed about it at the time. Marianne had left that morning saying she might do something about it. Aneka and Sebastian had both commented about it over breakfast when she appeared in a short-sleeved top. Jarrod had, in fact, had bursitis, but it was an inflammation in his Achilles some years back, and he knew that it was nothing to worry about. Still, he flicked back a text:

IN THE ELBOW? SHOULDN'T BE TOO SERIOUS. GLAD YOU WENT.

They would catch up late the next morning anyway when Jarrod was back, and while this was nothing to worry about,

Jarrod was glad that Marianne had done something about it. That over-sized lump wasn't going to disappear by itself, and she had a fundraising dinner on Friday where she would have to look her best. The coach was boarding now, and Jarrod shuffled alongside Connor Naughton, a young midfielder who had broken through this season from the relatively new academy and was on the verge of a first-team debut.

"Could be your night," said Jarrod, slowly putting his arm around him.

"You reckon?" came the surprised reply.

"If we get ahead and we're looking good for the win, no reason why not," said Jarrod, having the benefit of a chat with his manager and coaches earlier in the day.

Connor smiled but looked away sheepishly as if he was coy about his prospects. He had sat on the bench only a couple times as it was, and this was an important game. Jarrod let Connor board before him and they went off in separate directions, Jarrod choosing a seat near the front. He felt it more appropriate to leave the back seats to the young blokes these days. The front of the bus was where the coaches and manager would sit, so he wanted to be closer to the action. Coach Des Davis came on next and was deep in conversation with another youngster, centre-forward Willie Jevons, and took the seat beside Jarrod, still in mid-conversation, taking some time to finish his tête-à-tête and turn to greet his neighbour.

"Luck's out, Blackie," said Des, coining the nickname that had been bestowed on him at a team night out before the season had started. "You've got me."

"Four hours of one-on-one coaching, should be good," said Jarrod, chuckling.

Jarrod made a point of putting his earphones in when Des looked at him, suggesting that he wasn't looking for four hours of conversation, more like four hours of relaxation. Jarrod settled back in his seat and found his podcast episode, something from the BBC that had tickled him a few weeks back, and closed his eyes, his mind putting him in the studio with the panelists. He could feel himself relaxing with every breath.

The journey ended up being quite relaxing. The usual rowdy lads keeping it down until just after they had turned off the motorway, and that was when the excitement usually started anyway. Jarrod was happy to wake from his slumber to rejoin the atmosphere. As they came to the first sign welcoming them to Nottingham, a roar went up from the back and Mitch Short, right wing-back, began his usual routine, rattling off a series of carefully researched odd facts about the town they were visiting in a very articulate voice. He was getting more animated than usual this time though, rising to his feet with some random Robin Hood facts, regaling the coach with other useless information about the oldest pub in England and the oldest football club. Even the oldest haunted public toilet.

The younger players always loved Mitch's diatribes, and he was careful not to use the same line twice. Jarrod was thoroughly entertained by the faultless delivery of the comedy genius. Coach trips were very different to the experience he enjoyed at Gateshead. The bus was very League Two and hired for each game. There was less chance of an overnighter in a hotel, but the squad had become very close and were enjoying each other's company more and more as the season wore on. There was an element of the Crazy Gang among them. A feeling that the squad was made up of no-hopers, cast-offs, and criminals, but they had gelled into such a tight unit, taking every defeat personally and enjoying every victory as much as the first.

Life itself had changed since joining Darlington. Jarrod and his family had moved into a beautiful country house a few miles out of town. The kids had moved to new schools, and they had cleared out their old house in Gateshead; it was then rented out through an estate agent. Jarrod's Dad had insisted they keep the house to help towards their financial security later in life, in fact all advice they had sought pointed to the same thing – keep hold of the house as it would always accrue in value. They had bought the new house too, although the price was much more realistic than crazy Tyneside prices.

A mini-boom had priced a lot of young people out of the market, and Jarrod found himself owning two properties – he had started to get used to his money being tied up in something tangible. Marianne continued to work at the golf club in Gateshead, although her hours were now a little more constant – the short trips back and forth between home and work were no longer possible. She would find herself staying longer on some days and other days not being at the club at all. The winter had been horrible in the North East, and they were snowed in twice; no-one able to get in or out of their tiny village for a whole day at a time. Luckily, it didn't affect them too much.

The snow cancelled the majority of the golf and Darlington's home games were both postponed around that time. What it did mean, though, was a bit of catch up for Darlington, and they found themselves playing twice a week and not getting much training in between away trips of varying distance. With Easter now out of the way, there were five weeks to the end of season and everyone concerned with the club was ready for the fight for promotion.

Jarrod and Gary had a brief word before Jarrod entered the dressing room as the team filed in following the pre-game warm up. There were no changes to the team, no changes to the opponent's team, they would get straight on with the final tactical talk and general rev up. Jarrod held the door for Gary and he walked in, a hush coming over the room as he took a few long strides towards the back wall where there was a white board with some previous scribblings from half an hour ago, with the team formation. The clack of his heels against the floor was all that could be heard. All players, other than Jarrod, were now seated and ready to hear the team talk. Just as Gary reached his position, he put out his hand and leaned on the wall. It looked like he was deep in thought, until he slowly bent his knees and put one hand on the floor, his head bowed. Jarrod immediately rushed over to catch him before he hit the ground, obviously having passed out.

There was a mixed reaction from the players. There were a couple of shouts to physio, Sash, who they had left outside in conversation with his counterpart. Some players were watching on open-mouthed in disbelief at what was unfolding. Jarrod and another player, Raynor Gunn, cradled their fallen manager. Jarrod made sure that his head didn't crack off the polished cement floor, the door bursting open and the physios from both teams ran in followed by the doctor on call for the day. Sash took over from Jarrod and lay Gary in the recovery position, taking his pulse on his neck and confirming that he was breathing by holding his hand near his mouth. Thirty seconds of angst and all players had risen to their feet. There was a low murmur while Sash and the doctor did what they could to make their patient comfortable. Jarrod slipped out of the room to catch club administrator Jackie Furness and fill her in. She raced off to the referees' room to let them know, and Jarrod walked over calmly to the home dressing room and knocked on the door.

One of the home team's entourage opened the door quizzically, there still being five or six minutes before the allotted time to assemble. Jarrod recognised him as the assistant coach, a burly man who he had seen many times over the years but never here, and he had never known his name.

"Can I help you?" he asked. Obviously, the first thing that came to mind. The Notts County team talk continued in the background.

"Sorry to bother you," said Jarrod. "Our manager Gary's taken a bit of a turn, we're just letting the ref know too, and there might be a slight delay."

"Oh," came the rather ambivalent reply, "anything we can do to assist?" The assistant manager edged through the door and almost closed it behind him, still holding on to the door handle.

"We've got people in there already. Your physio is helping too. The ref will probably come and see you."

With a nod of the head, the assistant manager retreated to the dressing room and Jarrod turned to return to the away dressing room, the door open and people milling around. Jarrod's mind was working overtime. He asked a Notts County official if there was somewhere he could take the team before kick-off, and he was told there was an area used to store a lot of the match day equipment further into the bowels of the stadium that was open – it had a lot of room as all the equipment was out being used.

"Can you show me, please," said Jarrod. "Just a moment."

He raced into the dressing room where some players were chatting normally, others were sitting with their heads down, and Connor Naughton was looking on with tears in his eyes. He asked Sash what the latest was. Sash got up and softly answered.

"Gary's conscious," he replied. "He said he'd been struggling with a virus this week."

"Right," said Jarrod. "So, he's okay?"

"I think so, will keep you updated," came the reply.

Jarrod immediately stood on one of the benches at the side of the room and bellowed out, "LISTEN UP! Everyone follow me, we can use another room. Bring anything you need for the game. All players follow me, now."

Jarrod's manner was professional and direct, the instruction delivered in such a way that there was no doubt about it. Jarrod walked to the door while some players grabbed some last minute bits and pieces and joined the home team official at the door before heading off around the corner, his teammates following. It was only about thirty metres away, and Jarrod thanked the official and waited until everyone had arrived. This was a cold concrete bunker, obviously used to store the nets and goalposts and advertising hoardings. It was dimly lit but had plenty of room. Jarrod started when the last of the stragglers had arrived, conscious that they had barely three minutes until they had to reassemble back at the top of the tunnel.

"Lads," he started, clearly and eloquently in his least Aussie accent, "Gary's going to be okay. He's just had a turn for the worse after a bit of sickness during the week."

There were a few smiles and relieved looks. Jarrod was unconvinced at his own reassurances but pressed on.

"We have to switch on, right now," he continued, "we're here to play football and we're here to get three points. We all know what's expected of us, Gary expects us to be behind the ball at all times when we haven't got it and expects us to break quickly when we can. The team is as it was on the board, you all know what your jobs are, we all know what our fans expect from us, nothing but 100% effort and determination on the field."

That last statement saw a few chests puff out and Jarrod felt that bringing the supporters into the conversation, who were estimated to be travelling in their thousands today, was the perfect way of stirring some emotion. Coach Des, who had arrived on the scene and had put a fatherly arm around Connor, then interjected.

"And be safe at the back," he said, alluding to a horror moment the week before when Sam Basaan had opted to try and play out of trouble before being dispossessed and left on his backside as the striker raced through unopposed to score.

"Yes," affirmed Jarrod. "Safety first."

One of the referee's assistants had arrived on scene. Jarrod caught his eye and gave a nod.

"Time to go," said Jarrod. "Time to get out there and show what we're made of. Let's do this one for Gary."

There was a roar of appreciation and some back-slapping as the players filed into a line and made their way back towards the dressing rooms and out into the tunnel area. Jarrod jogged ahead and shook hands with the referee and his assistants, thanking them for their patience. It was just past the official kick-off time, but they were still in the tunnel. The dressing room door was open, and it appeared that Gary was still in there receiving assistance from the doctor. Jarrod tried to catch his eye, but that was never going to happen from such a distance, and the bark of the referee to move out on to the field took his eyes back to where he should be focused, on the field.

There was a huge roar as they came out of the tunnel. Jarrod collected his little mascot on the way out from her Dad, bedecked in a Darlo top that was two or three sizes too big. They walked confidently hand in hand towards the centre circle alongside the Notts County counterpart, giving his miniature partner a beaming smile as they reached their destination. The players filed in to their positions for the walk through of handshakes and the home players filed past them, each player shaking hands with their adversaries and with the mascots and referees.

Jarrod always loved this part of being captain, it allowed the players to square up to each other, share a smile with old teammates, and have a chuckle with the mascots. There was another roar as the Darlington players ran towards their bank of fans at the larger of the two end stands. The estimate of thousands being spot on, maybe two thousand, a sea of black and white reaching up to the back of the stand, all with hands in the air applauding. This game obviously meant a lot to the supporters, and the players would need to put on a good performance to repay their faith.

Jarrod called his players in for one last talk, the pre-match huddle being effectively only ever a token gesture as a show of strength to the opposition and to both sets of fans – he could never think of anything new to say in the huddle and always went back to the basics of '100% effort' and 'for the fans.' That 15 seconds together, though, did give the players focus, and that was very important before any game to make sure anything in the players' minds before the game was set aside for the opening exchanges. The players gave a shout at the end of Jarrod's Churchillian words and they disbanded to make their way to their allotted parts of the field to begin the game.

The nervous excitement that filled Jarrod at this stage always took him back to his first game at Carlisle, when he had filled in for the first team all those years ago, and it had never dampened over the many seasons since then. The crowd was buzzing, this was going to be a big game, and a big result was needed. The referee blasted on his whistle, lingering a little with the note, and the game leapt into action. County started with that tried and usually failed tactic of swinging the long ball high out wide for the first aerial duel.

Darlo held their own in a tense first half that was low on skill but high on effort, and the defence dealt with everything immaculately. The only criticism was the distribution, and too many times the midfield was missed out and the long hoof upfield was aimless. Sam Basaan was immense, and even afforded himself a moment of redemption when doing a Cruyff turn on the edge of his own area to get out of trouble, to the collective disbelief of the Darlington fans and players alike, but still drawing a smattering of applause and plenty of oohs and aahs.

The half ended with a massive long ball from defence that picked out the galloping Will Telfer, and his long legs got him to the ball ahead of his man and just as he shaped to shoot, he was clipped from behind and sent tumbling to the floor, making sure he reached for the penalty area to try and convince the ref of a penalty. Of course, the ref was having none of it, but the fact that it was outside the area meant that a red was the only option, and the defender was dispatched immediately, before any debate or remonstration from either team.

This was a big turning point perhaps, and Jarrod made sure his players stayed out of the discussions, a sending off at this stage of a game clearly worth more than a penalty. After some deliberation over who would take the free kick, which was just to the left of the arc of the penalty area, Jarrod made a dummy run to the left of the box, making it look like a training ground set-piece, surprising the defence and leaving Will to step up nonchalantly and bend the ball expertly around the bottom of the wall and into the net off the far post.

The absence of any Darlo fans at that end meant there was a delay before the noise came from behind them. Will already wheeling away to celebrate. Jarrod raced over to congratulate his teammate and there was a ruck of players before long, milking the moment and taking as long as possible to waste as much time as possible before half-time. There was no time for any further action, the referee wrapping up the half before the restart, and the Darlington faithful were jubilant as they walked off the field, the players visibly walking with a bounce in their step.

They walked up the tunnel and into the dressing room, and Jarrod waited by the door, giving out more pats on the back to his teammates as they filed in. The mood was buoyant. Jarrod checked outside and then slammed the door hard to get everyone's attention. Des was the first to speak and the players all listened intently — he had a way with words that made the listener know he was a knowledgeable man, and his overall assessment of the first half was spot on; bringing up two instances where he wanted things done differently and praising the players for a battling performance.

As he wrapped up, there was time to congratulate Will for his goal, before going over to Sam and grabbing him around the neck and warning him to never to do that again, after his heart-in-the-mouth moment on the edge of his own box. That brought a laugh from the team, and the laughter turned into a roar as the players started banging their hands on whatever was near. The idea was to make their opponents hear the war-cry in the home dressing room. Jarrod came in for a word at that moment, clearing his throat to make sure his voice was booming.

"Lads," he said. "How much do we want promotion?"

Again, there was a roar as every player shouted their own reply, ranging from an incoherent holler to an expletive-laden tirade that got everyone to their feet again. This was a game on a knife-edge, the sending-off having brought the home side down a notch and giving the impetus and the expectation of the victory to the away team. No-one mentioned Gary, there was not one word to take their focus off the task in hand. Sash did the rounds and checked on the players he knew were carrying knocks, making sure that he spoke to everyone by the end of the half-time break.

The players took on fluids and there was overzealous hacking and coughing as Declan Hines' energy drink went down the wrong way and he gasped for breath, red in the face and getting a hearty thump on the back from behind. The knock on the door came and it was time to get back out on the field. A surprised fourth official greeted Raynor Gunn as he opened the door quickly before the third knock. Darlo were keen to get out there, and they were ahead of the home team, no changes at half-time meaning that there was no need for any further tactical discussion, just a reinforcement of what they were already doing.

The Notts County players walked out onto the pitch to muted applause and their body language suggested there was disquiet in their camp. This served to pump up the Darlo players even more, and they got together for another huddle, something that came naturally even though they never usually did it before the second half – the extra thirty seconds out there had presented the opportunity to again show their strength. With the teams in fourth and fifth breathing down their necks and holding one and two games in hand, it was imperative that Darlo kept winning, and this would be a great opportunity to do so.

The referees were last out of the tunnel, but quickly found their positions for kick-off. The Darlington players quickly rushed to their posts. Wes Kellehar raced back to his position and waved at the man in black once he had reached the goal and had checked his gloves one last time. The man in the middle got the second half underway and the home team made their intentions clear from the off. The ball was played backwards and then launched forward by the goalkeeper in search of the nuggety centre forward who got absolutely nowhere near the ball.

Darlington found it difficult to make any inroads into the opposition penalty area, a wall of players keeping space to a minimum. As the half wore on though, the superior passing of the visitors began to take its toll on the home team and legs started to tire. There looked to be nothing on when Jarrod picked up the ball midway through the half, just outside his own penalty area, but a quick burst of pace to get away from the tackle saw the field open up in front of him and he galloped into the space, his teammates sensing the surge.

A blazing run from Dec Hines down the left drew his defender and left a lovely hole in the rearguard for Jarrod to race in to. His neat close control saw him evade the last defender, and as the ball skidded towards the byline on the left-hand side, he executed the most exquisite slide and cross. In one single movement he dinked the ball over the goalkeeper and to the far post, where Will Telfer found himself unmarked and let the ball drop to his knee and cushioned the ball into the empty net for a second goal, right in front of the travelling fans. Will ended up tangled in the net and was immediately set upon by his teammates.

The fans roared and bounced around with arms flailing. It was a good two minutes and a yellow card for Dean Minto, who was adjudged to have been time-wasting before the game restarted, and once Darlo had won the ball back, they were again on the attack. This time, Raynor Gunn lifted the ball into the middle from a free kick out on the right. Will leapt high and the ball was cleared to Jarrod on the edge of the area. His neat control and twist onto his right foot saw him create enough space to get his foot right around the ball and his searing shot arrowed into the top corner before the goalkeeper could even move. Jarrod knew he had gotten lucky; those ones rarely hit the top corner, and he raced over to celebrate with the black and white masses behind the goal who were still on a high after enjoying the last goal.

Jarrod signalled to the bench on the way back to the halfway line – they were three goals up and there was a good third of the half to go, but Jarrod made it known that it would be a good opportunity to bring on Connor, to which Des gave him the thumbs up and quickly gave the young midfielder a word in his ear. Jarrod watched on as Connor looked back at Des in amazement, awestruck that he was going to be given the chance, before quickly leaping out of the dugout and sprinting along behind the assistant referee for a warm up. A good eight or nine minutes later, after a period where Darlington maintained possession for what seemed like thirty passes, the ball finally went out off a Notts County player and the roar went up from the Darlington fans as the board signalled the substitution.

It was Jarrod who would be making way, and he had to double-take to realise it was him, so unusual it was to be substituted. There was ten minutes left, they were three goals up. Jarrod walked over to the sideline giving the fans applause as he went and gave Connor an embrace – this was time-wasting for dummies. Connor, though, was so keen to get on the field he pulled himself away and left Jarrod there smiling as he stepped off the field and watched the fresh, ginger-haired youngster race onto the field to huge applause.

"Nice touch," said Des, "and well played."

"Ha, I thought you'd take off one of our attackers," said Jarrod.

"Got to preserve the old legs," replied Des with a smile. They clasped hands and hugged.

There was always the risk that those ten minutes would see a complete turnaround of events, especially with such an inexperienced head in midfield, but the substitution served as an opportunity for all the players to pull together to make the experience memorable for their new recruit. Goalkeeper Wes shouted to Connor when he received the ball back from a stray through ball and elected to play the short pass to him, making sure that everyone knew the intended target. The rest of the defenders stood back and let Connor take the ball confidently out of defence, taking advantage of the space created by the tired legs of their opponents and their numerical deficit.

He ran with his head up, looking for options as the Notts County midfield finally closed him down. A sweetly struck ball out to the left wing was played with precision and found the feet of Dec Hines, and there was applause from his teammates and Dec himself, who played a first time ball back towards the defence and stood and applauded. Jarrod felt like crying, this was like the birth of a new superstar, the players doing their utmost to make him feel at home. It was only a split second before he was on the ball again, this time putting in a well-timed tackle to win the ball in a 50/50 situation, bouncing back to his feet and calmly stroking the ball out right before running into space to receive the return pass.

Darlington kept the ball for a good two minutes at one stage, eating up the time and affording their fans some relaxation, and even a few olés were heard. Just as possession was about to be given up, a quick burst of speed from Will Telfer saw him anticipate the pass from Connor and he was clear of the last man. His touch was poor for once though. The ball ran through to the keeper, but his first instinct was to turn and give Connor a clap for the pass.

The game drew to a close in a carnival-like atmosphere from the Darlington fans, the whole away area in full voice. The final whistle was drowned out in raucous applause. Darlington had totally controlled the second half, even more so when Jarrod had made way, and Jarrod was first onto the field to shake hands with the opposition and to congratulate Connor for a wonderful cameo performance. Jarrod ushered all the players to the Darlo end and they took in the acclaim, standing in front of the away end for a good minute applauding with hands above their heads and punches in the air.

Jarrod reflected on the coach ride home that he had gained a lot of satisfaction from the game that night, and a lot of it was due to the fact that he had been able to make decisions at a higher level than captain. He had taken the situation with Gary and turned it into a positive, coolly taking command when a lot of players and staff would not have been able to cope. He even gave himself credit for the substitution, although he would have liked to have stayed on the field until the end.

These thoughts were giving him the idea that managing a team one day might be a logical step for him. Gary had been checked out at the local hospital and was staying in Nottingham for the night – word got back soon after the final whistle, in the dressing room, that Gary was good. He sent his congratulations to the team, and that heightened the celebratory mood even more.

Jackie was staying down at the hospital, leaving Des in charge of getting the players and their kits successfully on the coach, while Jarrod had made his way to the low-key post-match press conference. There he started off by informing the press that Gary had been "under the weather" and that he was resting up, before lauding his players and giving Connor a big wrap. He explained he had to hurry as the coach was due to leave, and he shook hands with the Notts County manager as he vacated his seat for the next interviewee. Jarrod always had the thought he simply wasn't being convincing when downplaying situations, but felt he had gotten away with this one, none of the press grilling him any further about Gary after they had heard the news.

There was a ritual on the coach ride after an away game that he loved; the coach would be quite boisterous for the first half hour while they wound themselves out of the town or city they were visiting – all the players would be celebrating or commiserating with each other, and they would relive the game. Mitch would jot down some of the key incidents on an A4 pad. He was clearly up to something, maybe writing a book or giving a feed to a newspaper, but it served as a reminder and he made sure he gave an account on their social media page the following day.

Players would holler along the coach with their man of the match and their 'moment of the game' and they would erupt with laughter or disagreement or a bit of both. This would continue until the first service station, where they would usually stop for five minutes for a toilet break before the players settled down for sleep. This journey was really lively, Jarrod joining the discussion in the middle of the coach, Wes explaining how he thought he had broken the striker's nose when he missed a punch and collected the player, and plenty of speculation over what would come next in the season.

The radio had delivered the news that the two teams below them, Colchester and Lincoln, had also won and were still within striking distance with games in hand. Jarrod made a point of moving around the coach, as if a politician working the room in an albeit wobbly fashion, and he felt as though he had mysteriously hit the point where player and captain turned into something more. This was exciting.

The coach caught up with one of the supporter's buses on the way up the A1, waves and inaudible cheers coming from the darkened bus as the coach slowly edged past and the supporters realised who was passing. They made good time and it was around 2am when they were dropped at the stadium and they slowly made their way to their cars. The short drive from the stadium to home saw Jarrod slink in at around 2.30am and he softly pulled back the covers on his side of the bed, before realising that Aneka was in there. He picked her up and carried her to her room, the automatic snuggling of his daughter still giving him as much joy now as it did the first time she crept into their bed all those years ago.

Part Two
Clinic

Jarrod woke to the sound of a busy school morning underway. He must have been tired as it was rare for him to be able to sleep in while the rest of the house was up and about. After checking his various aches and bruises from the previous night and affording himself a good five minute stretch under the covers, he got to his feet and made his way to the bathroom. Aneka and Sebastian were there brushing their teeth – well, Seb was brushing, Aneka was doing anything else, messing around with her hair and pulling faces in the mirror which made Seb dribble toothpaste out his mouth.

"Daddy!" cried Aneka and gave him a hug around the midriff. "I missed you."

That was totally over the top – it had only been one evening – but it made him feel wanted. Seb gave him a smile and a fist pump, knowing that Darlington had absolutely romped the previous evening's game and Jarrod put his hand on his son's head to turn it to face him and planted a kiss on his forehead. Knowing he would not get any peace in there he left the kids in the bathroom and went down to the downstairs toilet, passing Marianne with a gentle pat of the bottom. She smiled and flicked her head, looking radiant as the morning sun streamed through the kitchen window.

"Just be a minute," said Jarrod. "Coffee on?"

"Just a press of the button away," replied Marianne, referring to the nifty Nespresso machine she had recently bought.

Jarrod returned to the kitchen soon after and Marianne was busy making sandwiches for the kids, the last part of the lunchbox jigsaw; making sure she put the right one in the right box, knowing that Seb was the fussiest of eaters and wanted everything as plain as possible.

"All good last night?" asked Jarrod.

"Kids were fine," Marianne replied. "Aneka was playing up a little, probably because her Daddy wasn't here."

Her tone was jokey. She put her hands on Jarrod's cheeks and pulled him in for a kiss.

"Hey, how's your elbow?" asked Jarrod, suddenly remembering and noticing that there was no bandage and still a lump.

"It's all good," said Marianne. "No drama. Dr Kinsella wouldn't drain it yesterday as she had a lot of patients in. Plus, I was ten minutes late to my appointment."

Marianne had refused to change doctors after the move to Darlington and had insisted on seeing her regular doctor back in Gateshead. It gave her an excuse to head back to see friends, and it wasn't too far from the golf club either.

"When's she doing that?" asked Jarrod.

"I'm booked in this afternoon. Can you get the kids from school?" asked Marianne.

"I'll have to let you know," said Jarrod. "Training is on, but I don't know what time."

"Okay," said Marianne, fully aware that she would have to do the school pick up then race to Gateshead. "Let me know."

Jarrod opened the dishwasher and began to unstack it from the night before, gradually taking over the kitchen until Marianne got the hint and left him to finish off the morning routine. Off she went to get ready to go to an event in Northallerton; a breast cancer awareness fundraiser that she had helped organise through the golf club. Jarrod flicked on the TV for a spot of morning news. He had timed it just right, a couple of minutes of weather followed by a wrap of the previous evening's sports.

The piece led with a story that Gary Hollister had been taken ill at the game and that coach Des Davis had been in charge of the game, before showing the highlights. A quickfire roundup of the goals followed with no replays in between, and Jarrod's goal looked an absolute beauty. The kids appeared, ready to go, and Jarrod quickly clicked back into gear and raced off to get his wallet and keys that he had left beside the bed and rejoined the throng at the door, both kids scrabbling for their shoes. Marianne came bustling into them, jokingly telling them to get out of her way.

"I am dropping the kids, aren't I?" she asked, as Jarrod joined the scrum at the hallway cupboard.

"Oh, I thought I would," said Jarrod.

"Awesome!" said Marianne, knowing that she was cutting it fine by having to go into town first before hitting the road. They all did their kisses, Marianne choosing to drop everything and concentrate on getting the kids ready now that she had a little more time on her hands.

"Let's go!" hollered Jarrod as he left the door. "Have a great day, Hun!"

Marianne watched as they all jumped into the car, affording herself a bit of a smile as the kids flung their bags into the back of the car. Aneka leapt in after hers, while Seb rode shotgun in the passenger seat. They screeched away out of the driveway, leaving two grooves in the gravel. The kids waved as Jarrod buckled himself in.

Marianne was happy and content. She had a great life, just the right amount of work and play, an awesome husband, and really loveable kids. She felt at that moment she was in a good place. This was a good mood to be in for a fundraising golf day, and she was ready to extricate the maximum cash out of the delegates, all in a good cause, of course.

Marianne opened the door of the doctor's surgery with a little apprehension as she had again mis-timed her run, leaving herself only just over half an hour to get there from the school pick up and was essentially twenty minutes late. The kids were in tow, Seb keen to get his homework done in the waiting room, Aneka full of her usual wonder when going somewhere new.

"So sorry for being late," she started.

"No, no," said the receptionist, who was filing things away. "Running about twenty minutes late."

Marianne smiled at Aneka, who smiled and nodded back, knowingly. Perfect timing!

"We had you in yesterday too didn't we?" stated the receptionist. "Mrs Black."

"That's right," said Marianne, impressed at the receptionist's memory.

"Dr Kinsella will be with you very soon," she said. "And you're the last patient of the day."

Marianne looked around and indeed there was no-one else there. Seb had made himself comfortable at a desk in the corner, Aneka was still standing beside her. The door to one of the offices opened and an older male patient came out followed by Dr Kinsella and they were in loud and jovial conversation. The doctor placed the patient's file in the 'in' tray and said her goodbyes while her patient began the paperwork process with the receptionist. She picked up the last file from the 'out' tray and looked immediately at Marianne.

"Marianne Black," she stated, knowing full well who she would be seeing. They smiled at each other, Marianne trying to stop herself from being apologetic for her late arrival – as far as Dr Kinsella knew, she had been waiting there for half an hour.

"Are you coming in Aneka?" asked Marianne to her daughter, who she knew would not want to be left alone.

"Okay," said Aneka, and followed her mother and the doctor down the corridor into the open door. Seb had spread his books on the table already and was in no mood to move again.

"Let's get this done," said Dr Kinsella. "You can lie on the bed and I'll raise it up. Let me just get something for you to rest your elbow on."

This was going to be interesting. Marianne's elbow was soft and squishy, it had the look of a gigantic boil, but was in fact simply an accumulation of fluid that had nowhere to drain to. The doctor pressed a button and the bed rose up quite high, this procedure was going to be done with the doctor standing up. Aneka stayed on her feet, so she could see what was going on. The doctor fetched a small table on wheels and wound it up to the desired height, resting Marianne's elbow on it, bending her arm into a ninety degree angle.

Out came a needle; an ordinary-sized needle much to Marianne's relief, but the doctor screwed it onto another component which was oversized, and the whole piece looked quite intimidating. Using a piece of cotton wool to conceal the point of entry from Marianne, she prodded around the area before quickly jabbing the needle in to the centre of the swelling. Marianne could feel it going in initially, but nothing as the needle went in. She had a brief nauseous wave as she saw the needle being pushed in further and further. A change in grip by the doctor saw her pull the 'handle' of the needle out, and a steady stream of brown liquid, much like the colour of rum, started to fill up the body of the needle.

Aneka could not believe what she was seeing, and Marianne looked at her and simply raised an eyebrow. The swelling didn't appear to be going down, but the needle was full. The doctor stopped and unscrewed the collection part, keeping the needle as still as possible, and put the full container on the desk. She screwed on a second container and let it lay down while she put the lid on the first container, and then returned to the needle, picked it up and with a quick glance at Marianne to see if she was coping, started the process of extracting the fluid again. She pressed on the swelling to move the fluid into a particular spot and kept going, eventually getting to the point where the fluid began to get clearer. This seemed to be the trigger for Dr Kinsella to stop, but she kept pressing and moving the swelling around, moving the needle around which made Marianne feel very strange, her childhood dislike of needles starting to return.

"That's all I can get today," said Dr Kinsella, in a way that suggested there would be another visit in the near future. "These things have a habit of returning as soon as you give it a knock."

"I'll be careful," insisted Marianne, hoping that her show of strength would convince the swelling not to return. Dr Kinsella put a small round plaster on the skin where the needle had gone in, although there was no blood, and then pressed over a bigger patch to cover the area completely.

"Please keep this on today, and it should be okay to come off tomorrow when you get up," instructed Dr Kinsella. Marianne was positive that Aneka would make sure she followed the instructions, after all she was sitting there taking it all in like a student nurse.

Dr Kinsella asked Marianne to get up off the bed and take a seat next to her desk where she started to tap away at her computer. She paused and looked at Marianne, staring deep into her eyes.

"Are you in good health otherwise?" she asked, suggesting that she was now starting a standard set of questions.

"Yes," said Marianne truthfully. She did feel good and would feel even better without this lump on her arm.

"When did you last get a smear test?" she asked.

"It's been a while," answered Marianne, stumbling first at the unfamiliar term and unsure as to why Dr Kinsella would not have looked that up on her computer.

"Yes, I see. Do you have time for a quick check over?" asked Dr Kinsella.

Marianne was slightly taken aback – perhaps this was one of the extra services offered to the last patient of the day.

"I, I guess so," said Marianne, unsure of the nature of the proposal. "What do you need to check?"

"Oh, nothing intrusive," said the doctor. "Just a series of standard questions that we go through with our female patients on a regular basis, and perhaps a check of your blood and a check of your breasts."

It all sounded very matter-of-fact, and Marianne was fairly ambivalent.

"Aneka," she said turning to her daughter who was sitting as still as she ever had. "Would you like to wait in the waiting room with Seb? I'll be ten minutes and Mum would like to talk with Dr

Kinsella alone."

Aneka looked at Marianne, then at Dr Kinsella, and eventually nodded.

"Okay, Mum," she said, and with maturity of a twenty-five-year-old she stood up, said goodbye to Dr Kinsella and showed herself out. Marianne could hear her school shoes taking the first few steps down the corridor and all of a sudden felt a little cold.

"We can do the smear test now, or you can do that next time you're in," said Dr Kinsella, knowing that it was getting late.

"We'll save that one," said Marianne. "I'll do that when I don't have the kids with me."

"Okay, do you mind if I take a blood sample?" asked the doctor.

"No, not at all," said Marianne. "The needle will be smaller than the last one hopefully."

"Oh, yes," said Dr Kinsella, reaching for a sealed packet from underneath her desk. "Here it is. Very small. Tiny."

Dr Kinsella smiled, and continued, "I'm going to take a sample from your finger, believe it or not, all you will feel is a scratch, I only need a very small sample."

After unwrapping the needle, which was indeed small, she took out a small implement that she could hardly see and gently took Marianne's little finger and pressed the implement to it. It did indeed scratch the spot and a drop of blood started to form on her finger, growing until Marianne was sure it would burst and run down her finger. Before that could happen, Dr Kinsella took the needle and drew the blood in, waiting for another twenty seconds before hoovering up the rest.

"All done," she said. "Would you like a plaster?"

"No need," said Marianne, feeling brave.

"I'll get that sent off this evening," said Dr Kinsella. "We'll get the results the day after tomorrow."

"What are the tests?" asked Marianne, and it was a good question.

"Believe it or not, it's a test for bowel cancer. And it is also a measure of your basic blood quality and cholesterol level. All that from a tiny drop. Amazing, eh?"

Marianne did that upside down smile action that only French women could do while maintaining any level of attractiveness. The doctor took that as a sign that Marianne was indeed amazed.

"Now," continued Dr Kinsella, "have you ever had a breast scan?"

"No, I haven't," said Marianne. "I've never been offered one."

"And I wouldn't expect you to either," said Dr Kinsella. "That's only for the OAPs. What about a breast examination? Do you check your breasts regularly?"

Marianne knew she didn't really bother, apart from when she had some aches from golf, or when Jarrod was being eager with his hands, but she still gave the answer.

"Yes, from time to time." A total lie.

"Okay," said Dr Kinsella slowly. "Do you have any concerns at the moment? Can I examine your breasts now? So I can be sure you are feeling for the right things."

Marianne started to take off her top and when she got it stuck on one of her earrings, Dr Kinsella helped her, leaving Marianne to uncouple her bra which let her breasts lower into a more natural position. She thought for a minute how funny it would be if Aneka was still in the room, she could imagine her chin dropping and eyes widening. She could also imagine the increased agitation of her husband, who would immediately be turned on by such a sight. Marianne could feel herself blushing.

Dr Kinsella took Marianne's first two fingers and started to press around underneath her left breast, showing her how to do so. Marianne then started to press under her right breast while the doctor pressed with her own fingers around the left breast and then seemed to take a moment before pressing in quite firmly at one spot just below the nipple. Marianne looked at her. She was conscious she could feel something pushing against the doctor's fingers. The doctor pressed in again, forcing her fingers into the soft tissue quite roughly and again Marianne could feel something a little unusual.

"You've noticed this before?" asked the doctor.

"I've had a little bit of tenderness there, but not for a year or two," said Marianne. She could hear herself saying the words and became very conscious of her voice.

"Let's keep going," said Dr Kinsella reassuringly.

They both continued, the doctor following Marianne's lead and she prodded heavily at an area at the top of the breast before moving on, taking the time to press each area flat as if feeling for marbles in the pocket of Seb's school trousers before putting them in the wash. Marianne had finished and watched wide-eyed as the doctor continued her examination.

"Marianne," she finally said. "You don't mind if I call you Marianne?"

"No, no," said Marianne, surprised at the question.

"I'm going to get you to pop in to the X-ray clinic up the road," she continued, "and they will perform a scan of both of your breasts. Just routine, we need to find out whether or not that's scar tissue or a milk duct. Or something else."

"Are they open now?" asked Marianne, suddenly remembering she had the whole school-night to come, homework, dinner; all that after the fifty minute drive back.

"They will be open for another hour," assured Dr Kinsella. "Let me just type up a form for you and I'll get our receptionist to call through and check that the right people are available to do the scan."

Marianne was relieved she would not be simply sent blindly to some clinic and she would be expected, but there was a nagging feeling of doubt about this whole situation. A stubborn denial that anything could possibly be wrong. Dr Kinsella finished tapping away at her keyboard. The printer whirred into action and spat out a single form, which was handed to Marianne.

"We'll leave the rest of the examination for now," she said. This suggested to Marianne she was cutting short the examination and was eager for her patient to make her appointment at the clinic. Thoughts started whirring through her mind. "Jayne on reception will have called by the time you get to the front desk and she will let you know if they are expecting you."

Dr Kinsella stood up and walked over to the door, remembering some key instructions before she opened it.

"Bring the scans back here and pop them into the letterbox by the door," instructed Dr Kinsella. "I'll have a look at them first thing in the morning and give you a call. Just make sure your phone number is up to date with Jayne." She put her hand on Marianne's arm as if to reassure her.

"Thanks, Dr Kinsella," said Marianne.

"Oh, please call me Sinead," said the doctor.

"Sinead," said Marianne. "Lovely name. We nearly gave our Aneka that name."

Dr Kinsella smiled and showed her the door. Marianne made her way to reception to see if the next visit was going to happen. Jarrod had texted, and Marianne glanced to see that he was indeed at training. As she reached the desk she saw a scene that all parents want to see – Aneka was sitting playing with some toys, albeit a bit young for her age, and Seb had his head in his book, writing furiously as if he knew that he would be interrupted at any moment.

The receptionist Jayne greeted her with a smile and let her know that the clinic were expecting her in fifteen minutes and there was an area just like the one she was in right now for the kids to amuse themselves. Marianne spent five minutes filling in some paperwork and Jayne checked her mobile number. Marianne walked over to Seb and placed her hand on his shoulder, which made him startle.

"Time to move on," she said, and Seb simply clapped closed his book, grabbed his pencil case and leapt to his feet. Marianne felt the urge to hug him for being so compliant, but also felt the urge to keep her calmness.

"Are we off home?" asked Aneka hopefully.

"Not quite yet," said Marianne and Aneka's shoulders visibly dropped. "Just one more visit and then I think we're going to have to grab some dinner out somewhere."

"McDonalds!" shouted Aneka.

"Subway!" yelled Seb even louder.

"We'll see," she said dryly. "Let's just get this next bit done and we'll see how much time we have."

They walked the short distance to the car and Marianne sent off a couple texts, first the kids old school friends, the Jones' who lived not far from where they were right now, then another to Jarrod letting him know she was going to be late and that she might not be there when he gets back from training. The kids' sat patiently waiting for Marianne to start away, and she did.

The car journey was only about four minutes to a newly-built clinic tucked away behind a row of gnarly trees that would have looked more at home in Greece. They found a car spot easily and the kids led the way as they entered the building. Seb had his same book and pens, Aneka seemingly without a care in the world and eager to see what was in this new place.

"Mrs Black?" came the question from a well-dressed older lady popping her head out from a doorway behind the reception desk.

"Yes," said Marianne. "Dr Kinsella sent me for a scan."

"I see," said the lady, walking over to the desk. "Yes, we'll be with you in five minutes. We just have one more patient to see and we'll call you in. Please, take a seat. There are some books and magazines for your lovely children."

Seb and Aneka were delighted to have been labelled as 'lovely' and instantly took a liking to the receptionist. Seb raced over to an empty chair at a low desk and opened his book up at the page he was at, obviously having been thinking about his homework in the car and very keen to get his thoughts into writing. Aneka thought he was racing her, and she ran after him, but was drawn instead to a TV showing some young teen Disney-style drama and was instantly spellbound.

Marianne walked calmly over to a seat near Aneka, took her mobile phone out of her jacket pocket and sat down, looking at the screen with a smile. There was a text from Catherine, and Marianne took the opportunity to give her a call.

"Oh my God," came the muffled voice at the other end of the phone. "I was just thinking about you when you sent that message."

"Freaky!" said Marianne with a laugh. "I'm just in the area with the kids and was wondering what you're up to."

"We're just leaving parents' evening at the school," said Catherine. "And we were talking about what to do for dinner. Hey, Chloe, Jack, the Blacks are in town. Do you want to meet up?"

There was squealing from down the phone and Marianne took her phone away from her ear, Aneka hearing it and bolting over to where her Mum was sitting.

"I'll just be another twenty minutes here," said Marianne. "I'm at the doctors, and then I'm ten minutes from the Trattoria. Meet you there?"

"Deal," said Catherine, known for her decisiveness. "I'll ring and book a table for us all, is Jarrod there?"

"No, just the three of us," said Marianne. "Training. Chris can be the driver."

"Deal!" said Catherine. "We'll see you soon!"

The receptionist came around the corner with a young lady in sporting gear walking with crutches, looking as though she had just been X-rayed for a nasty ankle injury, and she helped her through the front door and to her car where someone, presumably her Dad, was waiting glued to his phone. Marianne put her phone away as the receptionist came back through the door and beckoned her in.

"We're ready for you now, Mrs Black," she said in a low voice. "Come on through."

"Aneka," she said turning to her daughter who had snuggled up to her on the adjacent seat. "You stay here this time."

Aneka gave that pleading look, the one that usually made her Dad cave in, but this time it was non-negotiable and Marianne's body language suggested so, and she walked away from Aneka with a smile.

"Don't worry, "said the receptionist. "Carly's World comes on in 5 minutes and we can watch it together."

Aneka gave a laugh. Adults didn't watch those shows, did they?

The rather good looking radiographer, if that was in fact her title, was rearranging some equipment and gave the seat a wipe down as Marianne arrived.

"Hello there," she said with a cheer, quite a booming voice belying her petite frame. "I'm Martine, I'll be performing the scan today. Do you have the paperwork that your doctor provided?"

"Sure," said Marianne, handing over the paperwork that she had not even glanced at since receiving it.

"Ah, Dr Kinsella," said Martine, knowingly. "She is a fantastic doctor."

Marianne got the feeling she was following a path that had been well-worn by many.

"We'll get straight on with the process," she continued. "Please take your time, make yourself comfortable. We'll need to get your top and bra off, then come over and join me at the scanner." She pointed over to where there was an upright machine that looked a little like an exercise machine Marianne had used once at the gym. With a quick snap, Marianne had undone her bra and let it fall under her sheer black top, suddenly realising that it would have been easier to take her top off first – after all the goal was to get both off, but this was just force of habit.

She quickly pulled off her top, struggling a little as the bra straps constricted her shoulders, and then took the bra off and sat there for a moment to arrange her top so it wouldn't be all crushed. There was no time for coyness, and she confidently marched over to the machine, conscious not to stoop as if trying to hide. She did, after all, have a great body and was never shy to show it off on the beach or whenever it was appropriate.

"Okay, just move in towards the machine," Martine beckoned. "See the tape on the ground?"

Martine pointed down at a piece of tape; the type that a painter would use to cover the edges of the windows, and it was all dog-eared and peeling off.

"Just pretend you're playing darts," she continued.

Marianne laughed. They had recently been to one of the big darts events in Sunderland and it felt very relevant. She moved on to the mark and Martine took hold of a handle at the side of the machine, clicked a button and the whole top half moved towards her. It was on a pivot that made it easy for Martine to swivel and glide the machine into place before locking it again with a click, right in front of Marianne's chest. She lowered it to the desired height, and with a warning that it could be a little cold to the touch, lifted her left breast and placed it on the flat plate of the machine. Marianne gave a shake to signal the coldness, and Martine lowered the second plate onto the top of her breast and pressed a little to spread out the breast, so the plates had maximum coverage. It looked incredibly bizarre, but didn't feel at all bad, just a little uncomfortable for a moment as the plates warmed up with her body heat.

"Won't be a moment," said Martine, and she went out of the room for a second. Marianne heard a click and there was a hum from the machine for about a second. Martine walked back in and looked at the monitor. She then came over and lifted the plate and put her fingers under Marianne's breast to pull it outwards a little, Marianne aware that she could sense the radiographer's fingers running over the lump. She placed the top plate back down and her breast looked even more spread. She left the room again and returned within ten seconds to look at the results.

"Yes, that's more like it," she said with a smile, and released the left breast from its clamp before holding Marianne's shoulders and moving her body slightly to get her right breast into the correct position. She made sure she lifted the breast completely on to the bottom plate and squeezed a little firmer this time with the top plate, Marianne's breast spreading out like putty. Without a word, she left the room again and came back in after the now customary ten seconds and released Marianne from the machine. She deftly returned the machine back in its original position, careful to hear the click as it pushed back into its housing. Marianne was still amazed by the smoothness of the equipment and kept watching until Martine had let go of the handle.

"Okay, so what's next?" Marianne asked, suddenly feeling a little exposed.

"I'll need to check with my colleague," said Martine. "We need to process these and give them to you, and then it's standard to perform a biopsy. Dr Kinsella hasn't mentioned that though on the form."

"Does that mean I'll need to come back?" asked Marianne.

"We'll see," said Martine, quickly dashing out of the door before coming back in. "Oh, and, you can put your top back on if you'd feel more comfortable."

Marianne sat still and instead of putting her top back on, gave the lump a press. It was definitely a lump of some sort, a bit like a piece of gristle, but it wasn't sore, and she hadn't really taken any notice of it prior to today. Thoughts were running through her mind and her phone gave a 'ting' in her jacket pocket on the chair, but she left it, before grabbing the phone, ruffling her hair, arching her back to sit upright and taking a selfie. She checked the photo and gave herself a cheeky smile before sending it in a message to Jarrod with an even cheekier message underneath. Martine came in at this point with a colleague, an old-ish lady who had been ravaged by the sun in her earlier years, who she introduced as 'Dr Harrow.'

"Hello, Mrs Black," said the doctor. "Martine has filled me in on the situation and I would like to you to complete a form with me to allow us to perform a biopsy on your left breast."

Marianne had no hesitation. She was still thinking about the selfie and trying to imagine the reaction of Jarrod when he found the photo on his phone after training. Dr Harrow asked Marianne a series of questions and filled the form in as she went, able to skip over the majority of the questions as Marianne was generally in good health. They got to the end and the doctor passed the form over to Marianne for a signature.

"Will this take long?" asked Marianne. She was, after all, booked in for dinner very shortly.

"Not at all," said Dr Harrow. "About five minutes. It might be a little uncomfortable."

Marianne winced at the word uncomfortable as it clearly meant painful in this case, and when Martine produced a large needle from a packet, similar to the one that had extracted the fluid from her elbow an hour ago, it was clear that she would indeed feel some discomfort.

"All we need to do," said the doctor, as she continued to prepare everything, "is give you a numbing injection. That will take ten seconds to take effect and then we'll use the big needle. This will take a sample of the tissue and fluid around the lump in your breast, only a small amount, and you'll be on your way soon after. Does that sound okay?"

Marianne paused, and couldn't think of any reason why she wouldn't agree. Martine had already prepped the numbing injection and was giving it a light press, a little liquid coming out of the end.

"I guess it does," said Marianne. And with that, Martine found a spot near the lump and gave her left breast a jab with the small needle that immediately started to numb the area. It felt good and Marianne put her hand near the spot and could only feel with her fingers, the skin under her boob not feeling anything. Martine then distracted Marianne with a question while Dr Harrow pressed the big needle in hard, Marianne squirming when she felt it going in.

"Oooh," she winced. "That hurts!"

"Sorry about that," said Dr Harrow. "I'll be as gentle as possible." She flicked her thumb under the edge of the syringe part of the needle and drew it out deftly without moving the needle at all. It was all over in ten more seconds, the doctor pulling out the needle very quickly and Martine applying some cotton wool as a bead of blood formed.

"There now," said Dr Harrow, "All done. We'll get you a plaster and you can be on your way."

"Great," said Marianne, putting her left arm up and lifting her breast so Martine could stick the little round plaster on. She decided not to put her bra on and reached for her top, slipping it quickly over her head and standing up to straighten it out. She did have a good set of boobs, they sat very nicely, and two 12-month periods of breastfeeding over the years had actually given them a very pert shape that she liked. The top rubbing against her nipples gave her quite a sensation and she thought of Jarrod again.

Dr Harrow had packed everything away and labelled it all meticulously. Martine was closing the drawers and cupboards and started to turn out some of the lights. This was the end of the day for the clinic too and Marianne was ready to head off. As she grabbed her bag and jacket and edged towards the door, Martine rushed to the door and opened it for her and followed her to the reception desk to complete the final paperwork.

"Thank you for seeing me at such short notice," said Marianne as she reached the reception desk.

"That's why we stay open a little later than the doctor's surgery," said Martine with a smile. "It makes sense. Now, I will get a signature from you on the biopsy form to say that you have had the procedure, and we'll get everything sent through to Dr Kinsella in the morning, scans and all."

"Do I need to pay anything?" asked Marianne, unsure of how the process all worked.

"Nothing today," assured Martine, suggesting there might be some costs coming up soon.

"Fantastic," said Marianne. Aneka ran up to give her a hug and find out what was happening at the reception desk. Sebastian's books were closed, and he was still sitting at the desk, leaning as far back as he could on the seat to see the TV when he could have simply moved the seat. Marianne smiled as she knew that was not how his brain worked.

"Come on, Seb," said Marianne. "Thank you, Martine."

Martine smiled as Marianne walked to the door and opened it for the kids.

"Bonne chance!" said Martine, with a smile. Marianne looking back a little surprised. The accent sounded a little Mediterranean, a bit like some of Marianne's cousins. She thought about stopping and having a chat, but instead simply replied,

"Thank you," her accent as English as possible.

They rushed over to the car and jumped in. Marianne felt a sense of relief that the process had been fairly painless, and she was keen to see Catherine and the kids. Marianne started the car and the phone pinged as it connected to the console; the last text message appearing on the screen that Marianne quickly flicked away before Seb could catch the R-rated content. It was only a five minute drive to the Trattoria, a real family-favourite restaurant in a row of shops next to a big supermarket.

As they swung into the carpark, Aneka spotted the Jones' car and they spied the family in the restaurant. The kids fidgeted in their seats with excitement as Marianne parked the car. They both leapt out and ran towards the door, Seb leaving his car door wide open. Marianne was excited too – she hadn't made any friends as close as Catherine down in Darlington this year, not that she wouldn't in the future, and the history they had together could not be replicated. Marianne's phone gave a buzz and it was Jarrod replying to the text with an emoji of a devil, which made Marianne pick up her phone and call him.

"Woah, steamy!" he exclaimed.

"Hey, we're just about to have dinner with Catherine, Chris, and the kids. Fancy joining us?" asked Marianne, hopeful. "We're in Gateshead at the Trattoria."

"Wow, what are you doing up there?" asked Jarrod.

"Doctors appointment went a little longer than planned," said Marianne. "And Chris and Catherine are waiting there for us."

"It'll take me 45 minutes at least," said Jarrod.

"Oh, can you get up here without a car? Anyone heading this way?" Again, Marianne was very hopeful. She loved catching up with Catherine, but she loved even more catching up with Catherine over a wine or two and this was where Jarrod would come into play.

"I'll ask around," said Jarrod, cottoning on straight away. "Don't have too many vinos just in case."

"Okay, let me know," said Marianne. She hung up abruptly and quickly unbuckled herself from the car and strode purposefully along the path towards the door. She could see the kids in there already having accosted their old schoolmates, and Chris was now chatting to both of them while the Jones kids hung off them. As Marianne opened the door, there was a cheer from the table and Catherine got up and rushed over, arms outstretched for a hug, making the eighteen days since they had last seen each other seem like five years.

"This is epic!" said Catherine. "We were just wondering what to do for dinner and wham, here you are!"

Jarrod was keen to get up to Gateshead to join the fun. Training had been quite low-key, and the rain had started pelting down just before the end. The majority of the team skipped the set piece practice for a spot undercover as rain turned to hail, and the general consensus was to call it a day. He was now in the changing room, his mind still in two places after receiving Marianne's revealing text.

There were two players he knew who lived in the Newcastle area, and he managed to score a lift with one of them, Dan Collier, a young reserve team player who jumped at the chance to have Jarrod in his car for the trip home. Jarrod had minimal clothing, but he was sure there was a jumper in the back of the car that Marianne was driving, and if he was honest, he didn't really care how he looked, he was just ready to join the fun.

Jarrod texted Marianne to let her know he was on his way, and after an entertaining car trip with Dan, where Jarrod grilled his driver using all the interview techniques he had encountered over the years, he was dropped right at the front door of the Trattoria.

He could see his family in there with the Jones' and sensed the warmth and good nature of the evening he was walking in to, even more so when he opened the door and Aneka spied him. She moved chairs out of the way to run up to him and led him by the hand to the table. The kids were eating, the adults had a bottle of wine and seemed to have no interest in food; Chris was on the Coca-Cola, having been designated as the driver for the evening. Jarrod slipped in beside Chris, giving him a massage of the shoulders as he slid past, and the boisterous conversation from Marianne and Catherine stopped for a second as Marianne reached over and put her hand on top of Jarrod's hand and squeezed.

"Thanks for making it," she said, before turning and continuing the conversation with Catherine. Jarrod smiled and picked up an empty glass, poured in some of the brown fizzy liquid from the jug in front of the kids before clinking glasses with Chris and gulping back the icy drink.

The evening was excellent. The food came out almost straight away, Jarrod quickly ordering an extra salad, and the boys played with the kids while the ladies chatted like they had never chatted before. It was ten o'clock when they had finally had dessert and a coffee. The kids had started to wain with the electronics coming out signalling borrowed time and a quiet descended on one end of the table. Chris asked if they would like to come back for a drink, Marianne was as keen as the kids to continue the night, but a moment of clarity from Catherine saved Jarrod from being the spoilsport. She let the kids know in no uncertain terms that it was school in the morning and they had to get to bed.

Jarrod found himself driving South on the A1 about fifteen minutes later with all three of his passengers asleep and afforded himself a smile. What a great life. What a great wife, despite tonight's advertising on his mobile phone clearly not delivering what he had driven up to Gateshead to cash in on, and what smashing kids. They would probably all pay for it in the morning with a totally dis-organised school morning, but it was all about tonight and they had spent a fine evening in wonderful company.

Rumours were rife online when Jarrod reached home and had dispatched the kids and Marianne to bed – two upcoming Socceroos friendlies in preparation for a World Cup qualifier against a resurgent China had seen a squad of thirty players pre-selected, and Jarrod's name was on the list. This was completely against Jarrod's long-standing request not to be considered for selection but was in line with new Australia coach Mike Jerszek's statement that the slate was clean, and the door was open for players who showed form at club level.

Jarrod sat in the semi-darkness of the living room, the blinds still open, and only a light from the bathroom gave any brightness.

Jarrod was engrossed, flicking through all the websites from back home. The World Game went into the selections in detail. Fox Sports had a headline of 'Surprise inclusions prove Mike means business,' and further feeds from news sites leading with similar headlines. Jarrod had not been selected since just after his 24th birthday, when an incident curtailed his burgeoning Socceroos career.

Jarrod's rise to the Australian national team had followed a familiar path – selection in the younger national squads with minimal game time, until his second season at Championship side Gateshead saw him called into the full squad on the back of some solid club performances. Dad had always maintained that he would eventually be noticed simply because he was playing overseas, and whilst Jarrod didn't appreciate the way players playing in Europe seemed to gain preferential treatment, he wasn't going to turn down the chance when it presented itself.

A failed Olympic qualifying campaign was followed by a disastrous Asian Cup campaign that saw the Socceroos dumped out in the first round – two draws against much fancied Japan and Saudi Arabia meant a win against minnows Kyrgystan would see them through. That all turned sour when the green and gold went down a man in the second minute after a blatant handball on the line. Down a man and a goal from the resulting penalty and tempers flared sooner than usual, so much so they were reduced to nine men not long after half-time when captain Joel Thorn threw the ball away and was yellow-carded for the second time.

A comical, late equaliser looked to have given them a lifeline, but an even later goal in the other game that night between Japan and Saudi Arabia saw both of those teams advance and Australia dumped out in disgrace. Jarrod had contemplated quitting the national team to concentrate on club football, but the draw of trips back to Sydney made it all worthwhile. A rebuilding phase then saw new blood come in and the next World Cup campaign started in spectacular fashion, winning every game in the first round and then sitting on top of the group in the second round with two games to go and only one win needed.

That was when the incident happened, and it wasn't really anything to write home about, or so he thought. Taj Hamadi, a wonderkid setting the A-League alight at Adelaide United, had joined up with the squad and took part in a training game on the St Joseph's sports field out in the leafy Sydney suburbs. Jarrod was impressed with his enthusiasm. He looked the part as he made his presence felt and was eager to impress the coaches. It was only when he lost the ball clumsily, after some tight marking from Jarrod that he took exception and lashed out with an expletive-laden rant, squaring up to Jarrod and spitting in his face. Jarrod was known for his calmness and closed his eyes to think for a second before calmly drawing back his fist, and without a word, punched the young star in the face with quite an impressive hit.

Hamadi was sent sprawling on the ground, holding his face, some bright red blood trickling through his fingers as his split eyebrow began to seep. Jarrod was so shocked with himself that he reached down to see if the young man was badly hurt. Before he could get down to his level, two of the coaches ran over and grabbed Jarrod and pulled him away, making the whole scenario look a lot worse and making Jarrod out to be the instigator. Jarrod didn't put up any resistance as he was pulled away. He ended up being escorted to the dressing room and asked to get showered and changed, and to meet the coaches back outside. He took his time in the shower and even longer to get changed. The physio came in to pick up an extra bandage from the first aid kit and give Jarrod a disappointed look.

When he went back outside, the players had just started the warm down routine and the head coach asked to see Jarrod one-on-one for a moment. Jarrod was told in no uncertain terms that he would not be continuing with the national side for this World Cup campaign. As he stood there taking the news, he felt very close to wrapping his fingers in a fist and giving a second knock-out blow but refrained and simply shrugged. Without saying a word, he walked over to the team coach that was parked in the long driveway. The driver was sitting on the wall in the sun, and Jarrod put his bag down on the wall next to the driver and took a seat next to him to await the rest of the players.

Jarrod felt as though he had been hung out to dry – didn't anyone notice that it was Hamadi who was the perpetrator in this crime? By the time the rest of the players walked back to the coach and the baggage door was opened, Jarrod was seething. He had a couple of pats on the back, a couple of players asking what was going on, but he felt as though he had been given no support and felt there was no-one on the team man enough to stand up to the coaches or Hamadi and tell it how it was. He handed his bag over to the coach driver who was now crouched underneath in the bowels of the coach, making sure he thanked him, and sloped up the steps to find an empty seat next to the window.

They weren't going far, only over to the newly re-built Olympic Stadium, but he knew this journey would seem like an eternity. He was agitated and angry with himself. This was not like Jarrod at all. Hamadi was last on to the bus and Jarrod caught a glance, a big bandage covering his eyebrow and some swelling around the eye socket, but the youngster sat right at the front with the coaches and physios and seemed to be receiving a lot of attention. Asimir Brnic suddenly appeared by Jarrod's side and took the vacant seat next to him. Azi was one of the older players on the team, but not by much. He sparked a conversation with

Jarrod.

"Tell me mate," he started, turning to catch Jarrod's eye, "what was all that about?"

Jarrod looked up with very sad eyes.

"Azi," said Jarrod in a soft voice. "You'll have to ask young Taj about that."

"I have already," came the surprising reply. "He said you were giving him shit all afternoon."

Jarrod's fist clenched but he remained calm.

"Well, if marking a player tightly constitutes giving him shit, then guilty as charged," said Jarrod, with his eyebrows raised. "You saw what happened, and I'm not having someone spit in my face for no reason. That's outrageous."

"He spat in your face?" asked Azi again.

"He spat right in my face when he squared up to me. Then he realised what he'd done and started shouting in my face. Might have thought he was disguising the spitting as just having a verbal spray, but no, he spat in my face and for that, I had a swing."

Azi thought for a moment and was visibly torn between two differing stories.

"Mate," said Jarrod. "I don't think you need to bother getting involved. It's over and done with. I'll take all the blame and I'm sure there'll be some punishment."

Azi looked at Jarrod and took a while to reply.

"It's not like you to react like that," he said. "You're the last person I'd expect to clock a teammate like that."

"Well," replied Jarrod. "It is the first time I've been in that situation, and who knows it could be the only time."

"Take it easy, mate," said Azi and patted Jarrod on the leg before getting up and moving back to his seat as the coach roared to life and the aircon kicked in.

Jarrod smiled. A very, very wry smile.

The twenty minute ride to the hotel next to the Olympic stadium at Homebush was very hushed, none of the usual banter and a very sombre mood. There was a media session organised before dinner and a few of the players had been selected to appear, Jarrod one of them. However, a quick word from team manager Gaz let him know that he wouldn't be needed. That was when he decided to take matters into his own hands and made his way upstairs to the room he shared with Marco Terveris and packed up his gear, changing into some casual clothes.

He thought about leaving a message, but simply left the room with his uniform folded on the bed in a pile, headed down to the lobby, dropped his key in the late returns box and walked out the front door on to the street outside. The hotel was in a sparsely populated part of Sydney, the Olympic Park site having been transformed into a business hub. Very few people lived in the area and it boasted massive wide roads and big distances between all the main sites. Jarrod did know the area very well though, from all the bike rides he did with his mates around the area in his younger years, and all the events his Dad took him to at the stadium.

It was only about five kms to the front door of his Mum and Dad's house and he set out in the general direction, his bag immediately feeling heavy. He had already jettisoned quite a lot of uniform and the strap didn't dig in as much as it had on the way over. He flipped open his mobile phone and texted Marco that he had left and wished him good luck for tomorrow's game. Next text was to Marianne, letting let her know what he'd done, and finally one text for Anna, so she could fill in Mum and Dad and perhaps initiate a lift home – he was definitely not going to call Dad.

Feeling like an Aboriginal adolescent on walkabout, he eventually located a route through the new tower blocks towards the familiar path through the mangroves that he knew would eventually lead him home. He felt surprisingly liberated, but sad at the same time that he was choosing to totally throw away his chances of playing for Australia in the World Cup. It took him well over an hour to reach the front door of the family home. The 1970s graffiti on the Meadowbank bridge was still there after all those years paying homage to Deep Purple and other bands he'd never even listened to, lightening his mood. He had stopped for a chat with a couple of neighbours who were walking their dogs at the park en route and said hello to the shopkeeper on the corner of the road where he used to run and buy milk when they'd run out.

He hesitated to ring the doorbell, but he was hungry and the presence of two cars meant there was likely to be at least one person in. The door opened, and Mum reacted as any Mum would do at the sight of one of her children making a surprise appearance – she flung the door open and stood there with arms out wide, her head slightly tilted as if to say 'aaaaw' and let Jarrod rush in for a hug; like a little boy who had been brought home after running away.

"Come in, Jarrod," she said. "Anna's been on the phone. I've not told anyone else and your Dad's out playing golf."

"Golf?" asked Jarrod. "When did he ever play golf?"

"Ha, ha." Laughed Mum, giving instant relief from the angst

Jarrod was feeling. "Some corporate golf day he tried very hard to get out of. Anyway, I'm sure Marianne would approve."

Jarrod smiled and dropped his bag just inside the doorway and let his Mum close the door. She put her arm around his shoulder and led him to the kitchen. They sat down together at the kitchen bench and she put her hands on his and gave him a look of 'tell me everything.' Jarrod told her about the incident that had just happened, he told her he had been made the scapegoat and he just couldn't hang around with the situation the way it was. Maybe it was his youth, his lack of maturity in these situations, but he felt completely abandoned and very disappointed with himself and with his fellow team members. Not one of them had come to his defence.

Mum was taken aback by the sophistication of his conversation – it had been a few years since they had been alone, just the two of them – Jarrod was definitely an articulate man, who had principles that had been formed in part during his years in the family home, and she could see his frustration. Jarrod kept talking as she prepared dinner, a hearty fish stew with pumpkin and bok choy. As the smell started to fill the house, the memories came flooding back and he felt like he was back in year 12, discussing his worries about his exams.

Mum insisted he take a shower, to help him calm down and get his head clear, but not until he had called Gateshead and talked to someone official from the Australia team to organise his movements. He did it in that order too. First, calling Nigel Shackleton, the Gateshead manager, who he knew was an early operator and filling him in with the basics. Then he made a call to Socceroos team manager Gaz, who picked up the phone without it ringing. Gaz was a great bloke, but he was a little off with Jarrod, probably due to this being something that had landed firmly on his plate and the timing being so poor on the eve of a big game. Jarrod apologised for going missing and filled in Gaz with what had happened on the training field.

"Look, Jarrod," said Gaz. "This is a highly unusual situation. We're going to report that you have broken down in training and have been ruled out of the game tomorrow. I'll get onto Football Australia to organise a return flight for you tomorrow, so you can get out of the way and let this subside. Hamadi is ruled out too but he was unlikely to play any part anyway."

"Thanks, Gaz," said Jarrod. "I owe you one."

"I'll phone you when we have a flight organised," said Gaz. "Should be later tonight and expect to be leaving quite early in the morning."

"Good luck with the game," said Jarrod, and put the phone down, feeling quite numb. He made his way out to the back of the house to what used to be his room and was essentially the same as he had left it when he left to go overseas. He grabbed a towel and made his way to the shower, knowing that everything he would need would be in there already, and if it wasn't he'd just use Dad's stuff. A ten minute shower, which involved him simply standing motionless, getting wet, looking down at the ground deep in thought and he felt much better. So much so that stepping out of the bathroom and seeing Dad was as it should have been, a joyous moment, the two of them hugging happily.

The evening was great. Dad was in great form. Anna's perfect timing with a Facetime call just after dinner made it even more special. Gaz texted through details of a flight on Singapore Airlines at 10.30am. They ended up staying up quite late and talked until almost midnight. Dad not once talked about the incident and instead focused on Jarrod's burgeoning career in England, and Anna's emerging talent as part of the Sydney FC set up. Dad offered his son a lift to the airport, but Jarrod turned it down, knowing that it would be a total pain at that time of the morning, and instead asked to be dropped at the station at 7am and he'd make his way on the train.

There were tears the next morning as Mum said her goodbyes, and Dad was also teary when Jarrod got out of the car at the station. He was at the airport in good time and checked in at the relatively quiet desk, made his way immediately through the immigration gates and on to the Qantas lounge; a perk of playing for the national team he really enjoyed, if only to get out of sight. Unbelievably, he was told his card had been cancelled the previous day, and that brought home the ruthless efficiency of the national team set up, and also made Jarrod's mind up about how his chances were of getting back on the team.

The stopover at Singapore gave him enough time to catch the last forty minutes of the game playing in one of the bars, and Australia was struggling, down by two goals to one against South Korea. He was thankful for being incognito and ordered a coffee and sat down on one of the bar stools to take in the spectacle. A few other interested travellers tuned in, sharing common emotions and idle chat. The commentators mentioned Jarrod's name, saying he had succumbed to an injury at training and he joined Taj Hamadi and Nichol Greer on the injury list – the midfield solidity was sadly lacking as a result.

Jarrod was happy to hear his name, and for it to be used as a reason for not winning. The game turned though, and Australia equalised with twelve minutes to go and poured forward to get a winner, but it wasn't to be. A 2-2 scoreline was a fair result. Jarrod had finished his super-sized Café Latte by the end of injury time and it was time to make tracks back to the departure gate to rejoin the flight. A long, second leg of the journey saw Jarrod land at Heathrow and then a quick turnaround saw him on the next flight to Newcastle within the hour. The journey was over and he was glad to be home, but it was a definite end to his Socceroos career and there would be no going back.

Jarrod stared at the screen with amazement. Mike Jerszek's squad selection had been made and he had been selected in the initial squad of thirty. There had been no warning and no contact with any of the Australia coaching staff. He thought he had seen Steve Rickard, the head coach, at one of his games a few weeks back, but had dismissed it as unlikely, if not impossible. His heart was beating fast and he broke into a smile. Whether or not he would make the cut was another thing, but he was excited and a little nervous as to what lay ahead.

His phone had pinged a few times in the car journey home and he'd forgotten to check his text messages. It took a further ping to remind him, and there were a host of messages waiting to be opened, the latest one having come in from an unknown Australian number with the first part of the message showing: 'Wow, have you seen the n...' which was pretty much his own reaction.

He realised he was coming to the end of his career, but he was also aware he was playing some good football at the moment, and could still do a job, especially where a bit of experience and grit were needed. He sat back and started reading, glancing up at the clock and knowing he wasn't going to bed any time soon.

Part Three
Hammer Blow

It was May Day Bank Holiday, and Jarrod had finally joined the picnic in the park after finishing his post-match duties. With Gary back to full fitness after his health scare, the opportunities to speak to the media had reduced and Jarrod had reverted back to his normal captaincy role. He had given some punchy interviews following this game, talking up his team's chances of automatic promotion after they had clung on for victory after their two goal lead was halved only a minute after half-time.

With only two more games to play in the regular season they were still poised for a top three finish. Marianne had been invited to the park with the kids, who brought their scooters down and made use of the mini town-centre set-up at the park, with roundabouts and traffic lights for the smallest of road-users. They were having an absolute ball in the spring sunshine with their school friends. There was a big, marauding pack of girls and a smaller group of older boys, of which Seb was one of the youngest. Jarrod had left the car in town, walked down to the park, and had been stopped twice along the way for a chat with the locals. He was becoming quite well-known around town and with results going Darlington's way at the right time of the season, he wasn't cautious about walking down the street alone.

Jarrod recognised a couple of the Dads and made his way over to say hello after giving Marianne a quick squeeze of the arm to let her know he was there. She was in full flight, full of conversation and enjoying the company of this relatively new group of friends. The Dads were concentrating on the BBQ; a big bench built from fancy bricks with a sparkling new hot plate on top. They were deliberating whether or not it was lit correctly.

One of the Dads, Tom Rice, father of Aneka's friend Izzy, gave Jarrod a broad smile when he arrived.

"Jarrod," he started, as he checked over the BBQ, "you'd be an expert with one of these things being from your neck of the woods."

"You'd think so," replied Jarrod, with an air of doubt, before reaching down and pressing the ignition button and holding it for five seconds until he heard a click and a big whoosh as the gas that had built up in the block was finally ignited.

"Woah," said Tom. "Nearly took my eyebrows off there!" There was the familiar smell of burning arm hair as the heat belched out from under the hot plate and caught him unawares.

"Heh heh," said Jarrod. "You could have told me you'd had the gas on for half an hour already!" He turned and shook all the Dads' hands and made sure he'd given them all eye-contact, so he could try to remember their names.

"You're on a winning streak today!" said Kristen, father of Seb's classmate Thomas. Jarrod reluctantly declined the offer of a beer – after all it would have been well-earned today after he had covered a huge distance on the field in a pulsating 90 minutes.

The sausages and kebabs went on the hotplate and a drizzle of oil got the food sizzling. Jarrod instantly had memories of home and it gave him flashbacks of standing next to Dad, turning the snags for him on the grill outside in midwinter while Dad 'supervised', by cradling a red wine and telling stories. The food kept on coming and soon the whole hotplate was roaring away, with burgers being the latest addition, and a token portion of salmon wrapped in foil marking the presence of the 'pescetarian' in the group. The rolls were laid out and there was a production line of butter spreaders and napkin wrappers getting things ready for the tea-time rush.

This was fantastic, the Dads were in control of the food, the Mums were in charge of drinking the wine, while the kids were being kids and getting up to minor mischief in the afternoon sun. Conversation turned to holidays, as it often does at this time of year.

"We're heading to Croatia in the school holidays," said Tom, with a look on his face that suggested he wasn't exactly thrilled.

"Oh, fantastic," came one reply. "Absolutely stunning and really fun people."

"We're going to Tuscany just before the holidays," said another. "And the school said it was okay!"

There was a comical gasp as the group all played the part of the shocked parent, who had waited until the school holidays to go on holiday instead of taking the half-price option before the school holidays were underway.

"How dare you!" said one, smiling.

"Outrageous, "said another. "Little Tarquin will never catch up!"

The debate about taking kids out of school to enjoy holidays was one that had gone on since Jarrod's childhood – in his day though it was always just accepted that you would go to school, and it was only the posh people who could afford to go overseas for a holiday, even if it was outside the school holidays.

School holidays would be spent either roaming the local park, playing footie or 'soccer,' or hanging around the shopping centre, or heading up the coast on a camping trip with ten other families and going feral for a week. The current mood dictated that you weren't allowed to go on holiday outside of school holidays because it just wasn't fair, and if you did that you would be seen as a renegade, a rebel with no care for the future of your children. A bit harsh really. Jarrod and Marianne had not discussed their holiday plans. They knew they would be one of those families looking for a couple of weeks out of school to take advantage of the end of season break, but they just had no idea of when that would be.

They had set their hearts on travelling to Geneva for a holiday, renting a house on Lake Geneva, and spending some time over the border in Italy, but that had been holiday talk when they were down in Biarritz last summer. The subject hadn't really been touched since then. It had, after all, been quite a tumultuous time. Jarrod having moved clubs. The family having moving houses and the kids going to new schools. Still, Jarrod decided to test the water with his holiday plans.

"Hey," he started, by way of attracting attention, "has anyone been to Geneva before?"

There were a few surprised looks, before one of the Dads replied.

"Geneva is not really the sort of place I'd be taking my family in the summer to be honest," he said. "But I've been on Lake Geneva in Autumn with the family and it was absolutely beautiful."

"So, you'd recommend it?" asked Jarrod, hopeful.

"It's a bit left-field," came the reply. "I was only there because work sent me for a few days and I tagged on a family holiday, so I can't say we chose to go there."

"It's not Corfu," came one quip, which broke the seriousness of the conversation and it was instantly back to the high level, jokey banter that Dads of young kids seem to revel in.

Jarrod shrugged it off – he wasn't that keen on heading to the hot spots for sun, beach, waterslides, and fish and chips. He also wasn't keen, though, on wasting a good two weeks on a holiday they might not enjoy. He made a mental note to rekindle the holiday talk with Marianne when they had five minutes.

"Food's ready," declared Tom, and all the men moved into their positions as Kristen bellowed in his loudest voice that dinner was ready, and the kids should 'come and get it.' There was the usual apathy from all the kids as they continued doing what they were doing, not daring to be the first to break the trance of the great time they were having. One of the girls sprinted over and arrived on the scene unsure as to what to do. She took the time to survey the area and decided she could work out the intended production line. This would be a true test of the system the men had all but assumed, and they watched eagerly, almost guiding the young girl with their eyes.

She slowly grabbed a roll from the pile, placed it on a napkin, walked over to the barbecue and requested a burger, which was expertly placed on the roll. There was then a table next to the barbecue with a pile of lettuce on a plate, a bowl of sliced tomatoes, a small bowl of pickles, some of those orange, plastic cheese slices, and an array of sauces, or condiments as Jarrod liked to call them; the huge tomato sauce bottle looked battle-hardened after a few days like this in the past.

Their first customer worked the line perfectly. She constructed the perfect burger, walked three paces before stopping to shove the roll in her mouth and watching as the burger slipped through the lettuce and fell in the dirt. With a deep-rooted resignation that belied her nine years, the girl raised her eyebrows, picked up the burger and threw it into the bushes before making her way back with the same roll and snagging a second burger. The rest of the tribe started filtering in, and meal time was well and truly underway.

Jarrod loved this – the outdoor lifestyle he had missed out on for years since leaving Australia. With the nights starting to stretch and the sunshine bringing warmth to the spring air, there was a lot to love about living and working in Darlington. The men took their role as hosts very seriously as the kids had their final swoop on the barbecue. A sliced block of haloumi cheese was carefully prepared on the hot plate and the kids salads all tossed into one bowl, with the haloumi being deftly flung into the bowl. A perfect 'adults' salad was completed with some balsamic and olive oil sprinkled à la Jamie Oliver and a handful of pre-packed pomegranate pieces thrown, with the abandon of a high roller at the casino, over the salad.

The leftover burgers were packed away with a midweek Bolognese in mind, the sausages were arranged in formation as if being presented for show, and a big pack of thin steaks given a quick sizzle on the hot grill next to a sliced up hot salami. The kids meal had transformed into a feast for the grown-ups. The ladies needed no prompting and were lining up before the final steak had even gone on. A couple of the Dads instigated a quick walk around with garbage bags to show the ladies just how efficient they were. The ladies were definitely in a merry mood and the bright sunshine and free-flowing bubbles had turned afternoon into night and the volume had turned up. This was great!

Jarrod had a quick survey and spied Aneka helping her friend's little sister tie her hair back as she struggled to eat her dinner without taking mouthfuls of hair. That made him smile. Then, seeing Seb sitting on the edge of the big group of boys looking a little lost while the older boys all guffawed at some inappropriate joke or other, that made him wince a little. Marianne appeared beside him and slipped her hand into his and squeezed as they looked over at Seb. He clocked them looking and put his hands out as a 'what...?' Marianne mumbled under her breath in a resigned voice.

"Just look at him," she said, smiling and giving a wave.

Marianne rejoined the ladies in raucous chatter and the men simply enjoyed being the spectators, all of them with the same thoughts of how they might get lucky later on, with their wives all relaxed and carefree.

With the kids all done eating and back to their play with an extra bounce of energy, the adults sat around chatting. The first suggestion of night time came as the sun disappeared behind the really tall tree at the edge of the park, only to return in a blaze of glory a few moments later. Any thoughts of reaching for a jacket were swiftly dismissed as the warmth returned. They all sat in a straggling circle, some with plates on laps, others with steak sandwiches in hand, and the conversation grew more and more boisterous. The volume again cranked up as the kids also raised it up a notch.

Jarrod found himself starting to cramp up in the kneeling position he had adopted and quickly got to his feet, making out that he was heading to the barbecue to start the packing process. A few others took this as a cue, which it most definitely was not, but Jarrod went along with it and three of them made light work of the packing away. Janine Maddox wandered across as they finished with a bottle of red and three glasses, insisting that she pour the hard workers a glass. Janine was not the type to say no to as it would elicit all manner of questioning and forceful persuasion, which meant it was easier sometimes to simply comply. A red wine wasn't really high on his wish list at the moment, but he took a sip and got an instant kick from the aftertaste that suggested this was a bloody good tipple. He moved over to the group and sat down again, immediately joining a conversation as he did and genuinely felt as though he didn't have a care in the world.

The sun touching the tops of the rooves in the distance brought a couple of the ladies to their feet, making a bee-line for their children to give them some notice that the day was coming to a close soon and be ready to leave in fifteen minutes. Marianne was showing no signs of doing so, locked in a deep conversation with Janine about jewelry, so Jarrod took the initiative and wandered over to Seb, who was fielding in a game of cricket and grabbed him around the shoulders and whispered they would be leaving in ten minutes. Seb was clearly enjoying himself, listening to the cutting sledging from the older boys and chirping in with a few good ones of his own, but he was also more than happy to get back home and wrap up the fun and games in favour for some 'me-time.' Aneka on the other hand was full of questions, stalling for more time.

"We're in the middle of a game, Dad. Give us half an hour."

"Maddy hasn't had her turn, yet, and she'll be disappointed if she misses out."

"Can Elise come over afterwards?"

She was very good at manipulation, but Jarrod knew that his ten minute warning would never be ten minutes, especially with Marianne showing little sign of finishing her conversation.

"I'm just letting you know, Aneka," he said, making sure he used her name for emphasis, "that we will be leaving soon. In fact, everyone is going soon, so enjoy the last few minutes of play."

Aneka looked at Jarrod and held his stare just that little bit longer than usual to gauge the possibility of this playing out in her favour before turning her back and continuing her play with a curt but conforming, 'okay!' The spring sunshine then disappeared, and the parents began to twitch, reaching for jackets and then, as if a blanket was being thrown over the group, rising as one to start the actual real round up-process. The bottom end of drinks were tossed gaily into the grass, the loud and brash talk quickly subsided and gave way to regimented, well-practiced, practical instructions being bandied between the various couples, the powerplays evident. Jarrod and Marianne had always tried to keep things equal in their family set up, and this meant equally taking charge in such situations.

Marianne's relaxed mood and Jarrod's clear head meant that there was only one person in charge of everything today and Jarrod took to his managerial role with vigour. It was like a game to see which family would be packed up and ready first, then a game to see who would be the first to make the move and do the goodbyes. Tom, taking the lead when Izzy took a tumble, raced back to the group and gave a quick wave and 'see ya' before comforting his daughter and leading her off in the general direction of the road where the cars were parked. It was barely five minutes and despite Aneka's protests that Elise was coming for a sleepover, Marianne was happy to see Jarrod, Aneka, and Seb each carrying a bag walking in front of her as she followed behind with her iPhone out taking photos of her adorable family.

It was a short drive through town and out past the A1 to home, a journey which had never seemed as long as the first time those few months back. Jarrod withheld his door key and beckoned the kids to the boot to take the bags and scooters in the house before they all got too comfortable. The air was warm as they walked in the house. The chill outside was all the more evident now. Marianne came in last, stretching her arms up high and giving out a big yawn.

"Kids, showers," she uttered through the yawn, just managing to get the sentence out before the sharp intake of breath.

The kids obviously knew the drill and made a beeline for the upstairs bathroom. Seb easily swatted away Aneka as they reached the door. Seb was clearly the keenest to get the shower done to enjoy the rest of his night. It felt like Saturday night, but it was Monday. The home phone then rang, Marianne making the move out of the kitchen and up the stairs where both handsets had ended up, and Jarrod heard her answer with a cheery hello. Aneka appeared at the bottom of the stairs, clearly having rumbled with her brother and lost for the right to shower first, and asked Jarrod if she could help unpack.

Jarrod was always happy to have an extra pair of willing hands and they set about unpacking the picnic leftovers before moving on to emptying the perpetually full dishwasher and then putting away the bags themselves in their little hidey-hole under the stairs. Aneka raced upstairs when she heard Seb come out of the bathroom, and Jarrod followed her up to see if Marianne was still awake or had succumbed to the relaxed state and crashed out on the bed.

To see Marianne sat completely still and silent in the dim light, crouched over with the handset glued to her ear, came as a little surprise, and it took a few seconds to realise that she was actually still on a call. The person on the end of the line was also taking a breather before Marianne gave a 'mmmm' of agreement and Jarrod could hear the other person start away again. Marianne didn't speak and didn't acknowledge Jarrod as he walked around her and dropped his jumper in the washing basket. Jarrod put his arm on hers to get her attention, but Marianne simply listened and shifted uneasily on the bed, curling up even more into a ball. Jarrod left her to it.

The kids, now both showered and ready for bed, had snuggled up on the beanbag to watch the latest incarnation of the Voice.

Jarrod took a seat on the edge of the couch, unsure of what to do, and it didn't take long before he was swept away in the night time family viewing. A commercial break then startled Jarrod out of his semi-daze, and he reached for the remote and turned off the TV. The kids were resigned to their fate and didn't put up a fight as Jarrod leapt to his feet and shooed them upstairs to bed, never a quick task, before returning and secretly turning back on the TV with the volume low and watching the end of the show.

Marianne appeared at the kitchen counter and put her hands flat on it and bowed her head, looking as though she would rip into a rant at any moment, which made Jarrod lower the volume to a minimum and walk over to the kitchen. She lifted her head and her face was red, flushed in a way that Jarrod had rarely seen. Her eyes were heavy and red.

"They've found cancer in my breast," she said with a slightly broken voice.

"No!" said Jarrod, rushing around the other side of the bench to comfort her, "What's this about? Who have you been talking to? I mean..."

"That was Dr Kinsella," said Marianne.

"At 7pm on a bank holiday?" inquired Jarrod.

"Yes," said Marianne. "She wanted to tell me straight away. I had a check-up this week and a biopsy the other day."

There was a moment's silence as though Jarrod was being prompted to ask, 'so why didn't you tell me...?'

"Plus," she continued, "she has fast-tracked me for a surgeon's visit tomorrow and has referred me to an oncologist."

Jarrod had no idea what to say, let alone what to think, and just offered his chest for her to put her head against. She didn't, though, and peeled away with a calm and determined look on her face.

"I've got a lot of calls to make before it gets too late," she offered as she walked back upstairs.

Jarrod stood in the kitchen, processing. Surgeon. Oncologist. Cancer. What just happened? Cancer means dying. This can't be right.

Jarrod took Marianne a tea and a small slice of the cake they'd all had in the afternoon but left her to it. There was no time for Jarrod to be filled in with the details, Marianne was on the phone for an hour, at least. First, to a family friend who was a nurse in a hospital, then to her work colleague, Stella, who had been through breast cancer a few years back, and finally to Jarrod's good friend, Federico, who was a surgeon specialising in liver transplants, and over the years had provided a lot of knowledge on other health matters from his early years as a GP. Jarrod was impressed by his wife's tenacity – she had jumped right on this and was getting herself as informed as she could.

Jarrod was dozing on the couch in front of a late night movie, partly as a result of putting in a big performance today, partly knowing he had very little to offer from a medical perspective, when Marianne finally appeared. She simply curled up in front of him and put his arm around her and they lay there silently. Jarrod was not ready for answers, he just wanted to know that his lady was okay. Marianne gave some details of her multiple calls, her voice a little mumbled as she was facing away from Jarrod.

"Tomorrow at 2.15pm at Dr Groez in Newcastle," she said.

"That's the surgeon?" asked Jarrod.

"Yeah," said Marianne slowly, as if she was drifting off to sleep. "Then Jan Keever is the oncologist. She's someone big in cancer it turns out, Federico had heard of her."

"So, you'll be in good hands?" asked Jarrod.

"The best in the business."

Jarrod felt himself giving Marianne a tighter hug and they lay there for what seemed hours, drifting in and out of sleep.

Part Four
Scan

Training had been intense that week. The timing of the meeting with the surgeon, Dr Groez (pronounced Grooze, as Marianne had been informed), in his Newcastle office near the Freeman hospital, had worked well. Jarrod was able to do the full morning session after turning up early to explain the situation quietly with Gary, before jumping into the car and picking up Marianne well after midday.

They were there super-early to the appointment and sat in the waiting room watching the early afternoon runs of American chat shows. Jarrod tried to offer as much touching and holding as he could without being over-the-top. Marianne seemed to hold the high ground – she was the one meant to be vulnerable, she was acting anything but. However, Jarrod could sense that if he said anything that his wife didn't like, he would regret it. Jarrod was the one feeling sheepish, especially when another lady came out of the doctor's office looking pale and shuffling awkwardly, and the not-so-private conversation she had with the receptionist suggested she had only that morning embarked on her own cancer journey.

The receptionist, Harriet it said on her name badge, was as chirpy as could be, considering the subject-matter of the majority of the patients. She had that warm empathy that made you feel as though you were immediately her friend.

"Marianne Black?" came the announcement from the Doctor in the general direction of the only two other people in the room, both Jarrod and Marianne startled as they had found themselves concentrating on the conversation going on at the reception desk. Marianne gave a beaming smile at the tall, imposing doctor and leapt to her feet. Jarrod, simply toeing the line, was unsure as to what mood he should portray as the partner of the patient. He had already made a pledge to himself that he would let Marianne do all the talking, as he felt that as an unqualified male he could not offer any constructive information whatsoever. Dr Groez beckoned them into the office and closed the door behind them, giving Jarrod a quick handshake out of the view of Marianne and a friendly look, almost a wink.

"Well, hello there, Marianne," said Dr Groez. "Dr Kinsella has sent me everything – she never sleeps that lady, you should tell her to get some rest next time you see her, it can't be healthy."

"She's definitely dedicated," said Marianne, alluding to the call she received the previous night.

"Indeed, she is," said Dr Groez. "Now, I suspect you have a lot of questions for me, but I'm going to start with a lot of questions for you."

That led the doctor to a standard form the receptionist had given him as he came out of his room just before. It was a series of questions about Marianne's general health and well-being, past surgeries, history of cancer, and simple yes/no questions about smoking, drinking, and sleeping. These were all very generic, and Jarrod felt uneasy knowing the real subject-matter in hand was not being addressed, but it wasn't long before the doctor got straight to the point.

"Now, looking at the scans," he said, staring at the scan, "we have a lump about the size of a fifty pence piece that needs to be removed. We call this a lumpectomy, which is a term that sounds made-up, but in simple terms it is the removal of a cancerous growth and the tissue surrounding it."

The mention of the word 'cancerous' seemed to be like a hammer hitting a nail in.

"The position of the lump," he continued, lifting the scan, holding it briefly in the air then placing it on the illuminated box on the wall, "is cause for a little concern. It is quite close to your nipple and quite close to the surface. We need a certain amount of clearance around the lump, so you may find there is not much breast tissue left under the skin just under your nipple."

Jarrod looked at Marianne and she glanced back, horrified.

"We should be able to save the nipple though," offered Dr Groez in a compensatory tone. Marianne bowed her head slightly and the fingers of both her hands touched together nervously.

"Do you think you will be able to remove the cancer?" asked Marianne coyly.

Dr Groez thought for a moment and replied, "I know I will be able to remove the tissue and make as good a job as I can cosmetically, working with what tissue remains. Whether or not we get all the cancer depends on biopsies taken on the tissue removed. Now, just to be safe, I would like to remove two lymph nodes at the same time and get them biopsied to check for any further spread of cancer. "

This was a term totally foreign to both Marianne and Jarrod, and they both looked puzzled at the doctor.

"Ah, yes," he stuttered, remembering his audience, "the lymphatic system takes fluid around the body and is a primary mechanism for fighting infection. The fact that lymphatic fluid is flowing in and around your cancerous cells may mean that the lymph nodes themselves are affected. We'll be checking them just to be sure. You can live without a few lymph nodes, don't be alarmed, but there will probably be some chemotherapy to consider to completely remove the risk."

"Doctor, I will be putting my faith in you as a professional to do the right thing," said Marianne, with an air of resignation.

With that, Dr Groez smiled and produced more paperwork.

"Please take this out to the reception area when we're done and get them filled out."

Jarrod had already reached for the pen in his shirt pocket but left it there when he realised it wasn't going to be needed just yet.

"What I need to do right now, though," said Dr Groez, "is examine the affected area. If you could remove your top, bra, and sit on the table."

Marianne showed no sign of shyness and took off her loose top and bra and sat on the table in front of the doctor. Jarrod was in shock and awe at this, especially when Dr Groez began to touch and prod around the affected area. Jarrod didn't know where to look and ended up focusing on Marianne's marvellous breasts. Marianne caught him and jokingly gave him the two fingers to the eyes signal with a cheeky smile while the doctor delved around under her left breast.

"That's all for now," said Dr Groez, and Marianne put her bra back on and slipped the top back over her head and straightened it with a quick tug.

"What happens next?" asked Marianne.

"What happens next?" repeated Dr Groez to himself, before looking up at Marianne. "What happens next is that you take your form and fill it out with Harriet. You're going to have an operation in a week or so, and we'll organise that and any other visits required and let you know when and where."

"Thank you, Doctor," said Marianne and she got to her feet. Jarrod got up himself after a couple of seconds, after realising that it was time to leave.

They spent the next fifteen minutes in the reception area filling out the form, Harriet guiding them as they pondered. She could sense this was totally foreign to Marianne and Jarrod, and she probably had years of experience making a pleasant experience of a very haunting situation.

"You're in very good hands," said Harriet, once she had taken the completed form and filed it in the right place. "Dr Groez is a very thorough and particular surgeon and will do his utmost to give you the best results." She made a point of accentuating the 'oo' in Groez, just so they would be in no doubt about how to say it.

Jarrod had heard similar words before when one of his old teammates at Gateshead, Eric Neves, snapped his leg and Jarrod had accompanied him in the ambulance to the hospital from training. Eric was freaking out when they got to the hospital and it took some expert cajoling to get him into the hospital bed and ready for the operation. The surgeon then gave him every reason to relax by letting him know that he was the 87th leg break that he had operated on, and that he would be in good hands. Six weeks later Eric found himself having a second operation in the USA to remove the plate and re-break the bone to have it done properly. Jarrod had good reason to be suspicious of such throwaway words.

"So, what do we do now?" asked Marianne, echoing the question she had just asked Dr Groez.

"Okay, now that we have your paperwork," she said licking her lips as though she was going to be talking for some time, "your operation will be scheduled for the next week or so. It's likely that it will be a Tuesday, as Dr Groez tries to keep that day free for breast operations. This one will take a good two hours after you've seen the anaesthetist, and we'll keep you in overnight just as a precaution."

Realising that today was in fact Tuesday she doubled back.

"I see it's Tuesday today, so the chances are high that it will be next Tuesday, and you will have an appointment before the surgery at the Freeman for a scan, so we can pinpoint the location of the affected area. Prepare for a whole day from early in the morning. We'll confirm by the end of the week."

Jarrod looked at Marianne, who was taking it all in and processing. She was clearly thinking about what she had on, what the kids had on at school, what was in her diary, and even looked at Jarrod, probably wondering what he had on too. This was going to be an upheaval, but Jarrod got the feeling this would only be the beginning.

"Thanks, Harriet," said Marianne cheerily, snapping out of her thoughts. "You've been most helpful."

"Yes, thank you," said Jarrod, immediately feeling that his input was again superfluous at best.

Jarrod felt Marianne's arm slip around his waist as they walked down the corridor after leaving Dr Groez's office, and Jarrod stopped and pulled his wife in for a kiss. This was a lingering kiss and felt full of emotion. They were definitely off on an adventure here, whether they liked it or not.

In the car, Marianne flicked through her messages and returned one of the calls. The phone was picked up by the car's audio system and the name came up, and it was Nadine, his best mate Reggie's wife. The call was answered with a raucous "Saluuuut!" and to her credit, Marianne straight away announced en anglais that she was on speaker in the car with Jarrod, who offered a customary, "Ça va, toi?" in his best French. Nadine wasn't one to care who was listening, though, and just continued in French. Marianne made the most of the opportunity to revert to her mother tongue, with her strong accent and more frenetic pace of speaking. Jarrod made sure he was meant to head for home after a minute or so, butting in politely, but the girls didn't draw breath and Marianne simply nodded approvingly.

They were probably better off going straight to school pick up, but Jarrod was happy to head home for five minutes even just to change into some less constricting clothes. From his incredibly low base of French, Jarrod could make out that Nadine knew all about this and was offering some comforting words. Marianne teared up at one point and had to force out her words through the sobs, Jarrod placing his hand on her knee. This was definitely two great friends having a heart-to-heart and Jarrod was somewhat relieved he didn't understand the majority of it. By the time Jarrod clicked on the indicator to get off the A1 for the Darlington turn off, the call was wrapping up, numerous kisses were traded, and Marianne was full of smiles and glazed eyes.

"They're coming over this weekend," said Marianne, still smiling.

"Fantastic!" said Jarrod excitedly. "Reggie too? And the kids?"

"Yes," said Marianne, reaching for a tissue from the console between the seats, "The Westmann's are coming on Sunday. Reg can stay for two days and will then have to go back with the kids on Tuesday, and Nadine is good to stay as long as I need her. I think I might need her."

"Sure," said Jarrod. "Let's not go through this alone."

Jarrod was doing the calculations. The game on Saturday was going to be a massive one, and then they had the reserves in the Teeside Cup final on the Wednesday. Jarrod had been at every reserves game in that competition as a figurehead. This was going to be some week.

Jarrod had no choice but to maintain a level head and life was not going to stop for anything. The kids still needed their parents to be on form. Football was to be played, and there were even golf tournaments to organise for Marianne. Jarrod found himself trying his best to keep life as normal as possible; the same morning school routine and the same hands-on parenting he had always enjoyed, the same after-school activities, and meals.

Marianne on the other hand drew herself away from the hustle and bustle and was concentrating on making sure her mind was focused on work and the upcoming operation. They did, though, have to get through this Wednesday evening when Jarrod was due down in Doncaster to see Darlington's promotion rivals Chesterfield play their game in hand. Marianne would stay at home with the kids, going through the motions of a seemingly normal night.

Jarrod had caught the train with Gary and a handful of others from Darlington. It was a relatively short trip of just under an hour to Doncaster. They were met by a taxi, whipped off to the stadium for the full matchday experience, and a pre-match meal in the suite as guests of the home club. Gary still had a massive pull as an ex-England international and a household name to his generation, and this was one of the times when he used that to his advantage. They were joined on a table of eight by the wives of two local businessmen who had an adjacent table, Juanita and Alison tucking into the complimentary beverage package with gusto without having a clue who they were sitting next to.

With ten minutes to go before kick-off, and the sumptuous main courses being cleared away, it was time to head out to the stands and grab their seats in the main stand. The stadium was alive. Doncaster were looking to get one over on their local rivals, although they had very little to play for in reality, sitting in tenth spot. Chesterfield needed to win all their games to get automatic promotion, and this win would take them a point ahead of Darlington into third. Elsewhere, fifth placed Lincoln could push themselves into fourth with a victory at already-promoted Plymouth. There was a lot riding on tonight's results.

A first half of unbelievable intensity ensued, and the stadium enveloped in a descending mist as half-time approached. Neither team was able to find the final ball into the box despite some enterprising play. Every tackle from a Doncaster player was met with huge cheers. Gary had his little portable radio with him, and some mini headphones that made it difficult to tell if he was open to questions or not. Just as Doncaster romped forward and a good chance was spurned, Gary pulled his headphones from his ears and announced that Lincoln had sadly taken the lead. This news made Jarrod shift uneasily in his seat, and there was some rocking back in seats and puffed cheeks from Gary and his entourage.

The situation worsened when Doncaster tried to play themselves out of trouble at the back and gifted possession just outside the penalty area and were ruthlessly punished. The centre-forward drew the goalkeeper and slid the ball inside for his fellow striker to calmly roll the ball into the empty net. The Doncaster fans behind the goal were gesticulating angrily while the Chesterfield players went through their protracted goal celebrations right in front of them.

The half-time whistle sounded just as the restart was taken, and the Darlington contingency filed back into the suite where Juanita and Alison had been joined by two more glamorous older ladies and looked on a mission to cause mischief. News came through of Lincoln's second goal and the scene was set for Darlington to move down two places into fifth, making for an extremely tight and exciting run in to the end of the season.

A quick cup of tea and some sugary treats were served, and it wasn't long before the players appeared for the second half and the corporates all started to head back to their seats to catch the second half. Doncaster equalised a mere five minutes into the second half, and laid siege on the Chesterfield goal. The home fans were as raucous as Jarrod could remember in this division, and their collective roar was giving the team a massive lift – even Gary remarked that he hadn't seen such a vibrant home crowd in a long time. Jarrod was lapping it up. It seemed like one of those crazy games in Greece or Turkey, where the fans are in a frenzy and the atmosphere intimidating.

It all went quiet, though, with nine minutes left to play when Chesterfield broke from a corner and flooded forward en masse, at one point with a four on one advantage as they approached the Doncaster box. The initial shot was blocked, but it was a delightful chip from the rebound that capped off this flowing move with a goal of such cheek the whole of the Darlington group were off their seats applauding in front of disapproving glares and disbelieving home fans.

Jarrod sensed some hostility, and Juanita appeared in their section of seats, launching a drink in their general direction and bellowing something in Spanish while Alison held her up and offered her own fair share of abuse. It was cue for Gary to rally his troops and the Darlington mob retreated to the back of the members section and out into the depths of the stadium. They made the decision to leave the game completely to avoid the crush, and any further incident, and were quick to flag down a taxi which whisked them off to the station.

Gary was nervously listening to his radio. He put it down as the taxi arrived at the station and gave the final scores – Doncaster going down 2-1, as they had left it, and Lincoln winning by the same score at Plymouth. Not the scores they needed, and the trip home was a post-mortem of the night's results, after running through the station to catch an earlier train that was running a little late.

The evening had been therapeutic for Jarrod and quite entertaining. He arrived back home to a quiet house, creeping up the stairs to join Marianne in bed, who reached over with her arm, still asleep, and put it on his chest. Jarrod grabbed it and gave it a squeeze.

Life seemed to take on an eerie sense of normality. Jarrod likening it to that weird calm on a hot, cloudy afternoon just before the first clap of thunder rolls in, when the world seems to stop and it's only the birds chirping loudly that fills the still air. Before the weekend's crucial fixture at home to Exeter City, a team sitting in fourteenth and with only pride at stake, there were still two days of training. Jarrod found himself up and about early that morning, letting Marianne have a sleep in while he opened the kids blinds and tended to the morning rush hour.

He had thoughts running around his head, and there seemed to be one common theme – what happens if this is it? What happens if he loses Marianne and he has to bring the kids up on his own? Is he going to cope? He had always been very much able to cope, but he knew that, at the end of the day when he was tired and gristly, Marianne would step in to save the day and play 'good cop.' The same would happen when Jarrod sensed that Marianne was waning with her patience with the kids, he would simply switch modes and be the caring, sharing Dad even if he didn't really feel like it. That's what was so good about their tight family unit, there was always a parent in the right frame of mind and their children knew they always could trust their parents as a unit.

Jarrod drove the kids to school and was back by nine-thirty, pulling in to the driveway to see a couple of cars already there and the door ajar, as if whoever it was had just arrived. He walked past the cars, still ticking as the engines cooled down, walked in, closed the door behind him, and was met with a group of five or six school Mums. They were sitting around Marianne, who had taken centre stage on the couch and was doing all the talking, not in her usual energetic voice, but in low tones. This was a fantastic show of support, Jarrod felt, by some of the people they had only just got to know this year, but who were only too aware of what was happening.

Jarrod said his hellos and left them to it, taking a spot in the kitchen to run through his messages on his phone. Training was not for an hour, and Jarrod wasn't sure what to do with himself to fill the time. He overhead one of the ladies saying, "it's more common than you think," which made him wince – he had attempted that line of positive discussion while they were at Dr Groez's office and was shot down by Marianne with a tirade of abuse. His best intentions had been met with such scorn that he was sure there would be teacups launched any moment. This time though, with that statement came some back-up: "medicine is moving very quickly," "one in six of us will go through the same thing." Jarrod rolled his eyes when he heard Marianne agreeing with her new best friends.

Training was low-key, all the buzz was about the results from the previous night and how they found themselves knocked out of the automatic promotion spots. As a result the concentration just wasn't there. Jarrod had already confided in the management team about his situation, but he had not talked about it with his teammates. He couldn't bring himself to distract the team from their only objective, and he simply got on with it, keeping his thoughts to himself and allowing himself to forget Marianne's situation whenever he was around the lads. It took a casual comment from Wes Kellehar, who simply asked,

"Hey Blackie, how's the family?"

They were walking together into the changing rooms, to make him stop in his tracks and think about what he would say.

"Great, mate," came the reply. "Life is good. How's the young one?"

What a cop-out, Jarrod almost cringing as he heard himself deflect the question and hear the chirpy response from Wes, who was happy to share his news. No, the timing wasn't right. He kept it to himself.

Friday morning saw Jarrod doing something totally out of the ordinary. He had to take Marianne's place as chaperone for the kids as they made their TV debut on the BBC morning show as models for the new range of children's wear from Fenwick's. They had to be there at 7.30am in Newcastle, at the BBC studios up past St James Park. Jarrod chanced his arm at parking in the St James Park car park, using the Darlington badge on his windscreen as a means of getting past the car park attendant.

Much to his surprise he was waved through with a wink from the attendant and they parked and rugged up for the brisk walk up the hill alongside the busy road to BBC Newcastle. Jarrod was missing the morning training session for this, and whilst he felt that he was letting his team down and disrupting the preparations for tomorrow's game, he knew this gesture was going to make the kids feel pretty special, and he was more than happy for them to grab the limelight for once.

They were ushered through past the reception and into a waiting room, where they could see what was happening on live TV. They weren't due on TV until the daytime TV started after 9am. In the meantime, they had to meet and mingle with the other older kids who were professional models. They were walked through their steps and where they would get changed between walks. This was full-on catwalk stuff. Jarrod was loving being behind the scenes, and Sebastian seemed to have shaken off his 'too cool' persona to embrace the opportunity. The clothes they were wearing were very smart too and once they got changed into them, the kids were under strict instruction not to crush them by sitting down. It would then be quite a wait until their segment on the show.

Jarrod got to stand off-scene while the morning show got underway, and he was intrigued by what went on behind the cameras, and the concentration needed from everyone. There were people whizzing around, scampering quietly to get into position. The two hosts were as relaxed as they looked on TV as everything happened around them. The segment was only going to be a few minutes long, and the hosts, a sleek thirty-something in a slinky black dress and a middle-aged man with the body of a teenager, got to their feet to signal the start.

The designer of the clothes was beckoned on to the stage while the show was cut away to the adverts. When hush was asked for, the cameras started rolling again and the catwalk began. The hosts and the designer talking through the clothes as the kids walked on and off set. Jarrod chuckled as Aneka waltzed past the camera with the poise of a lady twice her age, in a summer outfit of white shorts and a striped blue and white top. Sebastian followed soon after, sporting a nice shirt, cravat, shorts, and a summer straw hat, and looked like he'd stepped off the pages of a magazine. The realisation was setting in very quickly that Jarrod actually had two soon-to-be-adults on his hands. The segment was over in five minutes. Aneka made it out for her second walk, while Sebastian got stuck trying to do up a pair of pants and missed the cut for round two, finally doing up the button when all the kids were asked to come on stage and surround the designer for one last shot.

The adrenaline pumping through the kids was unbelievable at that point. They were visibly on a high, and Sebastian seemed to have matured five years in that short space of time. Jarrod didn't know how to feel – he was so used to being the father of young kids, and he had taken a quick glimpse into the future of having teenagers and beyond. His thoughts turned to Marianne and how she would have really loved to have been there. She could have been there, in fact, but such was her fragile frame of mind, she had made the call to cancel the appointment before Jarrod stepped in. Jarrod was met in the off-stage area by Marianne's friend, the producer who had teed this up, soon after the segment.

"Oh my God," she said. "I had no idea."

She was clearly referring to having just heard the news, and probably from Marianne via a phone call that morning. Jarrod made sure the kids were otherwise occupied and out of earshot.

"Marianne's a strong woman," said Jarrod seriously but with a smile, and the producer put her hand on his arm and gave it a squeeze.

"You look after her," she said, staring into his eyes and holding the gaze for a moment while she welled up.

"Don't worry, she's in the best hands," said Jarrod and peeled her hand off his arm and turned to look for the kids. Sebastian was joking around with a pretty young girl about his age and making quite the impression, while Aneka was flicking through a rack full of clothes.

It was going to be like this for a while, Jarrod felt. Lots of sympathy and concern, and not much else on the conversation list. He was looking forward to Reggie coming over for some much needed banter and bravado.

It was the morning of the final home game of the season, and Jarrod was seeing to some duties in the media room when the Exeter team bus arrived, well ahead of schedule and with some weary personnel on board. They had obviously left in the early hours to make this game, but as is often the case, the extra hours allowed for traffic and unforeseen events was not needed and they were probably two hours earlier than anticipated. The reception party of the general manager Steve Gower, and head of media Pauline Huck, were yet to arrive, having duties at the under 15s game that morning. Jarrod took it upon himself to welcome the Exeter party to the Arena. He called upon a young steward, who he instructed to take off his hi-viz top and quickly asked his name. Jarrod strode confidently to the door of the coach and welcomed the first people off with a warm handshake and some quality small talk.

Turning to his new sidekick Jason, he offered some quick directions and let the away team know they should follow Jason to the changing rooms once they had unloaded and lunch was still being served in the canteen if they were in need of some pre-match sustenance. He felt as though he was in charge of the whole club at that point, and with a nod of the head to Jason who was giving him puzzled looks – clearly, he didn't know where anything was inside the stadium – he walked on to the front door of the stadium carrying a heavy kit bag and talking with the Exeter coach.

The opportunity for mischief was clearly not lost on Jarrod and the temptation to direct the team to the wrong place or to make off with some of the equipment was playing on his mind. In the end, he simply showed the Exeter coaching staff to the away changing room and gave them a quick tour, before making his way back to the media room where the BBC Radio Teesside had finished setting up and were waiting for their live interview for the sports update. Jarrod breezed in and took his seat just in time.

"We welcome Darlington captain Jarrod Black, to the show," said the relieved presenter, talking as he quietly and carefully clipped a microphone on to Jarrod's collar without touching the furry bit.

"Thanks for having me," said Jarrod, forgetting the name of the presenter for a moment.

"Tell us," said the presenter Kieran, "the Exeter team bus has just turned up very early, a lot of the Darlington players won't be here for an hour or so, how does that affect the lead-up to the game?"

"It's a long trip for the visiting team," said Jarrod. "They can take their time to stretch their legs after the long drive, have a bit to eat, but there'll be some sitting around and waiting. That's where the mind wanders, and the concentration turns off."

Jarrod knew the radio was being piped around the stadium and playing up to it.

"Plus," he continued, "we're confident. We haven't lost for a long time, and we're sitting just outside the automatic promotion places. This is a game that we've earmarked for three points."

Kieran smiled at Jarrod's surety before changing tact to a more personal line of questioning.

"You've been in this situation before with your old club, Gateshead," he said. "What can you take into these games from your past experience in the play-offs?"

Jarrod looked at his interviewer as if to say, 'what the hell are you asking?'

"The experience I can take from previous campaigns," Jarrod started, "is that it's not over til it's over. There's six points to play for and everyone else around us needs to get six points, or we'll be taking third spot and getting promoted."

Kieran shifted in his chair.

"Of course," he said, by way of correcting himself. "I'm not writing us off just yet."

"No, you'd better not, Kieran," replied Jarrod, remembering his name and using it in a slightly patronising way. "This is a club going places, and you'd better not forget that."

Kieran was flustered.

"No, no, sure," he said, searching for words.

Jarrod stared at him as cool as ice and didn't interject, waiting for the next question, even when the silence became uncomfortable. He could see that Kieran was struggling.

"Okay, back to you in the studio, Mike," said Jarrod cheekily. "Speak with you at 5pm when we've banked the points. Cheers."

Jarrod took off his microphone and threw it in Kieran's lap, making sure the fuzzy bit was well and truly ruffled in the process, and made for the door without even acknowledging the stunned presenter. He opened the thick soundproofed door and walked out in to the corridor where the receptionist was smiling and shaking her head, and a member of the catering staff gave him a thumbs up and a giggle. Jarrod was on fire today, he felt ten feet tall. If he had troubles on his mind, they were well and truly relegated to second place.

The rest of the players and the coaching staff were beginning to arrive. Gary breezed in with a determined look on his face, Steve and Pauline came with news of a triumphant display from the Under 15s, accompanied by the majority of the team, all hyped up by their surprise win over local big guns Sunderland. Jarrod took it all in as if this was his club. Everyone was keen to share their news with him. He was the centre of attention, even when Gary was around. It put him in the right frame of mind for today. With the majority of the players assembling in the canteen, he took the time to get a bowl and grab a small serve of pasta before the Exeter team began to file in to get what was left for their pre-match meal. Jarrod felt himself trying to resist staring them down.

As the teams stepped out from the tunnel onto the Arena turf, there was a massive roar. The sun was beaming onto the field and the ripped up newspapers floated through the air. Sunglasses and t-shirts were everywhere. The air was warm and still, and Darlington were ready to do battle with so much at stake. Gary was presented with his manager of the month award for getting the most points in April, partially due to the cancellations for the rain elsewhere in the country, but mainly due to a very good run of form, and the players needed no geeing up for this one after the raucous team talk in the dressing rooms just moments before. Jarrod recognised the referee from earlier in the season in a controversial game where two Darlington players were sent off. His last words to his teammates were to watch out for language. No need for silly reds today.

Exeter had brought with them a healthy following of about 250, despite the distance. This was their last away game of the season, typically a chance to dress up in fancy dress and have that one extra drink in the pub beforehand. They were in good voice too and just after kick-off, with the visitors keeping possession at the back and taking the wind out of Darlo's wet sail, they broke into song, filling the stadium with noise. The Darlington fans responded by continuing their version of No Nay Never which was so loud, a couple of players looked around curiously and the home team began to purr. Sam Basaan tricked his way past his opponent in his own half and launched a great ball down the wing for Will Telfer, who took the ball down with his instep, dragged it back, and set off down to the byline. He clipped in a gorgeous cross for fellow striker Nolan Parkes, who met it perfectly. The header cannoned off the bar and bounced through a bunch of players to safety. The crowd loved it and they were again in full voice, urging their players on.

There was only ten minutes on the clock and Darlo were again on the attack. Connor Naughton picked up a loose ball on the right and headed inside, faking to pass with his right before accelerating past his man into space. He drew the defender and jinked the ball into Telfer's feet. The tall striker turned delicately and reached with his extra-long legs to scoop a right-foot shot over the bodies in front of him. The ball took a dramatic dip over the outstretched hand of the keeper and clipped the underside of the bar and into the net for an outstanding opener. The players all rushed to Will, who was still in a tangle on the floor. He was lucky to get out of the resulting mêlée without any injury as the bodies piled on, the protracted celebrations matching the scenes in the stands.

Straight from the kick-off, Dean Minto's back pass to keeper Wes Kellehar was under hit, and the alert Exeter player nipped in to steal it. Wes hesitated, knowing that a foul outside the area would be an instant red, and let the ball run past him. He chose instead to lunge in for a tackle just as the Exeter striker entered the area, and he was nowhere near, upending the player just as he went to strike the ball past Mitch Short, who had made his way back to the line.

A definite penalty, and only a yellow card for Wes. The Exeter players were very vocal in their disgust at not seeing the red card. Their fans at the other end of the field were bouncing, their captain strode up confidently to the penalty and Wes guessed correctly, getting a palm to the shot and beating the bouncing ball away with his other hand before the Exeter man had the chance to finish it off.

The ball was still in play, and Mitch raced up the right, skipping past a tackle before offloading to Nolan Parkes, who took off down the right wing. The Exeter players were struggling to get back after the penalty. Nolan played it into the feet of Will Telfer, who in turn pushed the ball out wide to Mitch, who deftly crossed to the far post where time stood still for a moment.

The Darlington fans had seen Jarrod race the length of the field to get into the area and he was just about to meet the ball on the volley when he launched himself head first at the ball, powering a bullet-like header past the keeper. Every fan was on their feet in excited anticipation at this point, and when the net bulged the supporters went absolutely wild. The agony of a penalty being conceded, followed by the ecstacy of a penalty save, the rampaging build up, the measured cross, and the unbelievable finish, all within seven seconds of Wes getting his hand to the penalty.

Simply unbelievable. The Arena had never seen scenes like this before, Darlington were running riot. A good minute passed before Jarrod could get anywhere near his breath back, and still they pressed for another. Ghali Barbera, the wildly exotic sounding Brummie, then gave the crowd something extra special. He took off on a bamboozling run down the left, nutmegged his defender to a huge cheer before backheeling the ball into the legs of the same player to win a corner. He took the corner himself very quickly with the outside of his left foot, the ball curling in towards the goal instead of swerving out, and the keeper was totally foxed. The ball arched into the top left-hand corner of the goal past the despairing dive to make it three goals to nil. Exeter didn't stand a chance today, and the sheer dominance since that penalty save was suggesting a much bigger score than this, with five minutes still remaining before half-time.

Some clever tactics by Gary then took the sting out of the game somewhat. Darlington were told to keep the ball by their manager, and worked the ball to the keeper, then back out to half way, then back again, making the visiting players do the running in the warm spring sunshine. The half-time whistle sounded, and the contented chatter of the crowd accompanied the players down the tunnel. Jarrod made his way to the end of the dressing room and stood on the bench that went all the way round. He just wanted to be higher than everyone else. He looked down on his teammates, surveying the scene like a king, catching the eye of the odd player and giving them a fist-pump or a clenched fist. Gary was last in and closed the door.

"Goal difference, lads," he said. "We need to demolish this team. We can't rest on three goals, we've got to go for the jugular."

This was just what the players needed to hear. They were like caged lions who had just been released into the holding pen next to the Coliseum and they were fidgety and hungry for more. Players had abandoned their usual half-time rituals. The physio wasn't doing his rounds as usual. Gary joined Jarrod on the bench and put his arm around him.

"Let's do this, boys," he said calmly. "Let's do our fans proud and let's give ourselves a chance next weekend in the final day lottery. Make us proud, do it for Darlo."

The players rose as one and the roar went up. They took that mood back out on to the field and as soon as the game got underway, Connor thundered into a 50/50 challenge with his midfield counterpart and came out with the ball. Any doubt that the half-time break would stem the flow was dispelled at that moment, and Darlington began to stroke the ball around like a 1980s Liverpool team.

The defence was spraying passes around with absolute confidence. Every pass was controlled with precision and the fans lapped it up. A fourth goal took a good twenty minutes to arrive, and it was a screamer. Midfielder Jackie Thomas, picked up the ball in the middle of the park and strode between two tackles to open up the space. He jinked to the right as if to shoot, then came back onto his left and sent an outrageous shot searing in to the top right-hand corner of the goal before setting off into the corner to celebrate with the fans.

A fifth goal came, Sam Basaan, again making the overlap to the byline before scuffing his cross, but the goalkeeper was deceived by the pace of the ball and it ended up bouncing over his outstretched hand and into the six yard box where Will Telfer was on hand to bundle the ball in for the easiest of goals. Darlington 5 Exeter City 0. What a scoreline. What a performance.

With eight minutes to go, the subs started. Jarrod and Will made way to massive applause, then Mitch, replaced by young Steven Horton, making his first appearance for the club. Steven almost got lucky too. A long throw sent him away down the right and his cross ended up just clearing the bar to some oohs from the crowd. It was a truly carnival atmosphere. The last few moves of the game took place in the Darlington penalty area as the players strolled around to run down the clock. Gary signalled to his players to ease off and take it easy for the last few minutes. A huge roar greeted the final whistle.

The players all went to the home end, Bay 66, a reference to the main road just behind, and shared the love for five minutes, before a few of the Darlington players went to the other end to join the Exeter players in showing appreciation to the travelling fans. Jarrod found this quite touching and when he saw some of his teammates going up there, he rallied the rest of the team and made sure they all went up to shake some hands in the away end. The photographers had a field day, photos of Sam Basaan shaking hands with a mushroom from Mario Karts and Will Telfer posing with the two hairy blokes dressed in nurses uniforms. This is what League Two was all about, camaraderie, good honest players, and barmy fans.

Jarrod was still on a massive high when he came home that night. A prolonged lap of the field, the post-match press conference, and a TV interview making it quite late when he got in, close to 9pm. Everyone was still up. Marianne was snuggled up with both kids watching the movie Marley and Me, and Jarrod knew he wasn't going to interrupt such a tear-jerker. He simply went behind Marianne, kissed her on the head then wandered off to get changed out of his club gear into his lounge-wear of long sleeved t-shirt and flannel shorts. Jarrod had never worn tracksuit pants, preferring shorts even when deep mid-winter had set in. Something to do with the Aussie in him.

That got him thinking – he had a midweek training session in London with the Australia squad, and decided to use the time wisely to re-read the information he had been sent about the Socceroos. He was due there on Wednesday at midday, so he would miss the reserves game after all. It would be an early start, and that was on the back of Marianne's surgery on the Tuesday. A difficult balancing act coming up this week – he was anxious about Tuesday and felt guilty about his excitement for Wednesday. He was just hoping he could keep it together – he hadn't shared any of this with his teammates, and it certainly wasn't a news item. He was very happy to keep it that way too – much easier to deal with.

There was a knock at the door at 10am the next day. Marianne had been up doing a bit of cleaning around the house, making sure things were in their right place. She had picked some flowers from the garden and was arranging them in the heavy vase she used whenever people came to visit. Aneka raced to the door and flung it open, knowing exactly who it would be. It was Uncle Reggie, and he scooped Aneka up with his big hands and gave her a big hug, as Nadine tiptoed in with the kids Chloe and Massimo, before dropping everything and racing over to Marianne, letting out a yelp along the way. The tears had already started to flow. Marianne tossed down her garden scissors and they embraced in the longest hug ever seen in the Black household.

Seb had snuck up on Massimo and scared him and they greeted each other with their special handshake, and Chloe ran back outside to grab Aneka for a hug. Chloe was a couple of years younger than Aneka, Massimo was only just a few months younger than Seb. Everyone was so happy to see each other, and they saved the best til last, Jarrod appearing at the bottom of the stairs before striding purposefully over to the front door and locking in an embrace with Reggie.

Two of the tightest mates you could imagine, and they didn't need to be in the same country even, but the bond remained the same. Ever since those early days at Gateshead, they had been the best of friends, both moving to Tyneside at the same time and both breaking into the first team and enjoying some good years together with the club. They seemed more like family than Marianne and Reggie.

"We're so glad we're here," said Reggie, reaching in for a 'bise' with his cousin. "Nadi has been so upset."

Nadine indeed was sobbing and couldn't leave Marianne's side.

"Thanks for coming," said Marianne, visibly shaking. "This means so much to me."

Nadine led Marianne out to the back garden, chatting away at a million miles an hour as she always did with Nadine, Jarrod picking the gist of the conversation from the odd word he could make out.

"Kids," said Jarrod, reaching in to Chloe and Aneka who were jumping up and down in a frenzy and putting his hand on Massimo's head. "Kids, you know the score at our house, don't you?"

The kids looked at Jarrod, not entirely sure what he was talking about.

"Mi casa, su casa," he said.

They looked at him still puzzled, Massimo cocking his head to one side like a dog.

"Our house is your house," he said. "Make yourselves at home. Aneka and Seb will show you where your beds are, lunchtime in an hour, bathroom is just around here, and there's another upstairs. Go and have fun!"

The kids scattered excitedly, Chloe running out the door with Aneka to fetch her bag from the car and Reggie taking his place on the kitchen bench as he always did.

"Nice place you have here," said Reggie. "Rustic."

"We love it here," said Jarrod, reaching to fill the kettle. "Away from everything, but close enough to the town. And much bigger than our place in Gateshead."

"Yeah, isn't it?" replied Reggie, before changing the conversation immediately to the matter in hand. "Now, seriously," he said. "Is everything going to be okay?"

That changed the mood immediately. Jarrod had not talked about this face-to-face with anyone yet. He had poured out his heart to his Mum over the phone, but this was different.

"Reggie, we just don't know," said Jarrod frankly. "The doctor seems confident, but you know, there's just a nagging doubt, and it feels like we're on a knife-edge."

"My Ma has been asking me for updates almost every day," said Reggie. "I've not really known what to tell her."

"Just be positive," said Jarrod. "That's all we can do for now. Marianne's got the best people possible on her case and has done all the homework."

"And you, my friend," asked Reggie. "What are you feeling right now?"

That was a great question. Jarrod just hadn't really thought about himself at all – he had no time to do that anyway, and it just didn't matter in the scheme of things.

"Good, I guess," replied Jarrod. "Not a situation I have much experience with."

Reggie got up from the bench and took the few paces towards his dear friend and locked him in a hug. It was a gesture that gave Jarrod huge hope and made him feel loved. That's exactly what he needed, and he resisted the temptation to get Reggie in a headlock as they had always done in their younger years. They didn't even talk football, at least not for half an hour or so.

It was Tuesday, the day of the operation – Jarrod had dropped Reggie at Teesside airport for his flight back to Holland the previous evening and had arrived back quite late. There wasn't much sleep to be had anyway. With the kids all lined up for a day out with Nadine and family, Jarrod and Marianne had to be up and moving before six to be at the hospital for seven. Marianne had packed an overnight bag as if she was heading off for a conference. They made sure they had all the paperwork and directions where to go. They were due at the Freeman hospital for the scan, and after arriving in the empty reception, they were directed through what felt like a school building and into a laboratory where a middle-aged man with grey hair and an old jacket greeted them with the minimum of cheer.

The process was this: first, an ultrasound in an adjoining room, just like the ones they do when going through pregnancy, to precisely locate the lump. Once found, some drawing with a marker pen and a ruler to create a noughts and crosses pattern of the affected area, where the lines crossed presumably being where the injections were to be done. Four very long but very thin needles then followed, containing some local anaesthetic and then some kind of radioactive material that would show up under scans. The doctor, or professor as was later to become apparent, then showed Marianne how to massage the breast to encourage circulation of the fluid, a sweeping motion as if cleaning windows with a cloth. Jarrod took over as Marianne's arm began to tire, and the doctor left Jarrod and Marianne to continue the massage for five minutes. That process done, it was back on with clothes and into the waiting room, both Marianne and Jarrod scarcely believing how relaxed they were in the face of this totally foreign experience.

Only a minute later, they were called into a third room containing a big scanning machine and Marianne was asked to lie down. A younger doctor started to move the photo plates around to get some specific angles for taking scans. Each scan took three minutes, and each one was done in a different position; one of which was sitting up and effectively hugging the scanner to get a front on view. Marianne was pleased that she was quite fit and could hold the position for the full three minutes. There were a couple of screens showing the results of the scans in black and white, and it was a white blob of what must have been the lump area filled with the radioactive material.

As time passed, the radioactive material started to flow and settle in what looked like a hot spot, this being a lymph node. Dr Groez had described this, and this was what Jarrod was seeing. However, as the scans continued, there were more hot spots connected to the lump by thin lines, so there was no one obvious node collecting fluid from the lump.

These scans completed, they were moved into another adjoining room, where an older looking scanning machine on a long arm was used like a magnifying glass to see the affected area. After much conjecture and the introduction of another staff member to clarify things, Marianne received a number of dots and lines on her breast, and then was tattooed for a couple of them, as if they were the important ones that shouldn't be rubbed off. It took quite some time to complete this exercise and it was a little disheartening to Jarrod hearing the younger members of staff being baffled by what they saw.

What was hopefully the final room was waiting for them after that with a massive modern scanning machine, the one that you see on TV doing head and full body scans. Marianne had her hands put over her head, and strapped to stop them moving, before being eased into the machine and lined up. The machine was then programmed for a 15 minute setting, and off it went, ten minutes of what looked like a series of X-ray photographs from every angle, followed by a five minute full scan when Jarrod was ushered out of the room with the staff to watch through a window. The more experienced staff member then advised his junior to get Marianne's arms down straight away after the time was up, as they would no doubt be very sore from being in that position.

A fifteen minute wait in the reception followed, waiting for all the results. Jarrod was unsure as to how they would receive them or if indeed they would receive anything at all. They sat in silence, sending and reading text messages until they were asked for a couple of signatures for the ever growing medical bill, and they were dispatched to the RVI. They were both a bit edgy by then, and when Jarrod took a shortcut and had to pull over to get out of the traffic and re-set the navigation, Marianne was snappy. She was, though, remarkably calm as they arrived at the RVI, the Royal Victoria Infirmary, where Jarrod parked in the extremely tight car park and they found the in-patient reception area. There was a good half an hour wait, Marianne reading a travel magazine, Jarrod watching a bit of morning TV on the old TV mounted up high on the wall.

They were then invited to the ward and shown Marianne's bed, right by the entrance, in full view of the staff area for observation purposes. A familiar face was there to greet Marianne, a breast care nurse from a previous hospital visit, which made Jarrod feel at ease. Jarrod found it difficult to offer anything in the way of useful conversation but was there to help tie up the gown and stay with Marianne while they waited.

Jarrod took the seat next to the bed as Marianne got herself comfortable. There were lots of questions from the nurses, tags put on arms, and eventually Marianne was wheeled away, nervously, waving just like Seb used to do when he was dropped off in the morning in his first year at school. Jarrod had planned to stay, but the length of the op made the nurses decide he should leave and come back later. Jarrod felt very uneasy walking out of the hospital without his wife and had a dreaded feeling he might need to get used to this in the future.

It was still quite early in the day, Jarrod was told he should return in the afternoon at 2pm, so he made the decision to head back to Darlington and join in training. He had previously excused himself with Gary but was conscious he was going to be missing the next day too with the Socceroos squad. He arrived midway through the training session. After getting changed, and a short limber up with physio Sash, he joined in with drills.

The players were doing a simple one, practicing throwing in. The receiver playing the ball back to the thrower and racing to receive a return pass before swinging in a cross. Jarrod threw in first and laid a lovely ball to Dec Hines, who crossed a little too long. It was then Jarrod's turn to receive and his touch was exquisite. There was something about his state of mind that made him feel every touch of the ball, and he seemed to be as switched on as he had ever been. Perhaps there was adrenaline coursing through his veins, he wasn't sure, but the run and cross was sublime, and the ball was met with a fine header that swept past the keeper, Will Telfer acknowledging the service with a high thumbs up.

Jarrod couldn't stay around for the usual post-training lunch and banter with the lads and gave the excuse he had to be down in London the next day for a training camp, which was true. The players gave him a great send off, singing, "Tie me Kangaroo down," and shouting good luck and such delights as, "Say g'day to the sheilas will ya?" Which made Jarrod smile. He hadn't had time to take it all in properly, and this was a crazy opportunity to be part of something big for Australia in the twilight of his career.

If Tim Cahill could still do it into his late thirties, then Jarrod Black could too. He was still smiling as he reached the car, and then the realisation he wasn't actually going there yet dawned and he could feel the smile disappear from his face to be replaced by a determined but ponderous look. There was no time to call in at home, he had to get back to Newcastle and back to his wife before she woke from her operation. He decided to call the hospital.

"Yes, Mr Black," said the receptionist very formally. "Mrs Black is in being moved to recovery soon and we'd expect her to be back on the ward in about an hour and a half."

That was all Jarrod needed to know, and it meant he didn't have to drive pushing the limit but could take it relatively easy and still arrive well in advance.

Jarrod was at the RVI much quicker than anticipated and waited in the waiting room again, alone with his thoughts until he was called through. Marianne was awake and a little groggy. It took her a while to come around to her usual self and in about an hour she was sitting up sending texts, talking with her friends on the phone, and was generally chirpy. She was drinking so much water, after the prolonged period without anything in the lead up to the op. The conversation between Jarrod and Marianne was sporadic, Marianne lying back on her pillow for much of the time with her eyes flickering. The advent of meal time, which was super-early compared with their normal dinner time, brought Marianne to life and, whilst her face didn't light up, the idea of food after 24 hours without it was at the forefront of her mind. Jarrod helped finish the dessert – after all he was hungry too – but he would get something later at home.

Visiting hours came and went, but Jarrod was allowed to stay on. It wasn't until 7.30pm that Jarrod made the call to leave, after helping Marianne to the toilet for her first post-op wee. It was encouraging that Marianne was chatting with her next door neighbor, a middle-aged lady who seemed too vivacious to be overnighting in a hospital, and Jarrod was, as a result, less guilty about having to leave the hospital so early.

After an easy drive with no traffic to home, Jarrod came in to a lovely scene. Nadine had the two girls lined up and was platting their hair, while the boys were lying on each other on the couch in their pyjamas and watching the Sound of Music. Jarrod gave Nadine a kiss on the cheek and said hi to the kids before disappearing out the back to get his bag ready for the next day, finding all the paperwork he had been sent and packing a change of clothes; his travel toiletries bag, an extra pair of shoes, just in case he did end up staying overnight. He had a call from Marianne.

"Honey," she said, after clearing her throat. "Dr Groez passed by two minutes after you left. He said the operation went as expected, he got plenty of clearance and had to remove four lymph nodes."

"Sounds positive," said Jarrod in reply, unsure as to whether this was good news or not. "How are you feeling?"

"Exhausted. Dr Groez showed me the scar," she continued. "It doesn't look too bad, a golf-ball sized chunk taken out from under the boob, and it's kind of hidden anyway."

She sounded upbeat, so Jarrod went along with the mood.

"That's great," he said, slightly unconvincingly. "You'll be happy with that then?"

"I am Jarrod, I am." And with that she made noises as if she was ready to end the call.

"Okay, I'll not see you in the morning, remember?" Jarrod said. "Catherine said she was coming in, and Nadine will come up too mid-morning."

"Where are you?" she asked, surprised.

"I'm in London tomorrow, remember?" he exclaimed, "Getting

my Socceroo groove on."

"Oh, yes," she said, clearly annoyed to have not remembered. "Good luck with that. When will I see you?"

"Definitely not tomorrow but at some point on Thursday," he offered. "I'll pick you up from the hospital if they let you out."

"Oh, yeah," said Marianne. "They said I could probably go tomorrow. Anyway..."

She was yawning.

"Okay, keep me updated," said Jarrod. "Get some good sleep."

"Love you," said Marianne, and Jarrod returned the words before hanging up.

Jarrod felt that he should be there for her tomorrow, but he also knew she had more than enough people around her to help her if she indeed did get discharged. Time for bed for now though, and Jarrod peeked in to the lounge room to see where Sound of Music was up to. The girls had joined the boys on the couch, surprisingly without any ruckus. Jarrod filled in Nadine on what Marianne had told him before retiring to bed via the kids and giving them all a kiss on the cheek. There was still a while to go in the movie yet, and Nadine was firmly in charge. It was a big day ahead and a big day just gone, so sleep was needed.

Jarrod was up and gone before the kids had even stirred, but he made sure he had done the majority of the morning duties to make things easier for Nadine, unstacking the dishwasher in between mouthfuls of breakfast, then making the bits of the school lunches that needed to be made, noting 'butter' on the blackboard under the rest of the growing shopping list.

Nadine would be fine, she was always in control, and Aneka would be there to offer assistance if she couldn't find anything.

He had packed an overnight bag and set off in his dark blue tracksuit; he looked like a cat burglar, leaving the house with the birds beginning to chirp. Destination station, and he knew he would get a car spot nearby being this early. He found a space in the station car park and made his way over the bridge to the platforms.

They were surprisingly busy, Darlington perhaps being considered a commute from some of the other towns on the main line, and indeed the Northbound platform was full of well-dressed business people and a smattering of hi-visual jackets. Southbound was a little less so, and Jarrod took a seat after finding out which end of the platform his carriage would be. He only had eight minutes to wait, and he was conscious of a few eyes being on him. Being a fit, thirty-something man in sporting attire did tend to attract the eye. Sometimes it would be an inquisitive football supporter wondering if it really was him, sometimes a curious young Mum wondering why her husband didn't look that good in a tracksuit, most of the time it was just people surprised by the neatness.

The train arrived two minutes ahead of schedule and the platform sprung to life, more people getting on than getting off, and Jarrod found his way to his seat, finding an identically clad young man in the seat next to the window – Jan Haratounan, he knew the face, and the face was beaming back at him.

"Hey Jan," said Jarrod. "Pleased to meet you. I'm Jarrod."

"G'day!" said Jan, half standing. "What a pleasant surprise."

"I've seen you on the TV a bit this season," said Jarrod, referring to his breakthrough into the Hearts team and subsequent Cup winners medal. "Well done on the weekend!"

"Ha ha, thanks, mate," said Jan, a definite Scottish tone to his voice after what must have been at least five years up in

Edinburgh.

"Jees, you must have been up early," said Jarrod.

"Aye, it was bloody early," said Jan. "But you do it for your country, right?"

"Bloody oath, mate," said Jarrod. The first time he'd used that phrase in probably ten years.

The journey went remarkably fast. Jarrod and Jan getting to know each other and remarking on their similarities. Jan having led an alarmingly identical life but in Adelaide, leaving around the same age. Jan had signed for Kilmarnock before being snapped up by Hearts a couple of seasons ago. Jarrod was absolutely loving it. He'd missed out on many years of representing his country and felt a little bit like the way Manchester United legend Eric Cantona did about his place in the French team.

He knew this was an unlikely chance to represent his country, and his age and playing level were a definite disadvantage. He'd seen players like Mass Luongo, and Jackson Irvine, ply their trade at the lower levels of English football and still go to the World Cup, so that didn't seem to be a burden, although admittedly neither of them had played in League Two.

They were at Stevenage, and the empty seats in front of them with white tickets sticking out of the top suggested there would be more getting on. Sure enough, the dark blue tracksuits filed in, and two more Australian accents greeted the original two. Mitchell Moore, and James Bain, were also in the lower divisions with Luton and MK Dons. Jarrod had to admit he had not heard their names before. They both knew Jarrod though.

The four of them made their way through Kings Cross station to the tube, after taking a detour via Platform 9¾, which was just past the adjacent platform. They were like little kids, all getting

102

photos individually and then all together in a selfie. Jarrod resisted the urge to play Dad, and instead let the group make the call to move on. The London Underground was nothing new to Jarrod, but it had been a few years since he had been on it without kids, and he was surprised by the warmth in the carriages. The tracksuit tops were all jettisoned, revealing a smart dark blue polo shirt, each of the players having stuck to the protocol and worn the kit that had been sent via their respective clubs.

They arrived at Loftus Road after a bit of a hike from the tube station and checked in through reception to be warmly greeted by a party of coaches and admin staff, all wearing the same attire. Getting thirty-two players to Loftus Road, all arriving at the same time, was never going to be an easy task. Jarrod was impressed that whilst there were already a few players there, it was only a matter of minutes before more of the players arrived and they started to file into the media room and into the chairs usually reserved for the press.

There was still 15 minutes to go until the designated arrival time of midday, and this was a good chance to survey the room and catch a few eyes. Dane Radzinski sending a wave his way, and Zach Everett shouting a hello from across the room. The seats began to fill, and coach Mike appeared at the front and a spontaneous round of applause took over the room. This was the man that was going to revolutionise the Socceroos, or so was the hype surrounding his appointment, and Jarrod was more than happy to go along if he himself was involved in some way.

Introductions over and done with, the agenda of the day was spelled out – a quick bite to eat first in the adjoining room, medical checks straight after, pick up playing kit, and get fitted for missing or ill-fitting items, then changed and into a full afternoon training session. Jarrod was itching to get out there. He made sure he was at the front of the line for medical and kit and was one of the first to walk out onto the Loftus Road pitch. He joined the coaching staff and some other officials, who had set up a huge amount of cones in some intricate patterns on one side of the field, while the other side remained empty.

Maybe that was for game time and shooting drills, Jarrod hoped. His eagerness to get out there found him impatiently awaiting the rest of the players, juggling the ball near the centre-circle before trading long-range passes with his new mate, Jan. The training session got underway in familiar fashion with a light jog, stretching, and a run-through exercise, before they got into the simple yet well-thought-out drills that took him back to his early years at the academy at Christie Park in the Sydney suburbs.

Jarrod found some of them challenging, not from a technical or fitness perspective, but from a general concentration and understanding point of view. Some of the drills were against the natural way he played. One of the drills requiring two touches for every pass, another involving a pass, and then a close down of the receiving player, totally unnatural, and it really caused Jarrod a few problems. This must be what it's like to go senile he thought. By the end of the drills, every player was drenched with sweat, and Jarrod felt like he had done his first real training session in a year.

The cones and the rest of the equipment were cleared away and the players divided into three teams. Jarrod's team started off while the other two teams played each other on the full field. Only fifteen minute games, and they were punctuated with manager Jerszek, and coach Jim Grant, stopping play and manufacturing situations. A free-kick was taken and re-taken more than ten times, as the coaches began to lose patience and then started to find the funny side as the players finally got the idea and the set-piece routine finally worked.

Jarrod's team swapped on for the next 15 minute session and they started with a high tempo, which was quashed when Jim quite rightly repeated a goal kick routine a few times. The rhythm was back soon after though, and Jarrod found himself in familiar territory midway inside the opposition half with a bit of space ahead of him, and in confident fashion he stepped forward and unleashed a shot that sailed over the defence and crashed off the crossbar to involuntary gasps from some of the players.

Jarrod had his eye for goal and the extra excitement and the change of teammates made him concentrate that extra bit more. The next fifteen minutes saw Jarrod in ultra-defensive mode, as requested by the coach assigned to his team, and they were told to keep the ball as long as possible before trying to find the target man or the space behind the back four. Jarrod hoped that this was not a tactic and they were doing it to simulate a much inferior team parking the bus, but it wasn't obvious. Jarrod made a number of telling tackles, and the six man defence stood firm, keeping their opponents out.

A penalty session at one end of the stadium and a direct free kick session at the other was the half-time break they all needed. Jarrod having a go at the free kicks only, before they got back into the fifteen minute games. Jarrod was happy with his contribution and was happy in the final session to sit off for the last five minutes, his body starting to tell him it was enough.

The end of the session saw the players head back to the changing rooms and get changed, before a tactical briefing in the media room, where a video presentation helped the coaches explain the playing methodology. Gone was the 4-3-3 of old, and in its place was an exciting 3-5-2 formation. The diagrams showed the positioning of players as play went from one phase to the next. It was interesting stuff, very attack-minded, and a few remarks after the video from his fellow Socceroos suggested it was reliant on having some very skillful defenders who could play their way out of trouble.

That was the moment that it dawned on him – this is why he had been called up – they needed ball-playing defenders, not like the solid bone-crunching defenders of old, and not involving the ridiculous amount of running of a wing-back role. No, this was a back three of high-percentage pass completion and comfortable ball-players – a category that he liked to think he fell into. Jarrod convinced himself there and then that this was his role, and he craved one of the coaches to confirm his suspicions. The coaches, though, were still going through the technical aspects of the formation, and Jarrod decided he had to switch back on and listen intently.

The whole squad was invited to a nearby restaurant that had been booked out for the evening. They were invited to take all their belongings and take the short walk to Shepherds Bush Green and check into the Dorsett Hotel, apparently some sort of Australian pub in the past, but now a pretty swanky hotel. They were to meet five minutes later just around the corner on the main road at the venue, but Jarrod felt that he had to check in with Marianne. He fumbled in his pocket for his phone only to find that he had three missed calls already, all from Marianne, and this prompted him to sit on his bed as soon as he opened the door and called back.

"I've been calling you," said Marianne in a terse tone when she picked up. "Four or five times."

"I've been pretty busy..." he stopped himself from going any further – what would his wife, going through a cancer scare and sitting in a public ward in a hospital, want to know about his day. He immediately changed tact.

"Are you still in hospital?" he asked.

"Yes, I am," replied Marianne. "Nadine is doing everything with the kids. They've even been in to see me."

Jarrod didn't know which way the conversation was going to go. He could sense that Marianne was tired, and he could sense that he was in the wrong in her eyes, so he tried to be diplomatic.

"Great," he said. "Did the kids fuss over you?"

"Yes," she replied. "Yes, they did."

It was a weary voice.

"And you're feeling good?" he asked, hoping to lift the mood.

"Dr Groez came and checked on me ten minutes ago," she answered. "He says that he's happy with the wound and confident that the area will heal quickly."

"That's what we want to hear," said Jarrod, starting to feel a little more comfortable with the conversation. "And you'll be out tomorrow then?"

"I should be out in the afternoon," said Marianne, allowing Jarrod to mentally calculate whether he would stand a chance of being there.

"I'll come and get you," said Jarrod. "But for now, I need to go."

Jarrod looked at his watch and his roommate Jan had been gone for a while now. He sprung to his feet, still wrapping up the call as he got out a change of trainers and did them up the best he could with the phone pressed to his ear, before realising what he was doing and flicking the phone on to loud speaker. The wobbles and grunts in his voice from all the movement and effort as he left the room was evident, Marianne not sure what was happening.

He darted down the stairs and out past reception, taking

a second to work out if it was left or right, opting for right and then bounding around the corner and running past the restaurant before catching a glimpse of some dark blue shirts and screeching to a halt. He composed himself and walked slowly through the front door to join the two long tables. There was a roar as he approached the ends of the tables, and one of the coaches, Ollie Rescher, sprung to his feet and put his arm around Jarrod.

"You know the rules, Jarrod," he said. "Last one to be sitting down to dinner has to serenade us with a song."

Jarrod was relieved that he was not going to be slapped with a fine for being late and was quite happy that it was only a standard ridiculing he had to put up with. The initiation song was nothing new to Jarrod. It was standard practice for new arrivals in his time at Gateshead, but at International level he had never seen it. Best go along with it. As Ollie pulled out the chair and beckoned Jarrod to take the stage, the cries rung out.

"Jimmy Barnes!"

"Barbara Streisand!"

"Nah, it's got to be something Aussie. Slim Dusty!"

Jarrod was up on the table with forty odd pairs of eyes on him. He slowly started to sing in a low tone, getting louder as the first line got to the end and the realisation set in.

"Every-body-s doooo-in a brand new dance, now..."

He started to sway his hips and move his arms to the song,

"Come on baby, do the locomotion..."

There were howls of laughter as the rest of the squad joined in and a few got to their feet and were clapping along. By the time the 'C'mons' came around, everyone in the restaurant was singing along.

Jarrod had gotten away with it. He didn't really feel like playing the clown, but he knew it was easier to play along, and besides, it took his mind off everything else. He took his seat and the evening started.

It was around two by the time Jarrod arrived at the hospital. He got a cheap thrill by staying on the train all the way to Newcastle despite his ticket clearly saying Darlington, feeling like a teenage punk. Nadine was there waiting for him in the tiny station car park, her two kids beaming in the back of the car when Jarrod popped his head up unexpectedly at the window. They had time for a quick debrief on the way to the hospital and Jarrod offered to swap seats just before a set of lights, so he could drop her at the hospital door and park up. It was quite a funny moment as Nadine shimmied herself awkwardly from one seat to the other and Jarrod sprinted around the car to get in the drivers' side, just before the lights turned.

He knew that Marianne would like to see Nadine first – they were as close as any two friends could be – and Jarrod had received a slightly frosty reception the previous evening. Marianne was all dressed and packed when Jarrod finally got to the ward, and Marianne's body language suggested she had been waiting some time. She had organised after school care for Seb and Aneka, since she had been bound to the hospital and had plenty of time to set it up. Jarrod and the kids carried the bags, Nadine walking arm in arm ahead with Marianne, who had a drain still in her side, tucked under her shirt. The mood was good, and Marianne was clearly glad to be released.

After stopping to pick up the kids, and letting Chloe and Mass see the after school care centre, Jarrod folded up the back seats, so everyone could fit. Nadine took the wheel and they dropped Jarrod to the station to get his car. It had been quite an expedition and Jarrod was exhausted, but he knew he had one last stop, and that was to the supermarket. He got his phone out and punched the air when he remembered he had taken a photo of the blackboard the previous morning, making it a productive and efficient shop. The kids would be ready for dinner when he got in, and a quick and easy pasta dish was going to be on the menu tonight. He looked in the rear-view mirror when he finally rolled into the driveway, his sunken eyes telling the story. He took a sharp intake of breath, grabbed the shopping out of the car, and headed inside to join the throng.

Part Five
Tense

The final game of the season was tomorrow. The Football League had moved all games on the final day to the same timeslot, 1pm, so that meant an earlier start on Saturday and perhaps less intense training sessions today. Jarrod had been lying awake for some time, thinking through what was going to happen to Marianne in the next few days – there was a visit to the surgeon on Tuesday that he knew would be no problem to get to regardless of whether they sealed promotion tomorrow or had to go through the play-offs.

Jarrod's mind wandered over to football as it always did. The away game at Port Vale was a thoroughly winnable game and he knew that. With a bit of luck, they could leapfrog the two teams above them into the third and final automatic promotion spot. The thumping they had dished out to Exeter the previous Saturday had helped them bridge the goal difference gap between themselves and Lincoln to one goal, while on only one point more and an inferior goal difference were Chesterfield. It meant that even a draw might be enough, Lincoln hosting fellow play-off contenders Cambridge, who needed to win, and Chesterfield travelling to Grimsby, themselves scrapping to stay up with a win needed to guarantee safety. It was finely poised, plenty of interest at both ends of the table, and plenty of exciting games elsewhere in the country. At 1pm on Saturday though, all eyes would be on League Two. Jarrod could feel his skin crawl with excitement.

The heavy eyes from the night before were still there when he looked in the mirror and grasped both sides of the basin and stared into his own eyes. He was looking a little ragged. The tossing and turning through the night didn't help, and he was reluctant to nudge Marianne when the low hum of her cute snoring started. A quick shave and a shower got him perked up, and by the time he got out of the shower, Aneka and Seb were up helping themselves to breakfast with the TV blaring away. Jarrod quickly moved to the TV to turn it down before giving his kids a kiss. Aneka had finished her breakfast and handed her bowl to Jarrod, which Jarrod simply didn't take, and she huffed and got up and followed her Dad over to the kitchen bench.

"Aneka," he said softly, looking at his daughter who was wide-eyed and ready to listen, "It's going to be a tough few days for Mum, so can you please be kind and gentle with her and make her as comfortable as possible?"

"But we're going to school," said Aneka, and Jarrod simply smiled.

"I know that," he said. "But when you come home, if Mummy's relaxing or is still in bed, don't jump on her, just say hi and give her a kiss."

"Okay, I won't," said Aneka, remembering the time she jumped on Jarrod when he was in bed and almost cracked his ribs. Jarrod hugged his daughter, and the passing Seb was dragged in to the group hug too, pulling himself away as quickly as he could. It was good to connect with the kids as he was definitely not spending as much time with them as usual, and that fleeting moment gave Jarrod enough positive energy that he was ready to face the day. A light training session in the morning was going to be followed by set-piece drills in the afternoon, and a team-bonding visit to an aged care facility on the outskirts of town.

Jarrod was one of the first at training after dropping the kids to school en route. This was the usual story when they had early training sessions, and Jarrod was one of three players who had school-age children, all of whom would be at training way before anyone else. They coined it the Dads Club; Martin Howard having twins in primary school, Dario Reilly having three kids, two in the same middle school as Seb and Aneka, and they quite enjoyed a coffee and a chinwag before training. They swapped stories of schoolyard politics, youngsters and electronics and food strategies, it really was a Dads Club. Jarrod hadn't confided in any of the players yet and was keen to keep the subject-matter light and jovial, and quite enjoyed it being that way.

The majority of the players arrived close to the designated arrival time of 10 o'clock sharp, and they all got changed together in the white tiled changing rooms and it almost felt like match day. There was an air of expectation and excitement, even though the game wasn't until tomorrow. The session started in much the same way as any training session, a bit of stretching and warm up, a run through as a team, and then they got into some drills. A team favourite drill started the morning – a 1v1 duel, the winner being the one who got it through one of two gates, where they were faced with a 1v1 with the keeper.

This was a great way to simulate the situation where you break through and have a one-on-one with the goalkeeper after having already done a lot of work. The players always seemed to raise their game for this one and today didn't disappoint. It really set the mood. Jarrod could feel that his energy levels were not as high as they usually were, and felt like he was having an out-of-body experience; someone else living his life while he was inside his own head looking out. After the first round, where he was beaten easily by his opponent and gave out a petulant kick, he set off on round two of the challenge to see who would win the right to test the keeper. He pulled up after three steps, running off the side of the field, leaving his adversary to easily win the foot race, slip through a gate and draw the keeper out to make what was a fantastic one-handed save. Gary was watching on the sideline and could see that Jarrod was struggling. He had his hands on his hips and couldn't look up. He eventually took a few steps back and sat down on one of the advertising hoardings that surrounded the field, Gary ambling up slowly behind him and sitting right next to him.

"You're tired, Jarrod, is that it?" asked Gary.

"I think I must be," said Jarrod, unable to work out what was actually wrong with him. "I just feel drained."

"You've got quite a challenge on your hands," said Gary. "And with an ill-timed international call up put into the mix, I'm not surprised you're tired. Physically and emotionally. How is Marianne?"

"Marianne's recovering," said Jarrod, unable to state whether she was fine or not. He was pleased he had someone to talk to about it. "She has her best friend helping out, the kids are well looked after, and everyone is coping, but I'm finding it quite tough."

"If you need to talk to someone, let me know," offered Gary. "And don't feel as though you have to be here if you should be somewhere else. Maybe bed is the best place for you. Maybe you should head back home and get some rest or go and have a lie down in the physio room."

"Shouldn't I be here for the team?" asked Jarrod.

Gary thought for a moment.

"We would rather you be at the game tomorrow and be on top of your game."

They both sat for a moment in thought, watching the world go on around them, Gary showing no sign of getting up until Jarrod made the call.

"Okay," said Jarrod. "I'll get out of here."

"Call in this afternoon at the end of training, if you can" he said. "The aged care thing might do you some good too."

"We'll see. I'll let you know either way."

It was very unusual for Jarrod to leave training in this way. The last time he did, he had a bust nose and had to go off to hospital after colliding with a team mate. This time, though, he was not in a good frame of mind and instead of doing the rounds and saying goodbye to his teammates, he walked off back to the changing rooms, grabbed his gear, gave as cheery a goodbye as he could at the reception and walked off to his car that was just parked around the side.

When he got home, Marianne was up and about with Nadine and her kids. There were no questions as to why he was back – after all there was no set timetable that Jarrod worked to and as far as Marianne was concerned training was just whenever the coaches decided. Jarrod made small talk, then excused himself to go and get some rest, the bed still warm from Marianne who had obviously only just got up. He was out like a light in moments and didn't stir until Aneka came in with a cup of tea just after she had been picked up by Nadine from school.

Jarrod sat up quickly, unable to fathom he had been knocked out for over five hours. He got out of bed and walked with Aneka back into the hallway and down the stairs with the cup of tea she had only just carefully and skillfully negotiated the stairs with. It was Friday afternoon and the kids had finished for the weekend and were in a real Friday mood. Aneka was pumped up and doing a dance routine, Seb was rumbling with Massimo, and Chloe was trying her best to mimic Aneka's moves. Jarrod, though, was not in a Friday mood, and having just woken up after a Sleeping Beauty-esque slumber, his head was even further away from reality than it had been that morning. He quickly grabbed his phone and rang Gary, who surprisingly answered after only two rings.

"You're not coming in this afternoon?" asked Gary before Jarrod could speak.

"You guessed right, Gary," Jarrod replied. "But I can safely say I am well-rested."

"Good man," said Gary pensively. "Now, the coach leaves at 6am tomorrow from the Arena. You be there, and we'll have a chat on the way down to the game and I'll fill you in on what you missed."

"Fantastic, Gary," said Jarrod. "Thanks. See you in the morning."

Jarrod hung up and knew he was probably going to return to his bed in the near future, but also knew he had to get some food into him to generate some energy for tomorrow. He headed back to the kitchen where his cup of tea was sitting and made a point of saying how delicious it was in earshot of Aneka, who smiled knowingly without looking at him. Nadine and Marianne were deep in conversation in front of the TV that was providing the background noise.

Jarrod started to prepare the dinner, a tortilla bake he knew would be a hit and was a quick and easy meal that looked and smelled as good as it tasted. Aneka and Chloe appeared, as if by magic, to see if they could lend a hand with the cooking. They lived up to their billing as sous-chefs and helped get everything out of the cupboards, chop tomatoes, and work out the oven setting. Chloe, who was clearly not used to helping out at home, was in her element, stirring the mince as it cooked, using the step from the bathroom the kids had used when they went to the toilet way back when. The exaggerated motions of head chef

Jarrod had the kids in giggles.

He was sprinkling chopped tomatoes into the mince mix from a great height, arranging the tortillas in perfect unison in the baking tray, and using a big spoon to splat the remaining mixture over the rolled tortillas. The grated cheese went everywhere when he tossed a big handful from metres away with a basketball throw. Jarrod had completely forgotten how he had felt earlier in the day, Marianne and Nadine were watching on as their girls rejoiced in the kitchen and were then amazed at their willingness to clean up their mess as Jarrod placed the dish into the hot oven.

He declared the food preparation complete and gave the girls a high five. Fifteen minutes of calm followed as dinner cooked, giving Jarrod a chance to pack his team bag for the morning's journey. He felt he definitely had a spring back in his step, mainly due to the much-needed sleep he'd just had.

The boys, this time, had stepped up to the plate, mainly due to hunger. They had set the table, and made a salad, and were deliberating where the knives and forks went on the table when Jarrod re-appeared. Dinner was quickly removed from the oven and served, the boys taking the plates to the table as they were prepared, Seb even stopping to grab a serviette to wipe the edge of a plate, just like they do on TV. A bottle of red was opened, the TV went off, and a funny evening ensued. Everyone full of joie de vivre, the Blacks' house a very happy place to be.

The coach pulled up at Port Vale's ageing stadium at ten to eleven, a police escort having given them a speedy passage through the surrounding streets, and there was already a good crowd to meet them. The players filed off the coach, a few shaking hands with well-wishers and curious home fans. A small group of Darlington fans, bedecked in their black and white finery, roared approval at every player as they stepped out into the chilly morning. Jarrod had a few Darlington branded gifts ready and singled out some of the youngest members of the gathering, handing out teddy bears, pens, badges, and pyjamas.

Judging by the mood of the home fans, there was a good-natured afternoon ahead. Port Vale had finished the season mid-table after drawing away from the relegation places in March, giving them a relaxing final three weeks. Their form had been nothing short of amazing six weeks ago, but since securing their mid-table berth and coming up against some of the major powers in the division, the results had not gone too well. Last week's victory saw them score their first goal in four games, and it could be argued that the players were already on their post-season holiday.

Jarrod made his way with the rest of the team into the heart of the stadium and up some steps to a corridor, which took them to the dressing rooms. The doors of the home and away rooms were directly opposite each other, which Jarrod found a little strange. The doorways were a little on the compact side, bags scraping against the fresh paint of the door frame. As soon as all the players were in the compact room, the door was closed, and Gary put up a chart on the wall with blue tack, something the players had never seen in the past.

It was a hand-drawn set of permutations, nine of them in total, showing what would happen if Darlington were to win or draw with other likely and possible results, giving the nine different scenarios. Gary invited any of the players to come and help him explain what was on the wall. No-one was forthcoming, so he picked Dec Hines to come up, and asked him what he thought of the chart.

"It's very good, Gary," said Dec.

"Yes, it is very good, Hinesy," replied Gary. "But, what is it telling us?"

"Er...it's got today's fixtures on there, and..." he paused, "...and it shows whether or not we go up or not."

"Exactly," said Gary, inviting Dec to sit down. "Thanks, my friend. Yes, this is the whole set of possible scenarios that will play out today. Here, we see Darlington winning and everyone else losing, we go up. Here we see Darlington winning, draws, and losses elsewhere, we go up."

Gary was prodding the board. He had obviously spent a good while deliberating this.

"Here, we see Darlington drawing," he continued. "Everyone else loses, and by enough goals, we go up."

He held his hand on the board before finishing off.

"All of these other scenarios are meaningless. We don't go up. So..." he paused for dramatic effect, looking around the room, "...we'll remove this," he said, crossing out one scenario with his marker, "and this," crossing out another, "and all of these."

The big chart was now a sea of big crosses, leaving only two of the scenarios.

"A win," he said, turning to look at them, "is our only option today. If we win, then it's down to the other two teams to come up with results to stop us from going up."

Gary was conscious not to mention the names of the other teams. Jarrod was loving this, and it was totally unexpected and seemed to be against the ethics of his manager. Maybe it was reverse psychology, thought Jarrod.

"Now," started Gary, reaching into his bag and unrolling a second poster, which he place over the first, pressing hard in each corner, "who can tell me what this is?"

It was a photo of the Darlington away end at one of the games earlier in the season, when Darlington had scored a late goal, and were celebrating at the final whistle as the players came across. The joy on the faces of the fans was clear, some grown men were embracing each other, kids were on shoulders, there was even a lady with her top off, only in her bra, waving her shirt around her head. The photo was crystal clear, with the players not yet coming into focus in the foreground, facing the crowd, some with their arms in the air clapping. It looked like the cover of a magazine and it gave Jarrod a tingly feeling.

"Ah, yes," said Sam Basaan. "Look at that. Luton away. What a result!"

"Yes!" shouted Gary. "What a game indeed. Look at those fans, just look at what it means to them. They're going to be here in full party-mode today. They've travelled again in their thousands and we need to give them everything today. The results elsewhere are irrelevant. Today, it's all about these people. Today, is a celebration of their season. Some of them will have been to every game, home and away. We need to show them a reason for their devotion."

Jarrod could feel his chest swelling with pride, Gary was certainly pressing the right buttons with him, and he was pretty sure the rest of the team felt the same.

"Let's go get something to eat," said Gary. "I'm leaving this photo up. Look at it when you come back in and look at it again when you go out for your warm-up. See if you can recognise any of them."

After a quick café visit in what was a large portakabin out next to the main car park, the players came back in to the dressing room and Gerry Lincoln, the owner of the club, was there with his kids. He was an approachable man and a familiar face around the club, although some family health issues had seen him miss a number of games towards the end of the season. He was beaming with smiles and hugs and high fives for everyone. For an owner, he was definitely one that attracted much admiration and respect.

"Great photo, that," said Gerry, once all the players were inside. "We'll be seeing you all out there. Remember that today is about the fans."

And with that, he walked quickly out of the room. He probably would have stayed there if it wasn't for the kids, and they followed him out, the youngest girl skipping as she went.

The Darlington fans had indeed travelled in great numbers. There was a little bit of fancy dress going on, although not to the same extent as the Exeter fans the week before. One of the people leading the chants had a cardinal's robes on, complete with hat and staff, and he was working the crowd into a frenzy. The sun had just come out after an earlier downpour and the grass was letting off steam, rising in wisps through the warm spring air.

Jarrod assembled his team in a huddle for one last time, reaffirming four or five of the most basic instructions that had been passed on by Gary and the coaches. It was a call for simple football, hassling up front, but not pushing up too far, and above all a call for patience in what could be a very tense game. The crowd raised the volume as celebrity fan Robbie Williams' song came to its conclusion, and with a quick check of his assistants, the referee signalled the game to start. Jarrod loved this part of the game, both playing and watching.

It signalled the end of the anticipation and the beginning of the drama, and ahead of them lay 90 minutes of totally unpredictable action that could throw up any manner of excitement and frustration. Port Vale contented themselves with keeping possession and playing the ball backwards whenever Darlo threatened to make a tackle. The controversial maroon kit the team was wearing had never been a favourite with the fans, its round collar doing nothing for the fashionistas, but today it made Darlington look as though they had an extra man. The white and yellow shirts of the home team looking numerically disadvantaged. There had been six minutes of play already and not a sniff of a chance. Vale were executing their game plan to perfection, super-conservative football on a day when gung-ho attack would have been more appropriate.

Gary had already been out in the technical area and was now switching the formation from a 4-5-1 to a 3-5-2, Will Telfer, moving up front into his usual position, alongside the slightly inexperienced youth talent Jason Glenn, who seemed to be a fraction of his size.

Jason had been given instructions to harass the home defenders with his pace and acceleration, and he had been doing well so far. Bringing in Will next to him gave a more robust look to the attack, a target man and a player to play off. Still the hassling went on though, and Jason found himself charging down a clearance and coming away with the ball. He slipped the ball through to Dean Minto, who jinked to the byline and lifted a cross to the far post, where Will's bullet header was smartly tipped over from very close range by the young Vale keeper. That got the Darlington fans going, and the singing was as loud as Jarrod could remember. News was filtering through of a goal, Lincoln having gone a goal behind to seventh placed Cambridge, blowing the race for third wide open. The news spread through the Darlington fans and they began to celebrate as if they had scored a goal. A win was still needed here, though.

Jarrod was reveling being back in his familiar role in the middle of midfield, after the midweek session in London, and was finding a great deal of time and space, only the end product was missing. Wes rolled the ball out to Ghali Barbera, the midfielder dropping behind the defence to get a touch of the ball, and in an instant, he had raked an eighty metre pass across field into the path of Connor Naughton.

The young starlet took the ball down exquisitely in his stride and held the ball up on the edge of the area, waiting for his teammates to arrive. A feigned pass back to Dec saw Connor pull the ball back quickly and wrong-foot his marker, leaving him on the floor, before steadying himself and lifting the ball to the edge of the six yard box where Will had made a late run and met it with an almighty thumping header, which sailed through the despairing arms of the home keeper to give Darlington the precious lead they were looking for.

The whole team ended up surrounding Will in his moment of glory, and the fans could see what it meant to the players. Twenty minutes gone, one goal up, Lincoln losing and Chesterfield goalless against Grimsby, the live table would have Darlington promoted and the guys at Soccer Saturday would be frothing over the endless combinations of twists and turns still to come. Controversy then embroiled the referee, and it was from a low quality moment when Dec Hines miskicked a routine back pass right into the path of the advancing Vale striker.

The defence was totally flat-footed and the striker advanced to the penalty area where he was faced with the huge frame of Wes Kellehar. The seemingly oversized Mickey Mouse-esque gloves were no match though for the tricky attacker, who went to go around the Darlo keeper before cutting back and giving himself an empty goal to aim at. With the crowd rising as one to acclaim an unlikely goal against the run of play, Wes had other ideas and dived full-length towards the ball, only managing to bump the legs of the attacker sending him off balance. He regained his composure, though, to confidently stroke the ball goalwards before the defence swamped him, but the ball bounced off the post and was hacked away to safety.

Heads were in hands in the crowd behind the goal, but only for a moment, as the referee signalled a penalty with a shrill blow on his whistle and went to his pocket. The Darlington players raced to the referee at the perceived injustice – after all he'd had the advantage and stuffed it up – but the referee had made up his mind already and it was only the colour of the card that was the concern. When yellow was produced by the man in black, the ranting stopped from the Darlington players as the name was noted in the book. The bickering then started again when the ball was placed on the spot, words clearly being exchanged by the players as the penalty-taker waited for the whistle.

A less-than-confident run up saw Wes guess right and easily stop the ball, clutching it to his chest as the penalty-taker homed in and let fly with an almighty kick into the keeper's midriff. This was definitely not an attempt to play the ball cleanly, and the incensed Darlington players rushed over to haul the attacker away from the scene, Jarrod stopping to check on Wes. He looked white and wasn't moving. The referee moved over towards Wes and asked if he needed assistance, Jarrod answering for him and the grimace that came across Wes' face suggested he was either completely winded or had taken one firmly between the legs.

The red card was shown, and the attacker dismissed, walking hands on head to the tunnel and receiving only a smattering of applause amid the grumbles from the stands. Wes was winded as it turned out – never an easy situation to get over in seconds – and he took as long as he could to get up and even longer to straighten up, as the game couldn't continue without him.

A gingerly taken free kick short to Raynor Gunn started play again and Darlo were a goal up, a man up, and were heading for promotion.

A minute left of the lengthy injury time just before half-time, and the game had been a stalemate for a good ten minutes. Both teams were taking the safe route rather than throwing caution to the wind, and in Darlington's case it was justified. They had kept the ball moving quickly with the intention of tiring out their understrength opponents, and the passing was crisp and full of intent. That was until Freddie Asquith, out of his usual central defensive position, dwelt on the ball a little too long out on the right and had his pocket picked by the Vale wide man. He set off with the intention of racing to the byline, but when he found himself outpacing Raynor, he veered towards goal, drew Wes and slid the ball under his left hand and just inside the near post for the equaliser.

Vale Park was rocking, and what a great time for the home team to score, a timely lift going into half-time. The celebrations were over-stated for a team destined for mid-table obscurity, but it demonstrated that this game was being taken seriously by the home team and the crowd responded vociferously to the players' show of delight. The scenario then had changed, Chesterfield now in third place thanks to their continued stalemate at Grimsby, Darlington dropping to fourth, and Lincoln remaining fifth.

The players were in the dressing room and the mood was still up-beat. Gary was full of chat, and he was surprisingly positive having seen the last couple of minutes of the half. They had forty-five minutes to go, and they were up a player and all they needed was one goal. Gary was stressing the importance of keeping the ball moving and made a point of talking to his defenders to make sure they knew that the ball could not be still, not even for a moment.

The players had a look of concentration in their faces. This was different from the start of the game when there was much chatter and light-hearted banter. The players were focused, and Sam Basaan was standing chattering to himself, his head in the air as if looking to the heavens for inspiration. Gavin Selley, a midfielder who had come back from a lengthy injury and had been named as a sub today, was pacing the room and skipping into a trot every few seconds. If there were no nerves now, they certainly looked likely if the second half didn't get off to a good start.

Gary rallied his troops one last time. Jarrod repeated the basics and the players started to file out in to the corridor, where the home team were coming out. The players ended up mixing together in the tight corridor before running back out on to the field. The Darlington fans were a little more subdued – perhaps the pre-match beers were starting to wear off. The realisation was that the season could be over in 45 minutes, but equally it could be on for two, and hopefully three more games.

Darlington kept the ball moving quickly, and sometimes it was a little too quick. Dean Minto rushed to play a pass which bounced out of play with no pressure at all on him. Wes found himself on the ball a lot more than normal, playing as the last man in defence and leaving the goal unguarded when the away team were in possession. With ten minutes gone in the second half, he booted the ball clear and straight into the stands, which grew cheers from the home fans and disgruntled arm-waving from the bench.

The game just wasn't flowing. A substitution or a change of plan was needed, and Gary had one up his sleeve, moving Raynor Gunn up to partner Will Telfer up front. The tall target man now had an even taller partner for once. The instruction was to use them both as target men, and they would play with three across the back in a 3-4-3 formation, throwing a little caution to the wind. This gave Darlington a lift and they began to throw balls long up to the big men, while continuing to play some intricate tiki-taka football down the flanks.

Raynor was like a battering ram. Will was loving having a big unit alongside and able to use his skill rather than his physical presence to carve out the opportunities. A first clear cut chance came when Ghali chipped a long ball up to Will, who chested the ball in the air and took the ball down under control with his back to goal. The defender tried to reach the ball through his legs, but at that moment, the Darlington striker turned and left his marker for dead, skipped into the area and lifted a delightful cross to the far post. The inrushing Dec Hines met the ball on full, with a thumping shot that flew into the face of Raynor and knocked him flying, the ball trickling just past the post with the keeper and the defence completely beaten.

Raynor then flicked on a long ball to Will again, racing at full speed. He palmed off his defender and raced through on goal, placing his shot low just to the right of the keeper's leg, but the fingertips of the keeper were enough to deflect the ball wide for a corner and Vale escaped again. Up the other end, the Darlington defence were involved in the one-way wave of attacks, and it was only a piece of individual magic from the Port Vale midfielder that presented them with half a sniff of goal.

A swift break saw the wide man slip the ball inside to the wiry midfielder, who fended off his man, pirouetted to put his foot on the ball, and then pulled the ball back through two Darlington players to set off unchallenged towards the penalty area. A lob that Matthew Le Tissier would be proud of was carefully attempted. Wes pedalled backwards for what seemed like five seconds before reaching to tip the ball onto the bar. The sting was taken out of the ball and it fell perfectly for the Darlington shot stopper, who gratefully grabbed the ball and sprung to his feet to get the next move going.

Twenty minutes into the second half and nerves were starting to fray. Mitch Short let the ball run out of play and was about to pick up the ball and do a quick throw when a Vale player came in and smashed the ball into the crowd. The ball hit a fan in the head, the elderly gentleman ending up on the floor in front of his seat, all eyes turning to see while Mitch grabbed the Vale man by the front of the shirt and gave his opponent an up-front and personal verbal spray. That could have been a cue for a mass melee, but the sheepish Vale player held up his hands in remorse and made his way over to the advertising hoardings still with his hands up in apology to the victim.

When the players had eventually refocused on the game, the resulting throw in was touched on by Will, giving Connor Naughton a run on goal. The defender from the far side was across quickly, though, to block the shot. The assistant referee signalled a goal kick, and the Darlington players erupted in unison at the ridiculous decision. Two bookings later and some puce faces in the Darlo dugout, and the goal kick was taken. Time was definitely ticking.

Twenty minutes to go. The clock ticking over to seventy minutes was always the transition from 'midway through the game' to 'late in the game,' and with it came an increased level of tension. Darlington were having no luck. The players were starting to have trouble executing the basic skills, the ball seeming to have a life of its own. Connor was guilty of a lapse in concentration when he looked up instead of concentrating on controlling the ball, the pass rolling under his foot. A Vale player was on to it immediately and wasted no time in launching a long cross-field to the other side of the field where the gaps were starting to form. It took a momentous tackle from Freddy Asquith to avert the danger, sliding in perfectly to cleanly dispossess his opponent. This would be the only way Darlington would lose this game, Vale had otherwise stopped attacking and were playing with five at the back and a middle four with no-one seeming interested in attacking.

The travelling faithful were still chanting and singing, and Jarrod could sense them willing the team to get the all-important goal. A fantastic block by the Vale captain on his line then saw the home team survive. Dec Hines then chose placement over power but didn't get enough purchase on the shot to take it past the outstretched leg of the Vale man with the keeper beaten. Hands were on heads in the crowd, but there was still ten minutes to go. In a momentary lull in the action, Jarrod could hear talk amongst the fans that Cambridge still had the edge at Lincoln, and that Chesterfield were a man down but still level at Grimsby.

Jarrod roared at his teammates, a double substitution saw Gavin Selley come on for Dec in midfield and attacker Julien Favot replace winger Dean, in an attempt to go route one. Effectively, they now had a front four, and it was win or bust. Sam Basaan lifted a ball into the penalty area to Raynor who held the ball up, again back to goal. He kept the ball close to his feet attracting the foul and ready to crumple at any moment, but the tackle didn't come. He laid the ball off to Gavin, who lined up a thumping shot from the edge of the area that took a deflection and glanced off the post and behind for a corner.

Jarrod's corners had been delightful today, and this one was again spot on, inviting the header from Ghali, but the ball sailed over. Four minutes on the clock. A roar went through the home crowd. Lincoln had equalised. Grimsby had a penalty. It was all happening. A home substitution gave everyone a chance to check the other scores. Grimsby had scored the penalty and that left Lincoln now in third. On the same points, but an inferior goal difference of one were Darlington, while Chesterfield now slipped to fifth. This was unbearable.

Gary was on the touchline barking instructions. Mitch was pushed up in midfield. They were now playing with two at the back and just needed a goal. Connor Naughton then came up with the move of the game, trading passes with substitute Julien, before jinking past his man and swinging over a cross right into the danger zone. Will and Raynor reacted much quicker than their defenders but got in each other's way. The ball bouncing off Raynor's knee and falling perfectly for Jarrod, five yards out. He reached and connected.

The Darlington fans held their collective breath for an instant, but the reach meant he was leaning back, and the powerful shot flew just over the bar when everyone in the stadium expected the back of the net to bulge. What a chance! The time-wasting was starting to test the referee's patience by now – Port Vale had nothing to play for, but the players were more than content to spoil the party and take the point off Darlington, condemning them to the play-offs.

It was now injury time. The board went up: two minutes. The goal kick was straight to Freddie. He played it immediately to the feet of Will Telfer, who laid the ball wide to Ghali on the edge of the area. There was time to jink to the byline and lift in a cross. That was cleared. The loose ball was lifted back in, the keeper came and punched. Sam Basaan then joined the attack and, as the Vale defenders anticipated the lay-off, he just kept going and sprinted right through the defence and on into the area, the keeper coming to meet him. The 'aargh' of the Darlington fans was clear when he then blasted the ball high and wide, not an ounce of composure left in his body, and he collapsed to his knees in despair. The Vale fans kept the ball for a few seconds before the goal kick was punted long and the referee gave three blasts to signal the end of the regular season.

Jarrod couldn't believe it. He had been in similar situations before, but this one was a tough one. They had played the whole of the second half with a man advantage, against a team they were almost certain to beat on paper. The fans were looking around at each other bemused. The second half had been as long as any half of football had ever been. They knew that a draw was almost certainly not enough. The number of chances missed was outrageous, and the goals in the first half a distant memory.

Darlington had failed at the final hurdle. The scores were confirmed over the tannoy system, Grimsby winning one goal to nil to preserve their league status, and then the news all the fans had already known, Lincoln had snatched a late winner to win two goals to one, thus confirming their automatic promotion. That news was bittersweet − the win for Darlington would not have been enough, and Jarrod knew he wouldn't have been able to cope had his team won and still not gone up.

Jarrod ran over to Raynor, who had sat on the floor and hauled him up. He geed up his team mates to go and salute the travelling masses, the applause slow to start, but once it got going, it reached a crescendo in a huge roar. Darlington had not lost and were still in with a great chance of promotion. Only this time the opposition would be considerably stronger.

A slow walk to the tunnel followed, as the Vale players continued with their lap of honour, such is custom for the final home game of the season, regardless of how a team has fared during the season. Jarrod felt totally frustrated. The second half had exposed a perceived weakness in their armour. They were unable to kill off a team who were ripe for the picking. Raynor Gunn booted the door of the changing room as he walked in, sending splinters everywhere as the door knob hit the wood paneling behind. Mitch Short then followed it up with a punch to the same door, before Gary caught the door and closed it behind him.

"Lads," he said. "I don't know where to start with this one. We were better all over the park today, but my goodness we made tough work of it."

"We were shite," came the shrill Irish tone of Dec.

"Ah, no, I don't think we were shite," said Gary, coolly shaking his head. "They were shite and we played at their level. Any other day we would have scored four goals in the second half. Hey, that would have been enough to go up on goal difference…"

Gary couldn't believe what he'd just said.

"Ah, shit," he said, realising just how much of a glorious opportunity they had just thrown away.

The journey home was unpleasant. Travelling through the streets around Burslem, there were plenty of onlookers happy to goad the players and give them a heckle. Mitch wasn't in the mood for the usual banter and, as a result, the whole bus was quiet. The players sat in silence, unable to rouse themselves for any conversation. Jarrod was listening to BBC 5 Live on his headphones and they were midway through the second half of the League One games that had all kicked off in synch at 3pm.

The same tension was in play in the relegation battle; two teams from four destined for the drop, and the commentary was flicking between games whenever there was a goal or an incident of note. It was absorbing, and Jarrod could only imagine what it would have been like two hours ago for the Darlington fans who weren't at the game.

The post-mortems would be done after all the day's games had finished, although there was a moment where the host of the show recapped the earlier action in League Two, stating it was a dramatic finish with Grimsby ensuring their survival to send Barnet back down to the National League. Meanwhile, at the top, Lincoln had denied Cambridge a berth in the play-offs with that late, late winner and in turn had booked their automatic promotion.

The play-offs, which the Football League had voted unanimously to remain as a four team shoot-out despite the success of the lower league's six team system, would be played over the following weekend. Crewe Alexandria would entertain Darlington in the first leg on Friday, with the return leg coming quickly on the Tuesday, and Saturday would see Chesterfield travelling to Mansfield Town for an evening kick-off before a Wednesday night second leg to decide the play-off finalists.

Jarrod played around with the scenarios in his head. Darlington had enjoyed a thumping win at Crewe in the league game towards the start of the season but had then struggled to a draw, sharing four goals in a mid-winter home game at the Arena in the return fixture.

Play-off football was definitely different though, and Jarrod had a lot of experience of that with Gateshead. Some good and some not so good. In fact, it was only 12 months since he was standing on the Wembley turf holding his shin pads, head bowed in an award winning photo on the front of the local newspaper. The wounds were still raw, and despite a whole season having passed since then, it still hurt to think back to that day last May. What a chance to put it right.

Jarrod's thoughts turned to Marianne. To be honest she had not been out of his thoughts all day, and he got the urge to ring her, but decided to save it until he got home and saw her. The radio commentary was increasing in pitch and excitement. Barnsley handing out a thrashing against relegated Rochdale to keep them up, but the other three games coming to a head; all three begging for a hero to save their team.

In the end, the commentary game came to a close with no goals. Leaving a confused host to try and work out where they should go next, and they timed it perfectly. Peterborough had just scored, coming into the third minute of injury time, condemning opponents Bury to the drop, barring a miracle. That miracle didn't come. Shrewsbury managed to get their required draw and Tranmere played out the last five minutes with nine men, meaning that Fleetwood went down after being swept aside by runaway champions Burton Albion.

It was clear from looking around the coach at that point that Jarrod had not been the only one listening in, and the mood had definitely mellowed as they approached Scotch Corner and neared home. Jarrod moved around the coach, checking to see how everyone was feeling. The simple positive responses from the majority of the players was encouraging. He had a word with Dec, who was still a bit angry with himself, then sat the rest of the journey with Raynor, discussing the game coming up on Friday. Jarrod was glad that it had only taken three hours for the pain to start to subside, and he had renewed optimism about the play-offs, and in turn a more positive attitude when his mind inevitably wandered to his wife's cancer battle.

Jarrod arrived home at around eight to an empty house. A note on the table from Nadine told him they were out for an early dinner, and as soon as he had read the note, the gravel in the driveway crunched and flicked, signalling the arrival of the flock back home, and the silence was replaced by the din of hyped-up children and babbling Mums. They burst in the front door, Marianne making straight for Jarrod and hugging him.

"You'll beat them on Friday," she said, surprising him with her up-to-date knowledge. "And then you'll have your day at Wembley."

That was all she said before peeling away, leaving a whiff of white wine in her wake. Nadine whispered that Marianne had enjoyed a second glass of wine, against doctor's orders, but Jarrod was delighted. He hadn't seen a spring in her step for some time. Jarrod knew they had a big day tomorrow, swim squads early in the morning for both kids, and he would take them with Chloe and Mass and make a morning of it at the pool and let Marianne have a rest. Jarrod found himself swept up in the evening as he managed the night time routine and packed off Nadine to bed after she had spent half an hour getting Marianne ready for sleep and untangled from the drain bag she was still attached to. Jarrod didn't hesitate to get straight to bed himself after making sure that Seb and Mass weren't on their electronics, an exhausting day of high adrenaline and disappointment over and done with. His life was being lived one day at a time at the moment, and while he yearned for some stability, he couldn't deny that it was ever so exciting.

Part Six
Ready

It was Monday morning, Jarrod had excused himself quite early at training to go and pick up Marianne and they were due to meet Dr Groez at the hospital in Newcastle, at 11.45am. This was the day when the cancer scare would be quashed, and Jarrod was looking forward to life getting back to relative normality. They did a quick dash to the shops in Eldon Square to buy birthday presents for the upcoming weekend's kids parties, and just making it there in time. Jarrod, again, dropped Marianne at the door so that at least one of them could be on time, while he found a park.

Jarrod rushed through the door of the consulting rooms just as Dr Groez was saying goodbye to his previous patient, and it was only a couple minutes before they were welcomed into his room. Within a minute, Marianne had stripped off her top and was sitting on Dr Groez's table. She was looking very hot in tight jeans, knee length boots, and her boobs out. Jarrod felt as though he was in a dream, watching his wife sit confidently, bare-chested in front of the doctor, while he checked his handiwork from the operation. Jarrod had to take a few breaths in to remember that this was totally normal in his totally un-normal life. Dr Groez was happy with the healing process and checked the drain that was still protruding from Marianne's side. The bag was getting a little discoloured and he asked the resident nurse to come in and change the bag for a fresh one. Dr Groez gave the air of a happy and contented man.

Then came the pathology results, and his face changed from relaxed and smiling to a more serious and neutral look. He only had interim results of the pathology, but he explained that the results were not as good as he had hoped. Marianne would have to get more tissue taken out in a second op. Boom, a smack in the face. Their early optimism and unwavering positive attitude had taken its first big knock right there. Jarrod looked at his wife with hopeful eyes, Marianne stared at him with a look of despair and denial, but they both knew they were at the mercy of Dr Groez and they could do nothing but listen to his description of what he had to do next.

Regardless of the final pathology results, there would need to be another operation, and the doctor also suggested that the chemo that had been mentioned before the first surgery and not discussed since might need to be delayed a little until this operation was done. Marianne quickly got dressed and Jarrod opened the door to the waiting room, where Harriet was waiting to help Jarrod and Marianne fill out the paperwork for op number two. The waiting room was empty at this stage, so Dr Groez felt comfortable continuing their conversation. He said he was hoping to have the final results that evening and would phone to give the latest update. Jarrod had his hand on Marianne's shoulder and could feel her shaking a little. Marianne made out that she was cold, but the truth was it was not a cold day and Jarrod could detect the sense of helplessness in Marianne.

Jarrod made a point of taking a detour to Marianne's golf club – Marianne had said she wouldn't mind popping in to get a couple things but was now unsure as to whether she could face it following the appointment. She was quite relaxed when they got out of the car, and even more so when she met up with some of her colleagues, who were just finishing lunch in the clubhouse. They were all asking how she was – it struck Jarrod that they were all up to date with her cancer situation, and there were hugs and kisses. Everyone wanted to know the latest.

Jarrod excused himself, making a mental note that it was perhaps time to let everyone at his club know what was going on. He had only confided in Gary and asked Gary to only share it with the management team. He was pretty confident that none of his teammates were aware. It had not yet come up at all in conversation, and for all his teammates knew, he had sponsor engagements and international commitments that were taking him away from training.

Jarrod had a look around the club shop, saying hello to the friendly ladies who worked there before they got back to assisting their two elderly but fit-looking customers in the shop. He had no interest whatsoever in golf, something that frustrated Marianne but didn't entirely surprise her – for all he knew, Marianne was feigning any interest she showed in football, so it was a two-way street. Jarrod couldn't hold a conversation about golf and apart from a hit with the squad as a team building exercise now and again, he could still remember all the times he had played golf in his entire life. He could definitely see the attraction, the group of slim retirees he could see out on the 18th green having a great laugh a clear indication as to why people took up the sport. He returned to the clubhouse after exchanging pleasantries with the ladies in the shop and found Marianne still at the lunch table with her colleagues crowded around her listening. They were making moves to get their phones and wallets back in their pockets and a couple were standing up, as if trying to draw themselves away from Marianne's captivating stories, knowing that time was ticking, and they had places to be.

Jarrod's appearance signalled the end of the party. Jarrod left feeling as though his mere presence was enough to drive away Marianne's audience and he checked to see if Marianne was okay while shaking some hands and saying goodbyes. Marianne was smiling, but it was a vacant smile that would be wiped off her face the moment everyone had gone. Jarrod was beginning to know that look, the epitome of the brave face. They had to get on the road again to pick up the kids from school. There was some sort of presentation before afternoon assembly they were encouraged to be at, and whilst they were not in the right frame of mind, they would attend for their children. It was something to take their minds off the situation at hand.

Marianne had been making call after call since they got back in the car, and it didn't stop that evening as dinner time came around, Jarrod finding himself on dinner duty once again while Marianne's phone rang hot. The home phone rang around 6pm and Jarrod beat Aneka to it and answered. It was Dr Groez. He asked straight away to speak with Marianne without any niceties or small talk. Jarrod was immediately worried.

The nightmare scenario had come, the results were, again, not encouraging. More tissue was to be taken out and the choice was very simple: go through the op again, with a large amount of tissue taken out of one breast leaving it smaller and mis-formed or go through a mastectomy to remove the breast completely. Marianne was again in shock when she placed down the handset, but to her credit she was straight back on her phone to anyone she knew in the medical profession. Ash, their doctor friend, Wendy, a school Mum from Gateshead who was a nurse and even a lady who had been through the whole thing herself.

Jarrod left his wife to her calls. She was on a roll and didn't even acknowledge Jarrod being in the room, so Jarrod felt comfortable leaving her to it. She would make an appearance once she had finished. It was late, the kids had been in to kiss Marianne goodnight and Jarrod and Nadine had put them to bed. Nadine and her two were heading back to Europe the following day, and Nadine was keen to catch up for one last time with her closest friend. Marianne walked out into the kitchen as if nothing had happened, she had a steady resolve about her, a determined look and clearly the decision had been made.

She sat down with a fresh mug of tea steaming in front of her.

She explained that, of course, there are different opinions, but the main thing is to get the cancer out of the system. Then there is the minimisation of the risk of it returning, so the mastectomy would not only remove that risk, but it would allow Marianne to get on with her life without the worry of breast cancer affecting her again. It had been a very difficult day emotionally all round, but with Marianne able to tap on resources a phone call away, she was able to make very clear and informed decisions. Jarrod had already flicked out a text out to a few key people that afternoon, before the results came through, to say that another operation would be needed, and that Marianne was a little upset and not to expect a phone call. By now though, she had spoken to most of them already. The mood was again positive.

"I'm going to have a double mastectomy," Marianne stated, to neither Nadine or Jarrod.

"A double mastectomy. So, no more boobs?" asked Jarrod with a little cringe at what he had just said.

"No more boobs," stated Marianne.

"So what next?" asked Nadine. "Do you just go in for an operation and they take everything out and it's all over?"

"It's a big operation," said Marianne, very matter of fact. "They remove all of the breast tissue, they remove more lymph nodes. There's a risk of my arm being slightly paralysed where they remove the nodes. I'll then be able to get reconstructive surgery in a few months, but there might not be much they can do, the nipples will not survive the surgery."

"But you'll get the cancer out of your body," stated Jarrod, seeing the reasoning behind the decision. "There's no point in removing one breast, you might as well remove everything and with that you cannot possibly have breast cancer."

"That's how I see it," said Marianne,

"Wow, this is big," stated Nadine. They were all sitting around the end of the kitchen bench on the stools and there was a moment of silence, not an awkward moment, but a moment of reflection.

"We'll get there," said Marianne, putting one arm on Nadine's arm and her other on Jarrod's leg.

It was now Tuesday, Jarrod had been to drop the kids off at school and had then doubled back to home to get everyone else – Marianne choosing to stay at home instead of doing the teary airport run. Mass and Chloe were in the car all buckled in, Jarrod was finishing off the packing of the car, rearranging a few things, and then he sat in the driver's seat and enjoyed a good chat with his captive audience. Nadine and Marianne were getting louder and louder and then there was silence, Jarrod looking in his rear view mirror to see them in a big embrace, which seemed to last at least a minute. Jarrod took the opportunity to start the car to signal the end of the goodbyes. Nadine joined him in the passenger seat, eyes red but smiling, Marianne appeared at her window for one last kiss and they drove off, the back windows going down to let the kids wave to Marianne. It was a lovely moment, and Jarrod was happy that it wasn't being played out in public at Teesside Airport, with the risk of camera-happy onlookers.

The paparazzi was something that Jarrod rarely had to worry about these days, but it had not always been like this. Back at Gateshead in the early days with Marianne, when they were just married, they had somehow become the glamour couple of the North East football scene – Jarrod the dashing footballer, Marianne the fashion queen, the couple seen at every party of note around town.

This was simply because they scored an invite to everything, and the party scene was self-fulfilling. If you got an invite, you became famous, if you were famous, you'd get an invite, so the parties were a mix of semi-famous people like himself, not really that fussed if they were at the party or not, and people who were famous for simply being at all the parties, and who loved it. Driving around town or to the airport used to be fraught with dangers – jealous people, happy-snappers, who would bundle in front of a moving car to take a photo, newspaper journalists, and the bane of everyone's life, the paparazzi photographers.

There was always one at Newcastle airport, seemingly in a full-time role ready to snap anyone who was anyone for the local papers. Jarrod got to know him quite well – after all, there was no need to be on the wrong side of him, otherwise there was the risk of him sending in a dud photo. So, Jarrod learned to make sure he stopped for a photo, one time even seeking him out to embellish a story of him arriving back after getting a suspension at the FA, despite sporting a black eye.

The glamour couple tag soon went after the kids came along, and with it the party invites and the need to be seen, but they always had to be careful to look presentable or face the consequence of ending up on the front of the trashy mags with some made-up story alongside. The paparazzi didn't even know where he lived these days, the days of them casually waiting on his front wall before he left for training long gone. The drive to the airport was, therefore, an easy one, and there was no-one batting an eye at what looked like a couple with their kids walking through the airport. Jarrod gave the kids a big hug each and then saved the biggest one for Nadine. She had been a superstar, and Jarrod felt as though the love and warmth shown to him by his mate Reggie over the years was touching him in that final embrace. They all had a tear in their eyes, Jarrod feeling a drop welling up and falling down his cheek as they disappeared around the corner and into the short immigration line. Jarrod thought he saw a double flash, like that of a camera, at that moment, but couldn't be sure, and didn't think anything of it. Wouldn't be much of a photo anyway.

Jarrod found himself at home again, with plenty of time before training. Gary had given the first team squad the morning off. Marianne was ready and waiting when he returned, looking happy in her smart but casual outfit.

"Can you take me shopping?" she asked.

"Er, sure," said Jarrod, unsure of what this would entail. Marianne had never needed Jarrod around when it came to shopping. "Just let me get my gear ready for training."

They were in the car within five minutes.

"So, what are you shopping for?" asked Jarrod.

"I'd like to go to this shop in town that sells wigs," said Marianne, in a manner that suggested she had thought long and hard about it.

"Wigs?" asked Jarrod. "You want a wig?"

"Yes," said Marianne, very matter of fact. "Remember that I'm going to go through chemotherapy very soon, and it doesn't take long for your hair to fall out when that starts."

Jarrod had his eyebrows raised but was looking ahead at the road. He hadn't considered that, but it was definitely a reality. But a wig? Jarrod could see the fun in it, getting some crazy colours and mixing it up a bit. In fact, it might put a bit of spice in their lives, if that was ever going to be a thing while going through this.

"How about headscarves?" asked Jarrod. "I remember Jeannie, you know Felix's wife at Gateshead. She switched from a wig to a headscarf when she went through chemo for her cancer.

Looked great, you wouldn't have even realised."

Marianne had not considered that, and she knew that Jeannie was indeed a glamorous lady. She didn't say anything though, and they drove into town and found the hair salon, parked nearby and walked in. The owner was straight on her case, all the people in the salon having a hairdresser already fussing over them, and Jarrod browsed behind them as they chatted intently. This was surreal, even more surreal were the prices – some of the longer ones well over half way to a grand. That wasn't a concern, but what was more of a concern was the fact that Marianne was going to conceal her cancer journey. Jarrod felt a little contradictory, not having told his teammates, but he definitely thought it would be something worth knowing about yourself, instead of hiding away behind false hair and pretending you were not ill. Jarrod had lost a bit of concentration and sat down in one of the seats by the door. One of the ladies piped up.

"Jarrod Black, isn't it?" came the broad accent from an elderly lady, who had just had her hair washed, the grey hair as straight as it ever would be. "Club captain. Nice to see ye wearing something that shows off your muscles."

Jarrod smiled. He looked down at his top and it was indeed a tight t-shirt.

"If I was forty years older," Jarrod quipped in a broad Australian accent, with a grin.

"Eeeh, you cheeky sod!" came the reply, followed by a half-truth. "I'm not even old enough to be your Mam."

The lady turned to her fellow customers and they cackled and roared with laughter, Jarrod not able to catch what they were saying.

"Mind," she said, "you'd better get that hair cut, or you'll not be able to see the goal on Friday night."

Jarrod flicked aside the hair that actually was getting in the way a bit. Before he could say anything, the lady shouted.

"Margie! Can our Jarrod here get a hair cut? Margie!"

The owner, who had not drawn breath with Marianne since they walked in, was suddenly on the scene.

"Joan," she said, "are you making a scene again?"

"Whey no," she snapped back. "It's Jarrod here. He needs a haircut, don't you, Jarrod?"

Jarrod looked puzzled, just not sure as to what he was meant to reply. As bizarre moments go, this was definitely one of them, but everything was such a blur at the moment that he just couldn't help himself.

"Where am I going to sit?" he asked.

"Ye can sit here," said Joan, leaping to her feet. "I'll be a while anyway, waiting for me hair to dry."

Jarrod got to his feet and sat down in the warm seat. All eyes were on him. The hairdresser appeared with clippers in hand.

"We don't get men in here as a rule," she said. "But just this once, we'll make an effort for you."

Jarrod was strangely entertained. He smiled in the mirror back at the hairdresser.

"Number two back and sides," he said. "Leave a little on top, bit of gel, please."

"Ooh," said the hairdresser. "We do love a man who knows what he wants."

Marianne had come over to find out what the fuss was all about. The four ladies, who had been getting their hair done, had all crowded around and were starting to ask him questions. Why was he here? Why was his missus looking at wigs? Jarrod beckoned Marianne over to him and took her hands in his.

"This is Marianne, my wife," he said, squeezing her hands. "Marianne is just about to start chemotherapy to get rid of her breast cancer. We're looking at options for when her hair starts to fall out."

The ladies, and the hairdressers, were staring, open-mouthed at Jarrod, then at Marianne. Jarrod could feel the relief at talking about it.

"I'm sorry to hear about that pet," said one of the ladies. "It's not a nice time of your life, but you'll get through it."

"Aye," said another. "My Alison had breast cancer and had radiation therapy and chemo and all her hair fell out – eyebrows, fanny hair, everything!"

"And me sister-in-law, Anne," came another story. "She had a mastectomy, and then had the other one taken off too..."

Jarrod sat back and listened, still holding Marianne's hands. She was looking at him intently in the eyes, the ladies were all chuntering away around them, but they felt a close bond and it was a magical moment. Marianne joined in the conversation as the hairdresser started cutting Jarrod's hair. The owner came in with a tray carrying a teapot and some mugs, and they all talked their way through Jarrod's haircut, stopping briefly to admire the cut and to offer their opinion.

It was a shame when they had to go. Jarrod was keen not to be late after missing so much training recently, Marianne having bought nothing at all in the shop other than paying for

Jarrod's cut and tipping handsomely. They walked out arm in arm, Marianne putting her head against his shoulder and she waved at their new mates as they doubled back in front of the shop window.

Part Seven
Operate

Marianne had been out for a power walk with one of the school Mums, and Jarrod was getting ready to head to training. He had finally told everyone the night before about Marianne's cancer. He had waited until everyone had arrived, and with Gary's blessing, had convened the first team squad in the undercover section of the training complex, away from the youth players and out of earshot of anyone else.

The players had expected some sort of revving up before the big game on Friday, instead Jarrod started with a shaky voice and let everyone know the reason why he had been absent from training so much recently. The players listened without saying a word, some heads were bowed. Jarrod spelt it out, saying rather dramatically and perhaps unnecessarily that his wife was in danger and it was not guaranteed that she would make it through the journey.

This simple act of talking to the people that he spent the most time with was incredibly enlightening, and with a few tears starting to drop down his cheeks, he closed by thanking everyone for listening and hoping they could all pull together and make football the great distraction he hoped it would be. Jarrod got a few pats on the back, some heartfelt hugs, and tried to keep a smile on his face. Any fear that he had of dampening the mood was dispelled in the first five minutes of the training session, where there was a definite heightening of the senses and the players showed a steely resolve to get the job done in the most professional and efficient manner possible.

That was last night. Today they had media duty first up, and Jarrod was weighing up whether or not he should talk about it with the radio guys. The postman had been, and a few letters had dropped through the letter box. Marianne brought them in with her after coming in from her walk. One of the many junk mail flyers caught his eye – it was from the Younger Breast Cancer Network and was in there purely by chance. He picked it up and started to read. The wheels of thought started to churn in his head, and he could feel an idea forming. Marianne had breast cancer, she was doing the second of her charity fundraisers the following Friday, and he was sure the charity was another breast cancer trust. This could be a great opportunity to tap into his own audience and make a difference to a cause that was becoming something very close to home.

"Honey," he said, using a largely underused pet name that caused Marianne to double take. "You know that fundraiser you're doing next week?"

"Next week," she said, and thought for a moment before continuing. "I don't think I'll be up for much. I've told the golf club that I'm unlikely to make it."

"Oh," said Jarrod. "Okay. But, what's the charity you're fundraising for?"

"It's Breast Cancer Care," she said. "We've actually got three fundraisers in total, and they're all for different aspects of Breast Cancer. Quite ironic, really."

Jarrod seized the moment.

"You know, I'm talking to the radio today," said Jarrod. "And the guys from the local press. Do you think I should promote your fundraisers? I might need to break the news to the media though. Are you ready for that?"

"Ready for what?" came the reply.

"Ready to be in the spotlight again," suggested Jarrod. "And to be on the front pages of the papers again."

Marianne looked puzzled, she wasn't really following.

"If I break the news this morning," Jarrod said, and then continued softly, "then we can use that to promote your fundraiser and raise the profile a little."

"Do you think people would care?" she asked bluntly.

"I think people would be really interested, and really supportive," said Jarrod. "It would allow you to do your bit for a charity that will benefit cancer patients like you directly."

Breast Cancer Care was a charity with a focus of educating people on what to expect when going through breast cancer and a way of linking patients to resources. They had also just taken on their first Care Nurses, and Marianne had been fortunate enough to meet with one of them in the hospital when she'd had her recent op. The nurse was simply someone to ask questions to and someone who could offer a bit of advice about the practicalities of everyday life as a cancer patient, something that a doctor couldn't really do, and something Jarrod definitely couldn't offer.

"That's who Gharda works for," said Marianne. "She was a nurse at the hospital. I see where you're going with this now."

Marianne cracked a smile and nodded her head while thinking to herself.

"I'm meeting with our media guru first thing," said Jarrod. "I'll ask her if I should announce it today in my interview."

"Yes, do that!" exclaimed Marianne. "Can we maybe get some social media coverage too? This might make all the difference to this fundraiser. Imagine that, TV cameras at the event! A chance for our supporters to get some coverage on the news. I'm liking this."

Jarrod arrived at training, knowing he wouldn't be working up a sweat for at least another hour. Media duty was something he had grown to love, although only after having some very nervy moments in the early years. He would go in there with the sole purpose of portraying his club in a positive light, having been coached over the last twenty years on the subject by some very knowledgeable people.

If there was something negative in the news on the day of media duty, he knew it was his duty to put a positive spin on it and be forever the politician. This time, though, he had a different purpose, and he could feel his excitement. He knocked on Head of Media Pauline's door, which was usually open, and she answered, mobile phone pressed to her ear and beckoned him in. She was in full flight, gesticulating with her spare hand and giving some terse instructions to someone clearly not connected with Darlington. She still managed, though, to engage Jarrod with her eyes and somehow communicated to him to take a seat and that she would be a moment.

Jarrod listened without being able to decipher what the subject-matter was or who the unfortunate soul was on the other end of the phone, but they were sure getting a ticking off. The phone call ended abruptly with Pauline reverting to her business voice and thanking the caller courteously and ending with a cheery 'bye.'

"Jarrod," she said, checking that her phone call had actually ended. "Radio Newcastle are here as well as your friend Dominic, from Radio Tees. What are your thoughts for today?"

"Well," said Jarrod, preparing for a long spiel, "I have an agenda today."

"Go on," said Pauline with interest.

"Marianne, my wife…" he said, knowing fully that Pauline and Marianne knew each other, "…has breast cancer."

Pauline's face changed from inquisitive to slightly shocked. Jarrod continued.

"We decided to tell the team last night," he said. "To justify why I've been absent from training recently and just to let everyone know as a courtesy, so they don't find out from anyone else."

"Right…" said Pauline, unsure of where Jarrod was taking her.

"So," said Jarrod, shifting in his seat, "the news is out there, and I want it to become public so that: a, it comes from us and not some other source; and b, Marianne has a fundraiser happening next week, which just so happens to be for a breast cancer charity."

"And you want to turn a negative story into a positive. Love it," said Pauline, immediately grasping the storyline. "How does Marianne feel about this?"

"Marianne's good to go," said Jarrod truthfully, although he knew that she wouldn't understand the amount of fuss it would cause. "So, how do I bring it into the conversation with the radio guys?"

"Who do you think we should give the scoop to?" asked Pauline, referring to Jarrod's sometimes rocky relationship with Dominic Barrow of Radio Tees.

"Dominic will love it," said Jarrod. "Besides, he's always here. It wouldn't be right to give it to anyone else, especially that clown Kieran."

"Let me talk to Dominic first," said Pauline, looking at her watch and raising her eyebrows when she realised they were already a few minutes later than usual. "Give me two minutes, then come in. We'll start with football but move it quickly on to Marianne. Leave me to it."

"Okay," said Jarrod, and Pauline got up from her perched position on the corner of the desk and walked over to the door that took her into the soundproof 'studio.' She had a determined look on her face, and Jarrod felt confident she would make the right move. The door closed behind her, and Jarrod could hear nothing.

Jarrod gave it a few minutes and then made his way over to the door and knocked as hard as he could, knowing it was sometimes difficult to hear external noises from inside the room. The door opened, and it was Dominic.

"Jarrod, come in," he said, beckoning Jarrod in with a concerned look on his face, most unlike the cocky Dominic he was used to.

Jarrod walked in and was instructed to sit in the seat vacated by Pauline, who was happy to stand and take it all in. Dominic sat opposite, the microphone suspended from the ceiling. Jarrod could feel an electricity in the air. Pauline, who usually left them to it, didn't move. Dominic gave a few key words before starting his introduction. This was being recorded but would be going to air as soon as they could cut the recording into an edited segment.

"We're joined by Jarrod Black, captain of Darlington FC, freshly called up to the Socceroos squad for the upcoming friendlies and looking to lead Darlo to play off success on Friday at Crewe. Jarrod, how are preparations going for the big game?"

"Thanks for having me, Dominic," said Jarrod politely. "As you can imagine, games don't come much bigger than the play-offs.

After sitting in an automatic promotion spot for a good chunk of the season, and only missing out when our rivals played their catch up games, we're hungry for success. Preparations are going very well."

"We know the play-offs are effectively cup ties," stated Dominic. "How do the two results against Crewe already this season give you confidence going into these two games?"

The interview was risking entering the bland zone, and Jarrod felt the need to change the tone.

"We're the favourites for this one," answered Jarrod. "We're going on the attack in the first game to see if we can make the second game less nervy than these games usually tend to be."

Dominic nodded his head in approval.

"And your own preparation for this one," Dominic asked. "How are you feeling going into these vitally important games? I understand you've had a lot on your mind."

Dominic winked at him. Pauline rocked back on her heels in preparation for the answer. Jarrod would have the focus for as long as he wanted.

"You could say that, Dominic," he replied, before taking a deep breath and then continued, "it's been a tricky few weeks since my wife Marianne was diagnosed with breast cancer. She's going through quite a journey. We've been through numerous doctor's visits. She had surgery up in Newcastle, and now we're preparing for a major operation tomorrow that will hopefully give her a great chance of beating the disease."

"Wow," said Dominic. "That's a lot to be going through. How have your teammates reacted?"

"They've been amazing," said Jarrod, unsure of whether or not

Pauline had planted that one. "And, if anything, there's a resolve throughout the team. As if we're all in it together."

"That's great to hear," said Dominic. "How is Marianne, and how are the kids?"

"The kids are resilient," said Jarrod. "They know something is going on, but in reality, it's business as usual. Marianne's been keeping a low profile, but in a twist of fate, next week she is hosting a fundraiser for breast cancer at Northallerton golf club. Hopefully, she's up for it. Little did we know when she was organizing it that we would be needing the help of the Breast Cancer Care nurses, and I can testify that the cause is as wholesome as any charity we've ever been involved in."

"Well, if there's anything we can do to help," said Dominic, with sincerity, "let us know. Northallerton golf course is one of my favourites. I'll look forward to the invite."

"Consider it done," said Jarrod with a smile that came across in his voice, "hopefully we'll be getting ready for the play-off final by then."

That gave Dominic that required route back to football, which he happily accepted.

"All this happening while you get a call up to the Australia team," he said. "Are you surprised to be back in the fold?"

"Yes, wow, what a blast!" said Jarrod. "It's been many years since I pulled on the green and gold jersey, and I had effectively retired. This is such an honour, especially at my age."

"Age is just a number," said Dominic rather cheesily. "You've definitely made a difference this year and for that, on behalf of the supporters, we thank you for what has been a fabulous first season in the Football League. This has surely surpassed all expectations."

"Not really," said Jarrod. "I didn't come here to flounder around in mid-table, I came here to help Darlington establish themselves as a front runner in League Two. If anything, we've underperformed. We should have finished in the top three. We should already be on our summer holidays."

"Positive talk there from Jarrod Black." Dominic was wrapping up. "Thanks for joining us, and we wish you every success on the field. You have the best wishes of all of our listeners as you and your wife navigate a difficult time. Good luck tomorrow, and we'll chat again before the end of the season."

"Thanks."

Pauline had her hands together on her chest and seemed to have held on to her breath for the whole interview, Dominic threw off his headphones and swiveled his chair on an angle to face her.

"Thanks Jarrod," he said. "That's big news. Thanks for sharing it with us."

Jarrod stood up and shook Dominic's hand, holding on for an extra second when he realised that Dominic had no intention of letting go either. Pauline stood and organised them into a photo pose, clicking away on her fancy camera. Jarrod felt as though he had done a good thing. Pauline walked towards the door and opened it for Jarrod to follow her through. Wes Kellehar was on the other side of the door and they met with a hug as Wes made his way through to see Dominic and take the hot seat. The door closed, and Pauline turned and grabbed Jarrod's hand and placed her other hand on top.

"Jarrod," she said, with heavy eyes. "I'll only say this once, as I know you're going to hear it from many, many people over the next few days. If there is anything I can do for you and Marianne to help you through this, just let me know. We're all here to help."

Jarrod was taken aback and could sense that there was a story behind that. Perhaps she had been affected by illness in the past, or a family member had been through the same thing, but Jarrod could feel a sincerity in her voice.

"Thanks," said Jarrod. "That means a lot."

Jarrod left Pauline in her office and went to grab a bite to eat from the café before heading off to training. He knew the terrain had changed and that by the time training had finished, Radio Tees would have run their piece and it would be a topic of conversation. Pauline would have put those photos on social media too, and the wheels would be in motion for a wave of interest.

Jarrod wasn't sure if he was mentally prepared, but he knew that he would be giving it his all in the training session, knowing he had an afternoon with the surgeon to come and a nervous evening with Marianne awaiting the surgery tomorrow. Anyway, he had to be mentally prepared – he wasn't the one going through it, and he knew he had to be strong.

Marianne and Jarrod arrived at Dr Groez' office well in advance of their scheduled 2pm appointment, and despite being hyperactive with nerves, they found solace in being early and able to calm themselves before seeing the doctor. It also gave them a chance to have a chat with Harriet, the receptionist, who was quite possibly the most positive person you could ever meet. Harriet commented that Marianne was looking so much more relaxed than she did the last time they had been in, and Marianne was clearly moved to hear that. Harriet knew the whole picture, and she suddenly realised that she could probably save them a bit of time by signing a few more forms for the next day's operation. It took her a moment to find the paperwork, going against the logical order of patients, and she guided them through the papers.

"So, Dr Groez will measure you for the inserts," she said. "We have a range in stock here, so we should be able to fit you straight away tomorrow."

Jarrod and Marianne looked at each other before Jarrod spoke.

"So, as part of the surgery, there's inserts too?"

"Oh, yes," said Harriet. "That's the way we do it these days – you'll be under anaesthetic anyway," she said turning to Marianne. "Dr Groez can do the inflatable inserts after the mastectomy is done."

"So..." stuttered Jarrod. "So, Marianne will still have boobs?"

Harriet smiled.

"Yes, Marianne will still have boobs," she confirmed.

That was amazing news. They had expected the mastectomy to leave Marianne flat-chested, or at worst, concave before the reconstructive surgery later down the line. Spirits were, therefore, quite high, even before Dr Groez came out to greet them.

Dr Groez appeared from his room with a lady who was around the same age and had just found out the same news Marianne had found out a couple weeks before. She was clearly not in a good frame of mind, and in the crossover time between finishing the paperwork for the operation, and the lady completing her own forms, Marianne struck up a conversation. The lady kept a stiff upper lip, but Jarrod could tell that she was a broken woman. Marianne wished her luck and there was an acknowledging smile of support as she left, and Marianne and Jarrod were ushered in to Dr Groez's office.

The first thing Dr Groez did was drain the lymphatic fluid from Marianne's wound and checked out the area around the breast, with a risk of infection the main worry in the lead up to this major operation. He was happy with the healing and stated that she was sufficiently recovered to undergo the next surgery. She was measured for the prosthetic inflatable inserts she would receive in the operation, and then Marianne settled down next to Jarrod to chat about the operation and the procedure in detail.

It turned out that Marianne would be inflated straight away, not fully, but partially, and with pictures of previous operations being shown, Jarrod and Marianne were amazed that she would actually come out of hospital with a reasonable set of breasts. This still hadn't sunk in, as Marianne had read everywhere it would be a number of months before the reconstruction and had forewarned Jarrod of the fact. With potentially a whole day in surgery tomorrow, Marianne was relieved this was a quick visit. Dr Groez's positive and relaxed attitude was matched by Harriet as he showed them out to the waiting room; the next patient having arrived and already acknowledged. Marianne left with her head held high and her chest puffed out. All Jarrod could think was a mixture of 'wow, what a woman' and 'damn, she's hot.'

They were back in Darlington in time to pick up the kids from school. Marianne had organised with another Mum that if she wasn't there, could she take Seb and Aneka home, but they arrived right on pick up. Marianne jumped out of the car at the gates as Jarrod drove a loop to join the pick-up queue. When the kids bundled noisily into the back of the car with their oversized bags squeezed through the doors, Jarrod could feel the return to normality, and he knew that he would have to savour this last night of relative calm before they moved on to the next new normal.

Jarrod thought about suggesting dinner out, but then remembered that Marianne would not be eating anything before the op, so he kept that one to himself. Aneka filled them all in about her day at school, Marianne was smiling and laughing at her stories and Jarrod put his hand on her knee and squeezed.

The evening was great fun, Marianne and Jarrod making the most of their time as a family and despite the kids being aware of what was coming up, the enormity of the situation was totally lost on them. Marianne ended up in bed with Seb, scratching his back as he went to sleep, just like the good old days, as the rain started to bounce off the window sill. Jarrod read Aneka a story, something that he loved to do, and then they talked through what was happening tomorrow. He explained the logistics of who was taking them to school, and that they had to be up early, and after school they were going to Gabby Robson's house and Jarrod would pick them up from there after dinner. Jarrod knew that Aneka had already been through all this with Marianne and was supremely confident Aneka would remember everything.

Then Jarrod explained what was happening to Marianne, how she was getting her boobs removed and replaced with new boobs, and she would be in hospital until, at least, the weekend. And, of course, Daddy was away the next day and they would be sleeping over at Gabby's on Friday night, which Jarrod knew would fill Aneka with excitement. Jarrod felt prepared and gave Aneka a big hug before turning out the light and leaving her to settle down to sleep. He walked into Seb's room and woke up Marianne, who had predictably fallen victim to the back-scratcher's curse, and they finished off cleaning up together and made sure they went to bed together, not a mobile phone in sight. It was quite an emotional night, without really talking about the operation, and feeling very connected.

Marianne had been advised to be at the hospital at 6.15am; Dr Groez had one operation for the day and that was Marianne. The fact that it was so early told Jarrod it was going to be a long one. Jarrod had budgeted for five hours, so he calculated that, if it started at 7.30, Marianne would be in recovery at 12.30 and would be out by 1.30. Jackie, the admin lady at work, had organised her Mum Cheryl to come over to kindly look after the kids in the morning and get them to school. All this extra organizing was taking quite a bit of effort, and Jarrod had assumed the role of keeping tabs of who was helping out when. He had already made the call that there was no way of making training that day and was feeling guilty about leaving the team to prepare for tomorrow's game without him.

The roads were completely empty at such an early hour. They arrived at the hospital around six and waited a short while to be called up to the ward. After another short wait in the ward waiting room, they were shown to Marianne's room. She was told to strip off, wear the paper surgical pants she was given and get her gown on, one of those backwards gowns that are impossible to do up. She would then wait on the bed. It was quite a nervy wait while all the pre-op checks were undertaken, lots of questions over and over again to make sure Marianne was ready, and blood pressure checks, and an injection.

A series of different medical staff called in to the room, and finally Marianne was wheeled up to surgery. Jarrod left her at the door with a kiss, and with the customary wave and thumbs up, now a family ritual. Jarrod went into Marianne's room to settle in for the wait, but before he did, he stopped at the ward reception to ask their opinion about how long the op would take.

"To be honest with you," said the male nurse on the reception at the time, who was filling in some forms, "you're not going to be much use here. I'll give you the direct number here and you can call at about midday to find out how things are going."

"Thanks..." said Jarrod, while his brain started to calculate, and the nurse wrote down the number on a yellow sticky note. "I'll do that."

It was still early. Training wasn't on until 9.30 and he would easily make it there and back. What if the hospital needed to contact him though? He had given the number of the football club, but he would be an hour away if he was needed. He was torn between his club and his wife, and it didn't sit well with him. He quickly made his way to the car and set off over the bridge and through the traffic building up with the morning rush. He resisted the urge to call home in Australia. The time difference was not in his favour, so he instead made a couple of quick calls, one to Cheryl to see how it was going, and another to Gabby Robson's Mum Pippa, to check that everything was in place for tonight's pick up from school.

He was at a junction heading in to deepest Gateshead when he got the urge to take a different route and ended up fifteen minutes later pulling in to the graveled driveway of the guest house where he had lodged for a few months upon arrival from Australia all those years ago. He had kept in touch with the owner Doris while he was at Gateshead; he had even made himself available for meet and greets at the airport and train station for new players going to stay at the guest house, just so he could sit down for a cuppa with Doris. She was his English Mum, and ever since she had forced him and Reggie to clean out their rooms before they moved into their swanky pad, he had the utmost respect for her. He hadn't seen her this year though, not since he had left for Darlington, and he felt guilty walking through the crunchy gravel to the front door.

That feeling of guilt disappeared when he saw the look of happiness in Doris's face when he walked into the dining room. She was clearing up after breakfast but put down the plates she was carrying and made a huge fuss.

"Hello stranger!" she exclaimed. "Wonders never cease!"

They went in for a big, warm hug and it felt like the hugs he got from his Mum.

"I know, I know," he said, backing away. "I've not been to see you for a while."

"Whey," she said in her thick accent, "ye're not playing for the Heed any more are ye?"

Jarrod started to stack up plates on one of the tables and Doris didn't stop him. She got back to what she was doing, and there was a mutual understanding that if they divided the task, it would free up time to have that cuppa. Jarrod rinsed the plates in the big sink and started to stack the dishwasher, while Doris brought the rest of the stuff in from the dining room and took fresh cutlery and napkins out to the tables in readiness for dinner. Jarrod knew where the tea was and had already made a pot by the time Doris had finished the cleanup and setup.

"You're a good boy, aren't you?" she said, referring to either the cleaning up, the tea-making, or the fact he was there at all.

"Doris," said Jarrod. "Marianne's in hospital getting a big operation. Right now. I didn't know where to go while she's in there."

"I heard it on the radio yesterday," said Doris.

"Ah, yes, you would have done," said Jarrod, knowing the segment would be repeated throughout the region.

"Having a sickness in the family is not an easy time," said Doris. "Priorities are different and the things you found important beforehand just seem so trivial."

"I just don't know where my head is at the moment," Jarrod admitted. He hadn't taken the time to talk like this since Marianne had broken the news. "There's so much going on. Life seems to be writing its own path and I'm just along for the ride. I don't feel in control."

Doris pondered for a second then spoke softly, reaching out to put her hands on Jarrod's.

"You can't be in control of this one," she said. "You're just going to have to go with it. You can't decide the outcome, but you can decide how you and Marianne cope with this. You've got beautiful kids who are growing up fast, and you've got lots of support around you. You'll be surprised by the amount of human kindness that comes out in situations like this."

"You're right," said Jarrod. "The school and the parents have been so understanding. The club have been amazing. Both our families and Reggie's family have gone to massive lengths to help us."

"So, be thankful for all that love," she said. "Don't be shy if you need something. There's always someone who can help, and it's not always the people you expect."

Jarrod had no idea that Doris had been a social worker in the past, but he knew her harsh exterior masked a warm and loving heart. They talked for a good hour, reminiscing about his time at the house, filling her in about Reggie and his family, and he could even feel himself welling up at one point when he was talking about leaving Marianne at the operating theatre door. They ended the conversation when a delivery of fruit and veg from the local greengrocer turned up. The delivery man breezed in to the kitchen with two big boxes and exited after a quick 'hiya' and a wink. Jarrod still had time to kill, but he knew that Doris would have plenty to do, and they finished up.

"Doris," he said as they stood up and hugged, "I love talking to you. You make everything seem better."

"Aaah," she sighed. "Stay positive and be there for your wife. Your kids need you too and make sure you keep a level head. Pass on my love to Marianne, and good luck tomorrow for the big match."

Jarrod felt so much better now than when he'd left Marianne. He felt vindicated in his decision not to head back to Darlington for training and the mild panic he had worked himself into had gone. He made his way back to the hospital and up into the ward, where he took a seat in the waiting room and started to check his phone. He had, as usual, missed a hatful of phone calls and there were a lot of messages too. So, he used the time to get stuck into them. A lot were well-wishers, there were a few from Marianne's family in France, and one from Dad. A quick check of the news saw that Jarrod was on the main page of the news websites, and then a broader check found a preview of tomorrow's game which hooked him in and he got lost in time.

"Mr Black?" came a question, which startled him out of his concentration.

"Yes," said Jarrod, looking up at the male nurse from earlier in the morning.

"Marianne has completed her surgery, and is being moved now to recovery," he stated.

"Oh, thanks," said Jarrod, straightening himself up. "How did it go?" He didn't expect to get anything concrete by way of a reply.

"Sounds positive," said the nurse. "But you'll be in for a good hour's wait before Marianne wakes up and can come out of recovery.

"Okay," said Jarrod. "Am I okay to sit here?"

"Sure," said the nurse. "It might be a long wait."

Jarrod took the hint and went off to get a bite to eat, by now knowing the hospital quite well and knowing where to find the cafeteria.

Jarrod went back up at one o'clock and went straight to Marianne's room. It ended up being well after two when she finally came out, and there was a bustling as the door was opened and the bed wheeled in to the empty room. Jarrod stood up. Marianne was not in a good way, unable to speak, unable to close her mouth, dry around the lips, and totally spaced out. There were a multitude of tubes and wires, and Jarrod could sense some sympathetic looks from the nurses as they caught the look of concern on his face. Clearly there had been a tube in her throat and she was struggling to swallow and had no confidence in moving her head. Her eyes were trained on him and she was looking pleadingly at him as if he should be doing something about her discomfort. Jarrod had no idea what to say but started anyway in the absence of any words from Marianne.

"Thirsty?" he said. She nodded her head ever so slightly. One of the nurses nodded at Jarrod and tilted her chin towards the bed. He poured from the jug into one of the plastic glasses and offered it to Marianne. She had no intention of moving her arms, but he quickly realised why the straws were there and put one in the water and held it to her mouth. The water level quickly drained, life flickering into Marianne's eyes and he went to add more water, and again this was demolished in three or four goes.

"Can you talk at all?" he asked, trying to coax a word from her.

The pained look on her face gave the answer, so he continued.

"Just let me know when you've had enough."

This continued for half an hour. Jarrod basically talking to himself, throwing in a few questions just in case Marianne was ready to engage. Her eyes followed him, and they were getting brighter by the minute. Nurses were in and out, not that Jarrod really noticed. It was like one of those time-lapse videos where everyone else is beavering around in double time, but they were at normal speed. A few words were then uttered, Jarrod sitting his wife up a little and pushing in another pillow behind her neck, and Marianne started to loosen up. The push-button morphine dispenser was getting regular pumps on the button. Dr Groez came in to see how things were tracking, having changed into his civilian clothes after the surgery.

"Hello Jarrod," he said cheerily. "Everything has gone well. The procedure was a long one, but the double mastectomy is done, and we have the expanders in there. No chance of saving the nipples, but as I hope you'll agree, the result is pretty damn good."

"Thanks so much, doctor," said Jarrod, firmly shaking the hand that had just been carving and stitching his wife. "What sort of timeframe do we have for getting out of hospital?"

"Early days, yet," said Dr Groez. "It'll be a couple of days, at least. We'll see how things are going tomorrow. Your wife is very fit, that makes a big difference to the recovery."

"Thanks," said Jarrod, not really sure what to say. "We'll be taking all your advice."

Dr Groez checked over the notes on the clipboard at the end of the bed, and bid them both goodnight; making sure Marianne had no questions, instructing Jarrod to keep up the good work.

He walked out before taking a step back and leaning in past the door.

"Good luck tomorrow night."

Jarrod smiled. Marianne looked at him with a withering look that suggested she could never be the focus of attention for more than a few minutes without Jarrod stealing it back. Jarrod didn't like that and would never intentionally take the spotlight off his wife, and he hoped that Marianne would know that. At that moment, though, he felt like he had done just that, and his smile turned quickly into an apologetic look of sympathy.

"If there's anything you need, darl, you let me know," he said, and Marianne nodded and stared at him intently.

It was Friday morning. Jarrod had left Marianne at about eight last night – she had eaten some dinner at the hospital and was settled. He conformed to the normal visiting hours and made tracks for home, mentally exhausted, but physically in good shape. The pick-up at the Robson's was quite late, so he refused the offer of dinner but was glad when he was pushed to take a dish home with a big serving of leftover pasta bake, just what he felt he needed. The kids had enjoyed a great afternoon, the biggest surprise being Seb saying he'd had a great time. Aneka explained that Seb had a crush on Michaela, the Robsons' older daughter who was a few months older than him, and they had spent all evening in her room after dinner. This caused such a ruckus in the car, Seb frantically reaching behind him to try and get her to stop talking, but Jarrod was loving it. Total normality in a time when nothing was normal.

This morning had been tough getting the kids out of bed when they had not slept for long enough. Jarrod got himself ready for his long day, packing his bag at the same time as the kids packed theirs for the night. Jarrod checked in with the hospital, to see if everything was okay and was put through to Marianne, who was full of zing. She asked Jarrod to call back for a video chat, and the kids gathered round as the video came on the screen of their Dad's phone.

Marianne looked great, still a bit white in the face, but looking much better than she had when he had left her last night. They exchanged kisses and Marianne wished everyone a great day before Jarrod signalled it was school time and clapped his hands twice to make the kids focus on the final tasks before school. They were having a sleepover, so they had each packed an overnight bag, Seb's a Gateshead bag and Aneka's a small wheeled suitcase in a lilac colour. Jarrod would hand these over to Pippa when he saw her at school drop off. Jarrod had his own Darlington bag with a change of clothes and his toiletries, and was in full squad gear, ready for the journey to Crewe and the upcoming game.

Jarrod walked into the school gates with his old Gateshead sports bag, wheeling the flowery suitcase behind him, but somehow still getting away with it, looking trim and professional in his Darlington gear. He kissed the kids goodbye, Seb running off to join a football game that was developing on the grass, while Aneka kept close, unable to draw herself away from her Dad for fear of missing something. Pippa had walked in just behind them, and Gabby ran straight towards Aneka, put her arm around her and they walked off arm in arm into the throng, Michaela straggling in behind, looking awkwardly cool and giving Jarrod a wave. The Robsons had been so good to Jarrod and Marianne when they first moved to the school – they were an unassuming couple, Pippa and Richard, who kept well and truly to themselves. Their two girls, though, were the life and soul of the school, and Jarrod had unconsciously drifted towards their parents to make conversation when they were at their first school event. Richard ran a security firm, and Pippa was a physiotherapist. It was only when Jarrod ran in to Richard working at the Arena at a night time game, marshalling some stewards, that the friendship bloomed. When Marianne confided in Pippa what she was going through, she declared an open door policy – help whenever it was needed, and Marianne took her up on the offer.

"Thanks so much, Pippa," said Jarrod, handing over the bags, "can you guess which one is which?"

"These metro pre-teens," sighed Pippa. "You just never know..."

"Purple is the new black," said Jarrod. "It's probably full of contraband anyway."

"Ah, good," said Pippa. "I've been waiting for a new shipment to pass on to my distributors."

"Only the best, straight off the boat," stated Jarrod. It was a peculiar conversation that continued for a while, both Jarrod and Pippa not sure if the other was being smart, sarcastic, or taking the mickey, and Jarrod finally ended the bizarre conversation.

"I've no idea what we're talking about, but thanks for looking after the kids tonight. I'll be there in the morning at ten-thirty to take Seb to football."

Jarrod arrived at the Arena and parked his car, trotting over to the reception, knowing he was close to nine o'clock and risking a fine for being late. They weren't leaving until after ten anyway, but rules were rules. A number of players had fallen foul of the team fines system, especially early on in the season when the severity of the fines hadn't been experienced. It all started with Will Telfer's five-pound fine for a foul throw in a pre-season game. Will did not believe he had to pay it. That was when goalkeeper Wes introduced the rule, unopposed, of incurring a fine for not paying a fine within two days. It was light-hearted fun in the first instance and totally unofficial, and there were comical fines such as for foul throws or shots that went out for a throw-in.

There was also a serious edge to it – simple rules that needed to be put in place in order for the team to function as a team, and timekeeping was up there as one of the first rules in place, with the harshest of penalties. Connor Naughton, for example, was slapped with a twenty-pound fine for rocking up half an hour late to a team dinner in pre-season, and for a player breaking through from the youth team, that was not a small amount to pay. The system seemed to have been cemented as accepted policy after the final pre-season game when Raynor Gunn was fined a fiver for a needless foul that led to a penalty, then copped another ten for getting a yellow card for dissent in the aftermath.

Jarrod had never been in a team that implemented such a policy, and with Wes keeping a log book of indiscretions, there was no getting away with it, and no way of avoiding the sanction. No one, though, had decided what was going to happen to the bulging pot of money at the end of the season, but Jarrod knew he didn't want to contribute any more to it than he already had.

The whole squad was there, Jarrod coming through the door and pointing at the digital clock that read 8:59:52 as heads began to turn. Jarrod shook hands with all his teammates. That was another of the things he liked to do, and that went right back to growing up in Australia. It was social etiquette for the men to shake hands with all the men in a group, and then fumble when working out whether to shake hands with the women, kiss them on the cheek, or do nothing at all. He shook everyone's hand though, including the admin staff, ladies included. There were a few quick questions about Marianne, which Jarrod quickly answered before Jackie appeared and got everyone's attention.

"Great to see everyone," she started. "We're heading to Crewe today. The bus leaves at 10am. First, we're going to have a team meeting in the boardroom, please drop any bags you have by the front door and we'll see you up there in five minutes."

This was all very serious. As captain of the team, Jarrod was usually up to speed with any discussions, but a 'team meeting' was usually something that had been called to pass on some information from the board or from owner Gerry Lincoln. Jarrod was intrigued and so were his teammates. They all filed up the stairs and into the boardroom, a room they rarely visited, and the high-backed chairs gave it a grandiose feel. Gerry was there with his three-man entourage, and encouraged the players to take a seat, or find a spot to stand if there were none left. When everyone was in and the door closed, he started.

"I wanted to bring everyone in today to thank you all for your efforts this season. Whilst we have missed out on our ultimate goal of automatic promotion, the end result can still be achieved over these next three games."

There was no hesitation to say three games, and barring a disaster, they would surely be playing three games.

"Crewe Alexandria, a club steeped in tradition like ourselves," he continued as he looked around at the players, "a proud member of the Football League for nearly 150 years, stand in our way of a play-off final at Wembley."

He paused to swallow and regain his composure.

"Wembley. That place where magic happens in the FA Cup final, where England plays their home games, where a crowd of 80,000 singing Abide With Me can send a tingle down your spine."

He was at risk of going off topic.

"Who doesn't want to play at Wembley?" he asked rhetorically, and Jarrod was glad that no-one responded.

"Darlington FC wants to play at Wembley, that's for sure. So do Crewe Alexandria. We've got to want it more tonight. We've got to take our league form and stamp our authority in this first leg and give our fans a celebration in the second leg here on Tuesday."

"Are we all in agreement?"

That was semi-rhetorical, and Jarrod saved everyone's uncertainty by blurting out, "'Kin oath!" That brought roars of laughter and lightened the mood considerably. Gerry continued once the din had subsided.

"So, as an incentive..." he started, then louder to take control of the room again, "As an incentive, our sponsors are going to pay every person in this room one thousand pounds if we make it through to Wembley."

Jarrod did a quick headcount and that was a shit-load of money for a League Two team to be forking out. There was a look of approval from everyone. The bonuses this season had been good with a high number of wins and lots of goals scored, but this was taking it to a new level.

"What's more," he said. "Everyone in this room will receive two thousand pounds when we win the play-off final."

That set the tongues wagging. That was an extra three weeks wages for some, and an extra nine weeks for others. For Jarrod it was still a nice gesture, but the money was not the incentive for him, it was the fact that winning would give some of the younger players an absolute windfall to go with the accolades of winning the play-offs.

"Finally, lads," said Gerry, pausing for effect, "go out there and do your fans proud. It's not a very big stadium down there, but we've got about one-fifth of the tickets and they're all sold out. Make sure they leave happy tonight. See you down there."

Gerry stood up, his colleagues following suit, and they picked up their papers and walked to the door. An impromptu round of applause started, and he was visibly delighted. It continued well after they had left the room and some players were hi-fiving each other and a murmur came over the team. The scene had been well and truly set, the stakes had been raised, and despite a good four hours on a coach to come, this would surely set the mood for a victory tonight.

The Gresty Road turf was absolutely pristine when they walked out after getting off the coach, some two and a half hours before kick-off. The red seats and the red stands contrasted against the lush green grass made it seem a lot bigger than it was. It would look a lot more compact when the red seats had people sitting in them, and a sea of black and white would disguise the red at one end of the stadium. Indeed, by the time they came to walk out for a warm up, the Darlington end was already looking quite busy. The days of spending the evening in the pub until one minute to kick-off were long gone now that you could buy beer in the stadium – entrance in to any stadium always took a long time just before kick-off anyway.

Jarrod came out to a cheer and made his way over to the Darlington end, applauding as he went, which kept the cheers going. Wes had been out for a good ten minutes already, collecting high balls from coach Des Davis, who was lifting in some beautiful crosses. The sun was disappearing behind the nearby buildings, bringing an unseasonable chill to the air. The appearance of Gary to the pitch made everyone run into the section marked off with cones and start the warm up routine, two lines running through the standard set of exercises, culminating in a couple of sprints that got the lungs working and the blood flowing to the thighs.

The chants started coming up from the home end, followed immediately by some defiant songs in return. The atmosphere was growing, and the game was less than half an hour away. Jarrod could feel nerves in his stomach, taking him back to athletics carnival at school when he would always feel queasy before a race. Walking back down the tunnel he had the urge to go to the toilet but knew that it was just nerves. He knew that a little bit of nervous energy before the game was a good thing, and he embraced the feeling. Jarrod felt in control once again, and life outside of football was taking a pause for the next two hours.

The noise at kick-off was riotous. Both sets of fans had started to wind each other up, and a funny chant about Wes's unfashionable gravy-brown goalkeeping attire had his teammates laughing as they lined up to shake hands "He's brown and he's staying down..." rung through the stadium bringing a smile to everyone's face. Jarrod won the toss of the coin and elected to 'stay as we are' so Darlington would be shooting towards their own fans in the second half, a tactic only reversed when trying to rile up the opposition, or on a really windy day.

The blast on the whistle signalled the start of the game, and Crewe gave a taste of things to come by laying it back to the defence from the kick-off and then back to the keeper before launching the ball long down the left wing to no-one in particular, Mitch Short watching the ball out of play. There was a swagger already to Darlington. Sam Basaan won a ball in defence and feigned to play the ball backwards before skipping past the lunging tackle and setting off down the left. Dean Minto called to let him know he was covering, allowing Sam to take on his man and head for the byline. A clever drag back took out the defender and allowed Sam to steady himself for a cross with his weaker right foot, the ball taking the tiniest of glances off the defender at the near post, taking it just beyond the reach of the in-rushing Jarrod's head and also just past the outstretched right foot of Ghali Barbera at the far post.

That was a great moment that lifted the team immediately, the ball trickling out for a corner on the far side. Connor Naughton went across to take the set-piece as Jarrod trotted over to the corner of the box. He was distracted, though, by the Darlington bench. There was a flurry of activity, as if Darlington were getting ready to make a substitution, and he could see Jackie talking to Gary and the manager was not concentrating on the game in his usual way. Connor's corner was swung over viciously, evading Will Telfer at the far post and ended up bouncing out of play on the far side for a throw in. Jarrod turned again to see what was happening in the dugout. Gary called him over with a 'come to me, quickly' hand signal and Jarrod raced over to the sideline, standing sideways a metre from the line, ready to run back

"Jarrod," said Gary in a nervous tone. "It's Marianne, she's taken ill. You need to get home."

Jarrod did a double-take, his shoulders slumped and he looked at Jackie, who was at Gary's side, lips pursed and emotionless. The substitution board was being prepared and Jackie simply nodded her head as if to say, 'it's time.' Jarrod turned and gave the rolling arms signal to the assistant referee that a substitution was required. The flag was straight up, the referee quick to see it as the home team were still preparing to take the throw in, and Jarrod took the two steps off the field, clasping hands with his replacement Jack Thomas as they passed, the murmur of a bemused crowd turning to surprise when the board went up and the change was confirmed.

Jarrod stood with Jackie for a moment and the crowd was quiet, not a single acknowledgement for Thommo as he made his way across to the far side.

"Let's walk," said Jackie, and they made their way down the tunnel, bypassing the traditional high fives on the bench. "Marianne is in Intensive Care. She's had a reaction to her pain medication and her blood pressure is low. We need to get you to her."

Jackie had a serious and determined look. Jarrod didn't know what to say and was totally dumbfounded. They walked together to the dressing room, Jackie opening the door for Jarrod who made his way straight to his bag and sat down.

"Don't waste any time," said Jackie. "Just grab your bag and let's go."

Jarrod did as he was told, grabbing his shoes from just inside the wooden alcove that was his space, picking up his bag, and walking back out the door closely followed by Jackie. Jackie then led the way out of the stadium, past some surprised reception staff and into the car park, where a taxi was waiting. Jackie offered the front seat to Jarrod, but they both ended up sitting in the back when Jarrod realised that Jackie was coming with him.

"Can I speak to Marianne?" asked Jarrod.

"No," was the reply. Jackie was being a tower of strength and making things easy for Jarrod. "She is in Intensive Care and she's not awake at the moment."

"When did this happen?" asked Jarrod.

Jackie thought for a moment, as if thinking of the right reply and not the truthful reply.

"Just before kick-off," she said. "We heard from the hospital just as you were warming up to start the game. We made a few calls, got the taxi ready, and decided that you'd had better get back to the hospital straight away."

"It's a four hour' drive," said Jarrod. "Are we taxiing all the way?"

"I've called in a few favours," said Jackie. "I'm just waiting on some calls back."

Jarrod was scared. He didn't know what to do. Four hours from the hospital and no way of knowing what situation he would be in when he got there. Jarrod was more than aware of the network that exists between clubs, managers, and to a lesser extent, players. He was interested to know who was involved and what could be the favours that had been sought.

"Where are we heading?" he asked, hoping that it was straight to Newcastle.

"Manchester airport," said Jackie. "Gerry has a friend with a plane and is trying to contact him."

"Wow," said Jarrod. "That's awesome!"

Jarrod took the time to change out of his boots and into his trainers and put on his training top. The journey to the airport would take at least 45 minutes. He got busy on his phone, ringing Marianne's brother, who would pass on the news to his mother-in-law, to Nadine, and then his Mum. It was all very brief, just filling them in on the little facts he knew. He put his phone down on the seat and put his head back on the head rest before grabbing his phone suddenly and ringing Pippa to fill her in on what was happening.

Jackie asked the taxi driver to flick through the radio stations to find the commentary of the game, hoping to take Jarrod's mind off the situation. He flicked around the dial before a crackly station came on; the name Telfer immediately catching both their attentions. Darlington had just gone close and were piling on the pressure, according to the commentary, heavy accent and all. The half-time break had been and gone before they arrived at Manchester Airport. Jackie made a call and then looked despondently at Jarrod.

"No plane," she said, and without pausing to even think. "Plan B then."

"If you don't mind just driving around to the train station, please," she said to the taxi driver, "there's a direct train in eight minutes to Newcastle."

Jarrod looked at Jackie in disbelief. As if a train would get him home quicker than commandeering this taxi and driving right in to the driveway of the hospital.

"Trust me," said Jackie. "I'll leave you here. Get a ticket and get on the train, stand by for a call."

"Is this for real?" he said. Jackie just shooed him out of the taxi and the taxi sped off back to Crewe, leaving Jarrod to race up to the train station concourse. There was no queue at this time of day and he bought his ticket, racing down to the platform with 30 seconds to spare.

Sitting on a train with no way of speeding things up and no way of getting to the destination any quicker had a calming effect on Jarrod, when anyone else might start getting impatient at every delay and every stop along the way. His phone rang, and it was Jackie.

"Get off the train at Huddersfield," she said. "There will be someone waiting."

That was all she said, not even waiting for an acknowledgement, but Jarrod was quick to give her an 'okay.' That was about half an hour away by now and his mind was swirling. He tuned in his phone to Radio 5 live and hoped for some commentary. His luck was in, being a night with only one game, and there was crystal clear commentary from Gresty Road. Darlington had apparently equalised with a penalty after an own goal had given Crewe the lead, and the game was entering the latter stages. A draw would be enough, though, but a win was expected. The draw would sow the seed of doubt in everyone's mind. Jarrod found himself motionless on the train, transfixed by the action through his headphones. It wasn't long before the game was over, a 1-1 draw lauded as a massive success for Crewe, and a result that kept the tie alive.

The post-match comments were all about the home team and how well they had done, and there were plenty of comments about the mysterious early substitution of their captain. Jarrod's phone buzzed with a message to snap him out of his concentration, luckily it did as he was pulling in to Huddersfield station. It was a message from Dean Minto, telling him that the whole team was thinking of him and wishing him the best.

The train rolled in slowly to the platform, and Jarrod positioned himself at the door to make a swift exit, opening the door as soon as it unlocked and jumping down onto the platform with a quick glance around to get his bearings.

"Jarrod?" came a voice from nowhere.

"Yes," said Jarrod, to no-one in particular until he worked out where the voice was coming from. It was an official from Huddersfield Town, at least that's what his blue and white attire suggested.

"Follow me, please," said the young man, and Jarrod was

beckoned to follow him at quite a pace.

"Where are we going?" asked Jarrod.

"We're going only a couple hundred metres," said his chaperone.

Jarrod couldn't keep up with the pace of the brisk walking and broke into a jog. They had reached their destination in a matter of minutes, walking around a big car park, across a bridge over a main road and he found himself looking at a tiny helicopter, parked on a small patch of grass in the fading light. The official was actually a pilot, who had dropped the club owner up from London just half an hour before. The cockpit was indeed very warm as they climbed in, Jarrod taking all his prompts from his pilot and strapping himself in as the engine roared to life.

"Have you flown in a small helicopter like this before?" he asked.

"No," said Jarrod. "I've been in a navy helicopter for a team building exercise, but this is something new!"

Jarrod was feeling guilty about getting any pleasure out of the situation he was in, but it was very cool the way the helicopter lifted off the ground carefully and all the nearby litter was blasted away in the hurricane. It was nearly dark now, and the lights of the town got smaller and smaller in the distance until Jarrod could no longer see them. With his headset on, he could speak with the pilot, but he chose not to and simply braced himself as the machine reached some pretty amazing speeds, seemingly very low to the ground.

Jarrod had no sights to guide him, so he was very surprised when the pilot told him they would be landing in three minutes. The pilot explained that they would be landing on the roof of the RVI, the main hospital in Newcastle, and he would need to sit tight until he was instructed to leave the aircraft. It seemed an eternity before the pilot tapped him on the shoulder and let him know through the headset he could open his door now and head to the entrance to the left.

Jarrod turned and shook hands with the pilot before taking off his headset and opening the door, letting in the fierce noise of the engine and the blades. Along with the heat that was coming from the side of the helicopter it was a little overwhelming. Jarrod confidently jumped down out of his door, closed it behind him, and made his way over to the beaming light at the entrance. The whirr of the helicopter intensified, and Jarrod could feel the force of the wind as it took off behind him, wobbling slightly as it lifted and then quickly darting away into the night air.

The entrance took him into a long corridor, and he ended up following signs for the Main Entrance and then Intensive Care. He could feel his phone pinging and went to grab it, but it was caught in his pocket and he decided to leave it until he had arrived. He burst into the reception area of Intensive Care. The nurse on duty was quick to work out who he was and asked him to take a seat while she called for a colleague. A second nurse, a burly man in his forties, came through the big double doors and immediately clocked Jarrod in his Darlington kit.

"Mr Black," he said as he approached.

"Come along. Follow me," he continued. "I understand you have had a colourful journey to get here."

Jarrod ignored the question and asked, "Is Marianne ok?"

"Marianne is sedated," said the nurse, by way of a warning that he might get a surprise. "She is very pale."

"Can you fill me in with the details?" asked Jarrod as they walked through a labyrinth of beds, all hooked up with machines and hundreds of wires.

"Of course," said the nurse. "Your wife had an anaphylactic reaction to one of the painkillers that we regularly use post-surgery when we wean patients off the strong stuff."

Jarrod didn't like what he was hearing, remembering Pulp Fiction or Reservoir Dogs, whichever movie it was that had someone stabbing someone with a needle to get them out of their shock. He also recalled just how one of his allergy-ridden schoolmates had reacted when mistakenly biting into a peanut butter sandwich that had been mysteriously switched in his lunchbox.

Jarrod came up next to the bed with trepidation, slipping his hand into Marianne's, between the tubes, giving it a squeeze. Marianne looked very white, and was very still, Jarrod conscious of the heart monitor beeping next to the bed and not able to see any sign of breathing.

"Your wife got to us just in time," said the nurse. "She was lucky in a way that she was already in hospital. It would have been a different outcome if she was somewhere else."

Jarrod didn't feel any consolation in those words and shuddered to think what could have been if she had taken the medication at home.

"So, what happens now?" asked Jarrod.

"We wait until we see signs of improvement," said the nurse. "Then we can start to give your wife some antihistamines and cortisone to assist with clearing the airways and getting her back on the road to recovery. It's going to be a critical few hours, and we'd hope to see some big improvement very soon."

Jarrod sat down on the seat next to the bed, still holding

Marianne's hand, and still unable to see any movement. He immediately felt helpless – his wife was a recovering cancer patient who had just been through a massive surgery and was now in intensive care, waiting to either get better, or not.

He put his forehead on the bed next to Marianne's head and whispered some positive words in her ear, trying not to sound like the captain of a team giving a team pep talk. He could feel himself welling up from the sheer emotion of seeing Marianne all hooked up, wires from her chest to a machine next to him, tubes in her throat and in her hand, and he was very close to giving way to the urge to cry.

"Come on, Jarrod," said the nurse, knowing exactly who he was, and Jarrod felt himself being gently lifted by the arm off his seat by the nurse and helped over to a nearby couch.

"You stay here, and we'll wake you up as soon as we know anything."

This gave Jarrod time to take stock of what had just happened, and he started to run through some rather unhelpful thoughts in his mind. He had been whisked away from a vital game to be here, so it was definitely really serious. Marianne was in Intensive Care, was not responsive, and his squeeze of her hand had been met with limp fingers. His kids were tucked up at Pippa's place, not knowing anything, as far as he knew, and Marianne's family was preparing to fly over. Marianne might die, and he would be left as a widower with two kids to raise without a Mum.

Would they be happy? Would they be forever mourning their mother? How could he be thinking such thoughts already? This was truly a test of Jarrod's mental strength, and he sat there on the couch, head resting on his palm. A steely resolve came over him, as if preparing for the absolute worst.

Jarrod must have dozed off, as the next thing he knew, he was being awakened by the nurse and told that he should sit up.

"Jarrod," said the nurse. "Come on. You need to be with us now. Marianne appears to have got through the worst of this and showing signs of improved blood pressure."

"Where is she?" said Jarrod, unsure of his surroundings and sitting up straight.

"She's in the bed," said the nurse. "Where you left her..."

Jarrod jumped to his feet and made his way over to the bed, grabbing Marianne's hand quite forcefully and could sense that there was much more life in her. He squeezed it between his two hands and put it to his chest. His heart was almost jumping out of his chest. It was well after midnight and the hospital had a peaceful calm about it, the lights dimmed and less people fussing around. Jarrod felt a flick in Marianne's little finger, or at least he thought he did, and he looked at Marianne's face. It remained completely still, but there was another twitch. The heart rate monitor seemed to speed up. This was going to be a long night, but Jarrod was going to remain right there. The nurse could see what was happening, husband and wife communicating by some sixth sense, and she quietly walked away and left them to it.

A light cough was all it took to bring the nurse back, and she quickly brought the doctor. The beeps of the heart monitor were much quicker, life seemed to be flooding back into Marianne's face. The sunken eyes lost their dark rings, the lips brightened, and there were some flutters from the eyes, and Jarrod felt a light squeeze before one eye opened. Jarrod sat up with surprise, and then the other eye opened and a frown came over Marianne's face. She moved her head slightly to the side and focused her gaze on Jarrod, whose eyebrows were as high as they had ever been, a wide-eyed amazement breaking in to a beaming smile.

"You're back with us," was the best thing he could think to say. "Great to have you back!"

The nurse put her hand on Jarrod's shoulder and they smiled at each other, the doctor checking Marianne's forehead to see if she had some warmth.

"Tell me this is a good sign," said Jarrod to the nurse.

"Oh, it is," said the nurse. "You must be so relieved."

Part Eight
Coping

It was five in the morning by now, Marianne was sitting up against the raised bed and had been given a number of drugs and then unhooked from a few of the machines. The tube was taken from her throat and she was taking very small sips from a plastic glass that Jarrod held to her mouth. The tubes from her underarms were still there, and Jarrod had to remind himself that she had just had major surgery and her body would still be very uncomfortable. There were three nurses and a doctor around the bed.

"Marianne, what are you feeling right now?" asked the doctor. It was a strange question, and Marianne thought for a moment, unsure as to whether she could speak or not.

"What am I feeling?" she asked gently, with a wince at the pain of speaking for the first time since the tube was out.

"Yes. Are you in any discomfort?" rephrased the doctor.

Marianne tried to sit up a little more but then decided against it.

"Sore around both armpits," she stated. "Very dry throat... aching head. Really hurts to breathe. Feeling bruised all over."

"And do you feel nauseous?" asked the doctor.

"Yes," said Marianne. "But everything else is distracting me from it."

The doctor smiled. Jarrod knew that Marianne was back. That was a wry response.

"We're going to move you back into the ward," said one of the nurses. "The worst is over. We'll check you out thoroughly and you'll start to lose the nausea soon."

The medical staff left, and Marianne asked Jarrod,

"How did you go?"

"We had a draw," said Jarrod. "One-one."

Jarrod didn't want to elaborate and let her know he had done a mercy dash across England to be with her and was happy to leave it at that.

"You'll come and watch on Tuesday, right?" he offered, happy to continue the light-hearted tone.

"Wouldn't miss it for the world," she said, with no conviction whatsoever. "But you should go home and rest Jarrod. Mes parents arrivent aujourd'hui."

Jarrod now had an agenda. He had to first get himself back to Darlington to get a little bit of sleep. Then he was due to pick up the kids, then pick up Marianne's Mum and Dad from the airport, and they would then all come back up to Newcastle and spend a couple of hours towards the end of the day with Marianne. He kissed Marianne goodbye, slipping her mobile phone into her hand as left, and made his way out of the Intensive Care Unit to the main entrance. He was still in his soccer gear. He made his way out the front of the hospital and there was a solitary taxi at the rank. His first thought was to get a taxi to the train station, but with the station only a short jog away, jumping into the taxi meant he was going to taxi it all the way to Darlington. The taxi driver re-checked.

"Darlington Arena?" asked the silver-haired driver. "Might be quite a fare."

Jarrod wasn't a man for flaunting the wealth that he had

obviously gained from a career in the upper reaches of League football and was always the one for doing things the right way. If there was a bus going straight past where he was going, he'd take the bus. If the kids wanted McDonalds instead of a fancy meal, he'd do Maccas. If the pyjamas from Marks and Spencer were on sale, he'd buy them instead of the fancy ones from the boutique store across the road. This time though, he knew he was going against those principles and he confirmed.

"Darlington Arena, yes."

Jarrod got back to the stadium and got the driver to drive into the gates and drop him right next to his car, giving him a generous tip for his trouble. The car was on its own, whereas the day before it was surrounded by other cars. It wouldn't have been that long since the team all got back after last night's game, but all the familiar vehicles of his teammates were gone, only a handful of cars and a motorbike sitting all lonely in the usually busy car park.

He made his way back home, all of a sudden feeling the tiredness as he walked from the car to the house. A quick brush of his teeth and a big drink of water signalled the end of the day, despite it being light outside and he stripped off and climbed under the bed covers with a long sigh. What a day.

The kids were keen to know how Mum was when he got to the Robson's house, and after the quickest debrief with Pippa, he managed to get Seb to his football game in time to join the end of the warm up, the coach shaking his head at his lateness. The irony of Jarrod being under such strict rules for punctuality with Darlington was not lost on him, and he simply shrugged a 'sorry' at the coach from a distance. Jarrod was still a little groggy after his mini-sleep, and luckily Aneka had found some friends and was playing with the younger siblings of Seb's teammates.

This was the highlight of Jarrod's week, watching Seb play. It was usually a little earlier in the morning and Jarrod could usually make it before home games, but this one was a late kick-off and he was glad about it. The Bulls, as they were known, were a great club, and Jarrod felt right at home on the sideline as a parent, or sometimes running the line as a stand-in assistant referee if the referee found himself short of helpers. He had not once been asked for input to the team, and he intended to keep it that way. Today coach 'Hammo' – Jarrod never actually asked what his name was, but assumed it was something Hammond – was in a foul mood and was giving the boys a tough time, grilling them in the pre-match talk after a lacklustre warm-up and getting a little shouty. It seemed to do the trick though, and Jarrod found himself being swept away in the action as the Bulls swarmed forward from the off, opponents Blackwell unsure of how to cope with the onslaught.

A missed penalty followed by a miracle save by the opponents' goalkeeper from three yards out gave this the feel of a game of missed chances, but once the Bulls' young centre-forward had smashed home the first, the tap was turned on. Seb was playing as well as he ever had, Jarrod used to his lazy, languid play, but today he was switched on. Maybe something to do with spending the night at Michaela's, Jarrod chuckled to himself. The score quickly rose to four and by half-time the Bulls had a proud five-nil lead.

Jarrod had a glance of his watch. The thought of popping home afterwards to drop soccer gear and get changed was out the window, no time for that before the rendez-vous with Jean-Jacques and Mireille at Teesside Airport, so he could relax. He remarked just how filthy Seb was as the players made their way back out on to the field, and how much of the mud would end up in the car. Still, a small price to pay for seeing his boy play good football.

The second half was a procession. Seb getting on the scoresheet with a tap-in from a metre out, before coach Hammo changed it around, throwing his defenders forward and asking his strikers to make up the rearguard for the final quarter of the game. The score ended at eight without reply, Seb was delighted, Jarrod loved every minute of the game, even cheering on the Blackwell players when they made a rare foray into the Bulls penalty area, and Aneka seemed to be having a great time too.

It was perhaps a glimpse into the future he had been contemplating early last night, proud Dad watching his kids play with a feeling of sadness at his wife not being there. He couldn't shake that feeling, and the immense pride he was feeling at watching Seb blossom on the field before his very eyes was tempered by the fact that Marianne was not there to see it.

The final whistle blew, and Jarrod made a bee-line for Aneka to give her the heads-up they had to go. Seb was in a huddle with his teammates and the extended post-match chit chat from Hammo was as positive as Jarrod had ever heard. Seb could see that his Dad was keen to make a move and sprinted off after the round of applause for the man of the match to join Aneka and Jarrod and they jogged over to the car park.

"Are we going straight to the airport?" asked Seb.

"Yep," affirmed Jarrod. "We need to be there soon – we don't want to keep Mama and Papy waiting."

Seb was obviously keen to get back to base camp to get online with his school-friends who were all into the latest shoot 'em up game and threw his arms up in the air as if to say, 'why does it always happen to me.' He had a resignation about him though, and in any case, he was excited to see his exotic French Grandparents.

Teesside Airport was busy when they rocked up – the increased volume of flights in recent months had led to a renaissance of Newcastle Airport's poor cousin – so much so, they had to wait ten minutes to get in to the car park and then had a good ten minutes again to find a spot, stalking a couple pushing a trolley load of bags back to their car. Jarrod really enjoyed his in-laws' company, despite their language barrier, this time though he was a little apprehensive – nothing like a critically sick child to change your perspective and demeanor. He needn't have worried though.

"Sebastiaaaaan…" came the cry from Jean-Jacques as he came through the frosted auto doors from the customs area and clocked his young grandson. Seb felt the urge to run up and give him a hug, Aneka doing the typical thing of copying, and running up to Mireille and putting her arms wide around her. Mireille was the most attractive pensioner he knew, and she certainly knew how to dress. When she spoke, it was with an air of mystery, and even with her broken English, her cigarette-affected raspy voice was so engaging. Jean-Jacques on the other hand, with his nose smashed one too many times from his years as a scrum-half in the local rugby team and his little wiry frame was a bundle of energy. He played the buffoon really well and didn't have a bad word to say about anyone.

Jarrod liked to think that Marianne and himself would be like them when they got older, just loving spending time together, and getting out and about at every opportunity. They were very different to Jarrod's Mum and Dad, and it was Mireille, who was definitely in charge of everything. Mireille gripped Jarrod tightly when they eventually made their way through the metal barrier and out into the concourse.

"My girl," she said. "Is she being looked after?"

"Marianne is up and awake," said Jarrod, mindful that he

should speak a little slower than normal. "We have had a big fright, but she is feeling so much better."

"We're going straight there?" asked Jean-Jacques, keen to see his daughter.

"Yes, it's an hour or so from here," said Jarrod. "Your porters will carry your bags for you..."

Jarrod winked at Seb and beckoned Aneka to grab a suitcase. They looked heavy, but they were on wheels, and Aneka pushed it as hard as she could and watched it career through the crowd before bursting into giggles and racing after it. Jean-Jacques was straight after it, too, and they ended up colliding, Aneka bouncing off her Grandad and sliding to the floor on her bottom to great laughter as the suitcase came to a rest against a wall. Top quality buffoonery, only twelve seconds after they had met.

The drive to Newcastle took a little longer than usual. Newcastle playing at home and a steady stream of cars with flags and scarves tied out the windows made a bottleneck as they entered Newcastle off the A1. The proximity of the hospital to the stadium meant they had to get through some heavy traffic, but this well-practiced route and a bonus car spot right by the front entrance made things very easy. Jean-Jacques, riding in the middle seat at the back, made a fuss of getting out of the car, squashing Aneka as he stumbled out, laughing all the while.

Jarrod likened him to a slapstick actor that starred in the majority of French movies he had seen, and Aneka again was in fits of laughter. This was a good mood to be taking in to the hospital. Marianne had texted to ask where they were. There was no need to ask at the busy reception if Marianne could have visitors, they just made their way up to the ward and checked in at the desk. After a two minute wait, a nurse opened the doors and they were ushered through, up a long corridor and then left into a carpeted area, where there were a selection of different sized rooms off either side of the walkway.

Room 406, there it was. Jarrod peeked his head around the door, Marianne was sitting completely upright, looking almost 100%. She smiled, then when Aneka and Seb raced in, she seemed to burst with happiness. It wasn't until her parents walked in that her face cracked and she grasped her Mum and they cuddled for what seemed to be five minutes. Marianne was in a flood of tears, Mireille was in bits, not her usual self, and Jean-Jacques, who had bided his time by the door, made his way over to his little girl and gave her a big hug, being careful not to pull out any tubes or squash any tender parts of Marianne's wounds. Jarrod watched on, Seb and Aneka joining him as they took in the enormity of what they had just witnessed.

Jarrod excused himself with a wave, and they left the room. Jarrod walked with his arm around Seb, holding Aneka's hand. He let Marianne catch up with her parents and they waited in the waiting area until Aneka's curiosity got the better of her and she walked back up the corridor to rejoin the party. Jarrod took the opportunity to ask at the desk when Marianne might be discharged, and he was surprised to learn that she may be out on Monday morning, or even beforehand.

The roar of the crowd from the nearby St James Park signalled either a winning goal or the end of a winning game for Newcastle, as they stepped out into the carpark. The logistical merry-go-round was to continue – if they got out of the area in the next ten minutes they would beat the crowds and the traffic, and they would then make their way back to Darlington. They would spend the night all together at home, then Jarrod would offer his in-laws to stay at their old house in Gateshead, still fully furnished, which had just become vacant at the end of a lease. Jean-Jacques and Mireille would take Marianne's car and they would all go up there and give the house a little airing and a spruce up.

Marianne would base herself there with her parents, so she was close to the hospital for all her visits and Jarrod and the kids would head back to Darlington on the Sunday night before school. It was all a little difficult to manage, and Jarrod had to get to training at some point on Sunday, too. He was made of stern stuff though, and despite it seeming like too much in too short a period of time, he found the challenge exciting. Even finding enough sheets and pillowcases for the night was made into a game, and he enlisted Aneka to help. He felt like a real Super Dad and surprised himself just how smoothly it all went.

No sport for the kids on Sunday morning freed up time for the 9am training session at Darlington. A quick hour and a half was exactly what he needed, and he found himself there early, giving himself enough time to catch up with Gary for a brief chat. Gary had been very concerned for Marianne, and also for his prized asset, and he wanted to be sure he was in the right frame of mind to take his captain's role for the crucial return leg on Tuesday at the Arena. Jarrod explained what he had on between now and then, and Gary offered assistance 'whatever you need, however trivial, give me a call.'

After they had left Gary's office, the players started to stream in, and there were a lot of encouraging words from his teammates. Sam Basaan stopped and gave him a bear hug. The training session itself gave Jarrod a chance to catch up with the rest of the team, and they walked Jarrod through the incident points from the first leg, who the players were to look for from Crewe, and how they might counteract the attacking threat they now knew Crewe possessed.

The fifteen minute game at the end was just what Jarrod needed; an opportunity to get back to doing what he does best, and to break through the weariness he was now feeling. There was no time to hang around after the session. Jarrod was in his car driving back home less than five minutes after Des had dismissed the troops from the training field.

Jarrod stepped back into the old house with trepidation. It had been just over seven months since they had finally moved out and made the house rentable, leaving a lot of their old furniture while they bought a lot of new items for their new home. The estate agent had given Jarrod feedback last week that their house was in pristine condition after the cleaners had come through and given the place a thorough scrub after the short-term occupants had left. He wasn't taking any chances though and brought a bucket of cleaning materials just in case there were any nasty surprises. The house did have a slightly different aroma to their usual family scent, but Jarrod was pleasantly surprised by what he saw as he wandered around the house.

The kids ran straight up to their rooms to check things out, and the in-laws made themselves at home in the kitchen, looking through the cupboards for a coffee pot. The old radio in the kitchen was flicked on, and the house began to come back to life. Yes, this would be a great spot for Marianne to convalesce, and her Mum and Dad would love staying here.

Marianne was up and dressed when they walked into room 406 as afternoon turned in to evening. The meal service was coming around and she was sitting on the edge of her bed, looking fantastic in a loose black sweater and tight black jeans, toying with what looked like a roast Sunday dinner. She dropped her fork and moved the trolley out of the way when Aneka bustled past Jarrod to get first hugs. Marianne was quick to stop her in her tracks and slow her down. The jumper was hiding a lot of bandages, drainage bags, and pain, but Aneka took it slowly and snuggled in to her Mum. Seb came close behind and cuddled them both in a group hug. Jarrod let Mireille walk in next and she was visibly shocked to see how much better her daughter looked, and there were smiles all round. The intense emotions of last night, the floods of tears, were replaced with happiness and lightness.

"You look ready to check out," said Jarrod as he walked in and kissed Marianne on the cheek.

"That's exactly what's happening," she said with a smile.

"What a difference a day makes," offered Jarrod. "You look so much better!"

"Yeah, Mum," said Seb. "Who was that lady we saw last night?"

Marianne smiled, Seb enjoyed his moment of comedy gold and translations for her Mum and Dad could wait. The surgeon had been around mid-afternoon to check on her, and he could see no reason why she would need to stay any longer. As long as Marianne was able to come in and get the drainage bags checked and emptied, and there was adequate support on the outside, she was free to go.

The most pertinent question on Marianne's mind had been whether or not she could make her first oncologist appointment which was on Monday, any suggestion of delay not being entertained. Dr Groez had no problem with her making the appointment, and indeed he was more than happy that the shock she had been through in the last 48 hours had well and truly passed.

Jean-Jacques and Mireille stood looking patiently at Marianne, not having understood anything. Marianne realised and launched into French, translating the situation; the surprised faces confirming they really had not followed the conversation.

And so, Marianne then got out of bed, looking as though she was a visitor not a patient, said a quick goodbye and good luck to her roommates, and made for the door. Her poise was elegant, her pace was very slow, and Jean Jacques came up alongside her and she put her arm through his and they walked along the corridor towards the lifts, Mireille following close behind, Jarrod and the kids goofing around further back.

Part Nine
Poised

A late night getting home after making sure Marianne and her parents were settled at the old house meant a late morning, and Jarrod struggled to get Seb and Aneka motivated for the well-practiced morning routine. After a false start when Seb announced he had forgotten his homework book a good mile into the journey, they eventually arrived at school and it was a quick 'kiss and ride' as Jarrod drove off up to Gateshead to pick up Marianne for the oncologist appointment. He took a call from Dad on the way up, who was having his usual early evening routine and ringing at just the right time of the morning after school drop off.

"Jarrod," he said. "How are you?"

That question was as Australian as vegemite and kangaroos. The standard answer was, 'I'm fine, how are you?' but Jarrod had been in England too long and that polite start to the conversation was lost on him.

"Dad!" he shouted. "To what do I owe this pleasure?"

"Checking up on your beautiful wife," said Dad. "And checking up on my son. How are you holding up?"

That was tantamount to, 'R U OK?' and Jarrod unconsciously and needlessly had his defences up.

"I'm great," said Jarrod. A start to a sentence that wouldn't wash with Dad.

"Just tell me, Jarrod," continued Dad. "Do you have enough support around you to get through this? I mean, you're captain of a team gunning for promotion, you've got two kids to look after, and Marianne tells me that her folks are in town too. That's a recipe for stress surely?"

Marianne often bypassed Jarrod when it came to passing on news, circumventing the filter that was Jarrod's memory and trading texts with Dad when she thought they should know something. It was no surprise to Jarrod that Dad knew what was going on. And it was no surprise that he could empathise.

"We're on a bit of a journey here, that's for sure," said Jarrod. "We've got all the support we can possibly ask for, but it's just really busy. Never a moment to relax and take stock. Possibly a blessing in disguise."

"You sound a little croaky," said Dad, and Jarrod remarked that his last words did sound as though they were coming from someone who was coming down with cold.

"Maybe I was shouting a bit much on Saturday at Seb's game," said Jarrod changing the subject. "He had an absolute stormer. I think he's starting to realise that he can play a bit."

"Just keep the communication lines open, Jarrod," said Dad, seeing right through this attempt to deflect. "Keep us informed. I know we're on the other side of the planet, but we love you and we like to know if we can offer any assistance, whatever it is."

"I understand," said Jarrod, correcting the steering as the car veered on to the cats eyes on the side of the road and started thumping over them with that familiar flapping sound. "We're just off to see the oncologist, I'll call you with any news."

"Thanks, Jarrod," said a concerned Dad. "Speak soon."

They had an 11:00am appointment at the Oncology clinic, and Jarrod did the quickest of stops to pick up Marianne and wish his in-laws a good day. This was a clinic in the same complex as the hospital, so familiarity of the route and the car parks made it a very easy journey. They had time to grab a coffee at the hospital café before making their way up to the clinic overlooking the main road. There were a few souls in the waiting room, no-one looking particularly sick.

There were some friendly staff on reception busily taking calls, organising visits, and appointments. The receptionist immediately broke the ice, telling Marianne that she should not be so nervous – Marianne had simply been cross-armed from the cold outside, but it was lovely and warm in there and the warmth gave Jarrod a cosy feeling. They filled out a form together at the reception desk, and the oncologist arrived. They were soon ushered in to her room for the consultation. Jan Keever was a prominent figure in the treatment of breast cancer, and Jarrod had heard her voice on a CD that had come from the hospital, 'Breast Cancer for Partners.'

He already knew that she was well spoken, and she was very friendly. She took Jarrod and Marianne through the process so far, noting everything down as she went, detailed the procedure of chemo, and then invited them to ask questions. There were many. The positives taken from the meeting were that there were to be only four sessions of chemotherapy, and surprisingly these were only two hour sessions, an hour hooked up to each of the two drugs that would make up the dosage. They would be able to start on Wednesday, so it would all be over by the end of June, well before the expected mid-August timeline as indicated previously during early discussions with Dr Groez.

The other side of the coin was that there was discussion regarding the "receptors," resulting from the pathology results received from the operations. This indicated that the cells remaining in the breast, and there were not many, had an attribute that made them responsive to oestrogen, and the possibility of cancer reoccurring. Marianne would be taking medications for the next five years, and it may be wise to have surgery to remove her ovaries at some point. That didn't really dent the optimism after hearing they only had six or seven weeks of treatment to endure.

They left armed with an appointment date and time, Wednesday at 10am, and enough information about how Marianne would feel in the eight day cycle between treatments to begin to plan out the weeks ahead; the first day of the cycle would maybe be a slight high from the drugs, the following days would be tough with nausea, the expected effect. The lack of white blood cells later in the cycle would mean Marianne would be susceptible to infection and would be lethargic. Just as the side-effects wore off, she would have to go through the next session, but that was a small price to pay for getting the cancer out of her system.

There was a lot of silence in the car on the way back to Gateshead, broken by Marianne as she collected her thoughts.

"Let's go back to Darlington," she said. "We'll pick up my parents and head back. We'll get on with our lives as if nothing is happening."

All the preparation put in to getting the old house ready was forgotten, and Jarrod was 100% sold on the idea.

"Hopefully Jean-Jacques hasn't been on the Ricard and he can drive," said Jarrod, not even entering an argument one way or the other with Marianne. "I'm not going to deny that I'm very happy with that decision. It will make for a few more miles on the A1, but it'll be much nicer for everyone if we're all back in Darlington and all together."

"Deal done, then," said Marianne, and they reverted to the cosy silence they had enjoyed for the most part of the journey.

As if Jarrod had not had enough big days recently, this one was definitely one of the biggest. They were awake early, Jarrod toying with thoughts of the game ahead, as well as wondering just what was in store for Marianne. She was lying peacefully next to him, and he thought about making a move to satisfy his morning urge, but as soon as he rolled over to snuggle in, Marianne made it quite clear there was no chance. Fair enough.

Perhaps that pent up energy might come in useful later in the day with high concentration levels needed in a penalty shootout. Jarrod chuckled to himself, always looking on the positive side. They had run through the day's agenda last night with the kids and with Marianne's Mum and Dad, Marianne translating so that Jean-Jacques and Mireille would be on the same page. Once Jarrod had done the school run, he was out for the day and Marianne would be in the hands of her folks. This would give Jarrod a little time for reflection and then to turn his focus on to tonight's match. The motivation was there to get out of bed early and get the show on the road. He sprung from the bed, found his tracksuit bottoms and got stuck in to the morning.

Aneka asked quite a cutting question as they made their way to school, still running remarkably early.

"Dad," she started, deep thought written all over her face, "is Mum going to get better?"

"What makes you say that?" said Jarrod, rather bemused after bringing Marianne home from hospital in relatively fine form.

"We haven't seen much of Mum for a while," interjected Seb. They had obviously been talking to each other and had formulated this conversation from their own. "She didn't say much last night to us."

Jarrod was slightly taken aback but knew that his response had to be super-positive, if not totally truthful.

"Mummy has just had a huge operation, and then has been really sick afterwards," he said, outlining the facts. "She doesn't have much energy left, and we have to let her get better in her own time. You just have to show her all the love you can, and that will help her get better."

Jarrod surprised himself by how well that came out and how positive it sounded, and he didn't want to ruin it by saying anything else, so he waited for the next question.

"So, what happens if Mummy doesn't get better?" asked Aneka with a worried look on her face.

Jarrod quickly pulled over to the side of the road and stopped the car. He turned to Aneka and reached over to touch her face. She looked defeated.

"Mummy is going to get better, Aneka," he said. "But she might be very sick for another two months before things start to get back to normal."

A tear popped out of the side of her eye and started to roll down her cheek.

"Mummy's been there for you both, for all of us, when we've needed her," said Jarrod. "Now we have to be here for her. If Mummy asks you to do something, you do it, if she looks tired and needs help, you help her. We've got to get through this together."

Jarrod clasped her knee and clasped Seb's too. He was feeling a little sad as well, but a bit of volume on the radio, a quick clap of the hands, and a toot of the horn at no one in particular and they were off again. Jarrod smiling at his kids, which made them smile back.

With twenty minutes before the bell, Jarrod decided he

would come in and enjoy the delights of the playground chatter with the Mums and Grandparents who did the daily drop. The kids had already forgotten their troubles when they saw their friends, and they were quickly out of sight. Jarrod saw Kristen, one of the Dads from Seb's class, and sidled up to him as the bell sounded and the kids started to form lines.

"Tonight's the night," said Kristen.

"Sure is," replied Jarrod. "Excited!"

"So are we," said Kristen. "Thomas is going to his first game tonight. He says Seb has been talking it up. Is Seb going?"

"That's the plan," said Jarrod. "I think Marianne's Dad is keen to bring him along. Don't think Marianne's up for it just yet."

Kristen didn't take the opportunity to ask how Marianne was, and Jarrod knew that it was because he simply didn't want to talk about it here and now in the playground.

"Say," said Jarrod. "You free after assembly? Fancy a coffee?"

"Sure," said Kristen. "I do a reading group here at ten with the young kids, and I've got a bit of time to spare."

The kids were all lined up now and the deputy head teacher started the morning assembly. Jarrod zoned out at this stage, but zoned back in when he heard his name mentioned.

"...and we have Jarrod Black, father of Sebastian and Aneka, here this morning on this important day for Darlington FC."

Jarrod hoped that he hadn't missed anything and was relieved when the eyes weren't expecting him to walk up to the front of the school. He nodded his head in acknowledgement at the teacher.

"Good luck to our town's football team this evening," the

teacher continued. "We hope to be able to follow the team down to Wembley in ten days' time for the final."

Jarrod enjoyed Kristen's company that morning. It gave Jarrod a chance to hear from someone at the same stage of life as himself, and someone who seemed to be more than happy to give his time back to the school community. It was only a quick coffee at the café just down the road, but Jarrod felt as though he could call on Kristen if need be just to have a chat. He had resisted going in too deep, and they kept it light, agreeing they should do coffee again very soon once things settled down. After all, Kristen could be going through all sorts of chaos himself, how would Jarrod know?

The rest of the morning, Jarrod kept himself busy. He had a few errands to run, a new thermometer for the pizza oven, batteries for the Xbox remotes, a decent food shop to tide them over a few days, and a quick stop at the off-licence to pick up some Ricard for Jean-Jacques – he couldn't get it at the supermarket and his father-in-law would be lost without it come five o'clock. He dropped the shopping off at home at one, and the house was empty; a note saying they had gone to check out a new coffee house nearby.

A great opportunity then to get some rest; lie on his back on the couch and flick through his insurmountable list of text messages. He went back to messages he had received after the train journey on Friday when he last had a good look, and the main themes were the interview with Dominic, concern for Marianne, messages from Football Australia regarding the upcoming friendly games, as well as the usual school app texts that flooded his inbox every week. This was just what he needed, peace and quiet, and a chance to catch up. He would hopefully run in to Dominic Barrow tonight and give him an update and plug the golf day on Friday again.

Meeting time was two-thirty for pre-match preparation, and Jarrod realised that his phone had absorbed a good hour of his life and he should be making his way now to the stadium or face a fine for being late. It wasn't far to the stadium though, and it wouldn't take very long especially at this time of day. It was game time, and Jarrod switched into game mode. A collection of thoughts came into his head, a list of things to do, and he started to tick them off. Remembering how he had to return home to get Seb's homework book yesterday morning gave him a resolve to make sure he would forget nothing.

"Jarrod," said Pauline, putting her arm around him as he walked into the stadium.

"Pauline," replied Jarrod. "How's your day going?"

"You know what I'm going to ask you, don't you," she said, ignoring his question.

"You want me to go on air again with Dominic Barrow," he replied with one hundred percent accuracy.

"Then come with me," said Pauline pulling his shoulder so he made an arced entry into her office, as if he was being press-ganged into something he didn't want to do.

"Dominic is already in there with Gary," said Pauline. "They'll be done any moment now. In fact, I think that's them finishing up."

The door opened from the studio and Gary walked through looking content with his work and shook Jarrod's hand on the way past, as Dominic appeared at the door.

"Jarrod," he said, much in the same way Pauline had addressed him.

"Hello Dominic," said Jarrod. "What can I do for you?"

"Jarrod," he started. "That interview we did last week was golden. We've had so much positive feedback from that. It was a serious bit of radio content, and it started a huge story that's in the national papers. How is Marianne?"

Jarrod knew that question was an after-thought but was impressed it had come so early in the conversation.

"Marianne is recovering," he said, and that was all he needed to give away.

"So, can we give our listeners an update on how things have been going since the last time we spoke?" he enquired hopefully.

"Look, there's nothing to hide," said Jarrod, playing the part of someone who didn't want to speak at all, but knowing that he had some spruiking to do. "But I can give you five minutes right now."

There was no hesitation from Dominic, who turned to the door that had closed on itself, opened it and offered passage to Jarrod and Pauline to get the show on the road. Pauline sensed Jarrod's agenda and played along, winking at Dominic as if they were on to a winner. They sat in the same places they had done just a few days ago, Pauline perched on a table, Dominic and Jarrod sitting either side of the microphone as if they had an audience.

The sound engineer was in the corner with his headphones on. Dominic chatted to the presenters of the show that was running at that moment; a song obviously playing on the radio allowing them to talk. There was excitement in the studio. A jingle was playing, Dominic looked at Pauline and then at Jarrod. It was clearly the biggest moment of Dominic's career, and Jarrod felt nervous for him.

"We're joined this afternoon by Darlington captain Jarrod

Black," started Dominic after some muffled words came through in his ear-piece. "Jarrod, thanks for joining us."

"Great to be speaking with you again," said Jarrod, playing the role of perfect interviewee.

"Jarrod," said Dominic, repeating his name for effect. "Last time we spoke, you were off to Gresty Road in search of a first leg victory. Your evening didn't quite turn out the way you had planned..."

"That's right, Dominic," said Jarrod, shuffling closer to the microphone, "unfortunately, my wife Marianne's health took a turn for the worse as the game kicked off, and with many phone calls, and thanks to the generosity of many people in the football world, I was by her side before the evening was out."

"How is Marianne?" asked Dominic, then butting in and continuing before Jarrod could collect his thoughts. "Is everything heading in the right direction after your scare on Friday night?"

"Marianne has had one hell of a weekend, that's for sure," said Jarrod. "And she's feeling a lot better, thanks. On the back of major surgery, she had an allergic reaction to some medicine and that was the reason for the mercy dash."

"Our best wishes go to your wife, Jarrod," said Dominic, keeping it cheery. "How has that affected your preparations for this evening's game?"

"I have to be honest with you," said Jarrod. "This has made me even more determined to win tonight. When the going gets tough, as they say, but anyway..."

Jarrod sat upright.

"Anyway, this Friday," continued Jarrod, "we're at Northallerton

Golf Club for a fundraiser for Breast Cancer Care. Come on down and support this fantastic cause, sign up for a hit with the professionals, get a table for lunch. This is going to be huge!"

Dominic wasn't expecting the plug but played along with it as if it was part of the script.

"What a fantastic cause," said Dominic. "One that I am sure is close to your heart."

"I'll admit," said Jarrod. "It's even closer to my heart now that I understand the good work they do. Look forward to seeing you there, Dominic."

The interview turned to football thereafter, and Jarrod relaxed, knowing he had gotten his message across. They talked for a good ten minutes about how they were going to line up, what they had learned from the first leg, and what the fans were to expect from Darlington tonight. The excitement was clear in Dominic's voice, he was a proper fan, and Jarrod found himself caught up in the fervour. This was exciting. Make or break. Jarrod shook hands with Dominic as the interview ended and the radio cut to some adverts. Pauline was delighted, some great radio there, and Jarrod was free to head off and get ready for the game.

A big crowd had been anticipated at the Arena that evening, but nothing could have prepared the players for the reception they received when they came out for kick-off. The club had been busy giving away tickets to local schools and businesses, and as the teams walked out of the tunnel, Jarrod was pretty sure he was in a sold-out stadium. This was football fever at its finest. A massive roar greeted them, ripped up programs showering down on them, toilet rolls launched as streamers, the place was a sea of black and white. Jarrod led his team to the centre of the field. The referee team greeted him and his opposite number, and they went through the coin toss routine. The Crewe players then filed past the Darlington players, handshakes for every player, and the scene was set for a massive game of football.

This was no ordinary night of football, and that was clear from the first moments. Mitch Short took the kick-off, despite being right fullback, slightly disorienting the Crewe team when they fell into positions in the ensuing passage of play. Darlington seemed to have a spring in their step and were playing the part of the dominant home team to perfection. Connor Naughton received the ball down the right and checked back just when the crowd was urging the team forward. This gave Mitch a chance to race past him on the overlap and drag his defender with him. Connor took the risk and jinked past his man, giving himself a massive gap to run in to, and blustered into the box with the look of a player ready to hit the ground with the slightest impact.

To his credit he slipped past the covering defender and lifted the most inviting ball into the area. Will Telfer had sensed what was happening and brushed off his marker to make the run to meet the cross, but Dec Hines came from nowhere and flung himself at the ball with a bullet header that caught the keeper out and crashed square against the cross bar. The ball made it to the edge of the area, such was the ferocity of the header, where Jarrod controlled, swiveled on to his left foot and curled a shot just past the post to a chorus of ooohs from the crowd, especially those just behind it, who watched from Jarrod's perspective as the ball skimmed the far post.

A quick glance at the sideline near the dugouts and Jarrod saw Marianne, her folks, Seb and Aneka taking their seats, whether it was after jumping out of them at these two moments of quality or just arriving, Jarrod couldn't tell. It was a moment though that gave Jarrod a massive lift. The away goal they had scored on Friday night was very important, and the message from Gary before the game was to make sure the away goal counted, a roundabout way of saying 'don't concede.'

This was an attacking team though, and their desire to score one more than the opposition was highlighted when a deft break by Crewe caught Darlington upfield. Some crisp passing in midfield gave the right winger a chance to run at Sam Basaan, who slipped and seemed to clip the winger, who kept his feet and swept an out-swinging ball into the area. The Crewe cavalry was racing to join the attack and watched as the ball bounced agonisingly across the edge of the six yard box.

Raynor Gunn finally collected the ball out wide and boomed the ball up into the Crewe half to ease the pressure. This was a game of sustained attack from Darlington and breakaway moments from Crewe, and Jarrod had to admit that the visitors were doing a good job of stifling them. It took a moment of class to get the crowd on their feet again. Dean Minto raced back to hook the ball away from the attacker with a Beardsley-esque tackle and emerged from a pack of players with the ball at his feet and his eyes on his next move.

Connor had made the run right to left, holding the line, and Dean found him with a slightly overhit through ball. The young Darlington midfielder kept his run going to the corner flag before slowing up and inviting his defender to lunge in. That was enough for a burst of pace to take him away from his man and he continued to the byline, looking for options. Will had made the run to the near post but was heavily marked, and there was Ghali Barbera, having checked his run to stay onside earlier in the move, and in the perfect position, sprinting towards the penalty area.

Connor's ball was low and hard and Ghali didn't have a second to think about it. The Darlington crowd held its collective breath as he caught the ball absolutely plum on the half-volley and the ball seared past the goalkeeper and into the side of the net for a fabulous opening goal. The stadium erupted. There were fans on the field. The place seemed to be shaking. Ghali raced off to the corner flag and punched the air, his teammates racing over to congratulate him for the picture-perfect photographer shot.

Jarrod grasped the goal-scorer by the shirt and saluted the fans with a roar. The energy was amazing, and Jarrod could feel his heart pounding as they made their way back to the halfway line. A goal to the good, but the players knew that it would mean nothing if Crewe were to score next, and in fact they would be back to square one. Two minutes to half-time though, surely there would be no cock-ups. Wes booted the ball long to be greeted by the referee's whistle for half-time. The crowd was raucous as the players made their way down the tunnel. Little incident in the game had meant no injury time, and Jarrod could feel the crowd were ready to carry them to victory.

The door closed behind Freddie Asquith, the last one in the changing room, and Gary was straight into his half-time talk. He wanted the players to step up a notch, be first to every ball, contest the tackle as if it was the last tackle they would ever make. The threat of yellow cards to miss the final was not lost on him though, and he made special mention to Wes, who was one yellow from a suspension, to play it cool but not too cool. Gavin Selley had been named again on the bench as he continued his comeback came and sat next to Jarrod, something white in his hand. It was a thin t-shirt. He unfolded it, and it read, "Doing it for you, babe!"

"Put it on under your shirt," said Gav. "You never know when you'll need it."

Jarrod was sceptical, but he had to admit that it was a great idea. He could whip it off if he scored, he could take it off just after the final whistle. If he was substituted, he could take it off as he came off. Jarrod gave Gav a hug and took off his shirt as Gary continued with his half-time talk. The feeling of t-shirt against sweaty skin made it quite a task putting on the extra layer. Mitch helped pull it down at the back, and it felt a little unusual under the material of the normal playing shirt. Still, he was going through an uncomfortable period in life, so what did it matter? It would be such a good look if he got some coverage for it though.

Gary started getting a little agitated and was singling out Dec for letting his man roam free in the middle of the park on a couple occasions. The players were focusing. A hush descended on the room and Jarrod could feel the concentration. Des then bashed on the wall, making a thumping sound, and shouted that it was time to get out for the second half, which brought a big roar from the players. This was a collective yell to signal their intent for the second forty-five. The door was opened, and the players filed out with one single objective – to win and to put this game to bed.

A ridiculous back-heel from the Crewe winger gifted Connor the ball early in the second half, and he shaped to shoot. Just as he corrected his stride to strike the ball, he was bundled off the ball. A free kick was the obvious outcome, and it was just outside the area. A little wide for a direct shot on goal, but a possible goalscoring chance all the same. Jarrod grabbed the ball and strode up to the referee to place the ball. The referee showed him the whistle to let him know to wait for the signal. A murmur went around the stadium. Jarrod had scored a couple of free kicks earlier in the season, but his radar had been off since the turn of the year.

Raynor Gunn's power had been preferred to Jarrod's failing precision, not that the goals were flowing for him either. This was Jarrod's free kick though, and a two man wall showed just how little Crewe feared the direct shot. The main action was on the far edge of the box though. A clump of players was ready to make the run to meet what would surely be an in-swinging left footer. The whistle sounded and the mass of players on the left-hand side of the box readied itself for action. There was pushing and pulling. The referee looked on with interest. Jarrod started his run up with purpose, but then slowed down and knocked the ball slowly to his left − Raynor Gunn had broken forward from his defensive position and was travelling with some speed. The wall realised what was happening and reacted, but Raynor was there already and he met the ball with an almighty shot that arrowed up and away from the keeper and into the very top left-hand corner of the goal, an amazing finish.

Pandemonium at the Arena as Raynor raced over to the Darlington end and leapt into the crowd. What a moment! It took two minutes for play to resume. Raynor was totally dishevelled after being man-handled by the crowd and his teammates. Two goals up, and forty minutes from Wembley. Crewe kept the ball for a minute from the kick-off and steadied their ship, letting the fervour die down, and seemed to start to play with abandon. This could go one of two ways, thought Jarrod. Either a spirited comeback by Crewe or an absolute annihilation by Darlington, and he pictured the latter.

Will Telfer was starting to make his presence felt up front and was playing the target man role to perfection. A raking ball from Freddie gave Ghali some space out wide on the left and his control was immaculate. This allowed Dec to make a run into the corner, but Ghali took the opportunity to hit the space, drew his defender and slipped a lovely little ball through for Will to race on to. The goalkeeper was committed and spread his arms wide to make the save. The ball bounced invitingly back to the tall striker, but he was off balance and the ball bounced off his shins and away for a goal kick.

Darlington just needed to keep their heads. Just as they were settling into cruise mode though, the curse of 2-0 struck. Sam controlled a long through ball with the poise of a ballerina and decided to take on his man instead of clearing. A cheeky steal from the attacker meant Darlington were caught out. Sam's lunge to try and win the ball back was fruitless as the Crewe man continued into the box, and with a shuffle to sort out his feet, he drilled the ball past Wes to bring the scoreline back to 2-1. The Crewe fans celebrated vociferously, a red and white sea of arms punching the air. The attacker was straight into the back of the net collecting the ball, and it was effectively game on again. Crewe knowing that one more goal might be enough to clinch this tie on away goals.

Jarrod had been in this situation a number of times, from both sides of the coin, and knew it would be a nervy last twenty minutes. Gary was out of his dugout raging at his players. Sam had his head down and was kicking the ground in anger. At least the fans could see what it meant, but nothing would ease the tension until either the final whistle or a third goal sealed the game. Wes fluffed a goal kick with ten minutes to go and got lucky when the striker failed to control it properly. Freddie was on the scene quickly to steady the nerves, and when Dean raced down the left on to a lovely through ball, there were groans when he slowed to a walking pace and trotted towards the corner flag. Time-wasting with eight minutes to go, not a good look, but at this stage of the game, the corner that he won when drilling the ball into the legs of the defender was a good return and bought more seconds.

A good four minutes of inaction was then played out as the corner kick became a throw-in and then another corner was won. The pantomime time-wasting enraged the Crewe coaching staff. They finally cleared the ball away, and won a free-kick on halfway, allowing them to send players forward in search of an unlikely winning goal. It was effectively all or nothing at this stage, and only the Crewe goalkeeper remained in the visitors' half as the long ball was boomed towards the far post area.

The ball seemed to hang in the air for an extended period while the players prepared to jump for it, and all of a sudden the ball ended up at the Crewe striker's feet, bearing down on goal, but in came Sam with a firm tackle to thwart the attack. The relief around the Arena was obvious. Jarrod found himself on the edge of his own area, looking up for options, but decided to keep the ball, and started moving forward, breaking into a sprint. The Crewe players were all camped up field, and two of them raced after Jarrod, who by now was over half way. A final defender was stuttering and wondering whether to commit or stay as Jarrod raced straight towards him.

In the end, the defender was flat-footed as Jarrod simply jinked and knocked the ball past him, finding pace that he had not felt for many years. He could feel his chest tightening as the length-of-the-field run continued into the box. The goalkeeper advanced to meet him and narrow the angle, huge gloved hands blocking the way to goal. Jarrod employed the same tactic as he had shown against the last defender and simply poked the ball past the keeper, and with the ball threatening to run out of play, reached with one last desperate lunge and hooked the ball with his left foot and sent it perfectly into the middle of the goal from quite a tight angle.

Jarrod was straight to his feet as the crowd rose as one to acclaim a mighty goal, and he lifted the front of his shirt over and behind his head to reveal the shirt he had accepted from Gav. He stood on top of an advertising hoarding, arms wide, facing the home end, and lapped up the joy. His teammates eventually joined him, pulling him down off the hoardings, and Jarrod collapsed on the ground, chest heaving from the lung-busting run he had just done.

The final four minutes were played in a haze. Crewe were unable to get anywhere near the Darlington goal. Gavin, on as a late substitute to huge applause, took the ball to his own corner flag to waste time, before the whistle went and the arms went up. Darlington had done it. They were Wembley-bound. Jarrod had his moment in the spotlight to support Marianne. Gary was surrounded by his staff and they were jumping around as if they had won the FA Cup, it was totally surreal. Having played all season to an average crowd of six thousand, a good atmosphere despite a relatively empty stadium, this was a sign of what it could be like. The sleeping giant that was Darlington was undergoing a right of passage, and the twenty-five thousand fans at the stadium that night knew they had been part of something very special.

Jarrod made his way over to the dugout, Gary lifting him off his feet in a joyous embrace, and then he found Marianne and gave her a hug. Aneka and Seb joined them. Jarrod quickly remembered to take off his shirt to show the t-shirt underneath and made sure he was in shot of the photographers. Seb took his playing shirt, rolled it up, and launched it high into the stand. They walked on to the field and the players all got together at the home end to applaud the fans and take in the cheers. Aneka joined in, her hands high in the air, clapping. Jarrod made sure the team had all celebrated together with the supporters before the players were inevitably hooked for interviews. Jarrod made his way over to join Dominic, who was trying to interview an excitable Wes, and made his way into the range of the microphone, simply shouting, 'Get iiiiiinnnnn!' before walking off arm in arm with Marianne. What an evening. This was the stuff of dreams. Darlington at Wembley! One more game and they could achieve the promotion they had set out to win.

The previous night's elation was still in the air. Jarrod had just dropped the kids at school and was skipping across the driveway with a spring in his step, a bag with two croissants from the bakery near the school in his hand. He felt as though he didn't have a care in the world. Marianne was up and about, and frantically cleaning the oven. A simple scenario that made him double-take, but he decided not to comment. Things were beginning to feel almost normal. Today, though, was the day, the first chemo session, and the event that Marianne had been anticipating the most.

Marianne had taken her first steroid pills the day before, which were beginning to give her a very odd kick, hence the oven getting its first clean since they moved into the house. Marianne hadn't noticed her slightly odd-ball behaviour until her Mum grabbed her by the shoulders the night before and stopped her mid-conversation and told her to be quiet. It was all said in jest, but she couldn't stop talking, and couldn't finish a sentence before starting the next one. She had also been most demanding to her mother, which was a little strange, and Jarrod pulled her up mid-conversation.

Marianne was due at the clinic at eleven. They set off in good time at about ten to ten, no traffic of note, arriving at the clinic in Newcastle with ten minutes to spare. The clinic was actually a converted terrace house in the inner-city streets not far from the hospital; a new facility was being built right next door as a replacement. They rang the doorbell, but the door was open, and they were met by the friendly receptionist and then given a seat by the front window, a nice comfy looking recliner seat for Marianne with a wheel-able table like in hospital. The only thing that suggested this was used for medical purposes was a drip by the seat.

There were four similarly comfortable-looking seats in what

was either the front room or a bedroom of the house, very quiet and intimate. There was even a middle-aged fellow dishing out cups of tea and coffee. They were made to feel right at home and the nerves were calmed. They were finally greeted by Anne-Charlotte, whose accent had them slightly confused, Irish mixed with something else. She ran them through the procedure, talked at length about the symptoms and after-effects of the treatment, and gave Marianne some pointers for staying healthy.

Marianne had to look away while the canular was put in, but within a few seconds it was in place, and she was hooked up to the anti-nausea drug. It gently seeped into Marianne's hand. Once that bag was empty, out came the chemotherapy drug, which was hooked up while they were talking with Anne-Charlotte. It seemed like the most natural thing in the world. The sun streamed in the window as Marianne relaxed and the drug flowed into her veins.

The expected descent into total incapacitation did not happen. There was no throwing up, no days in bed, nothing to suggest that Marianne had, in fact, gone through chemo. Whilst that could be attributed to Marianne's overall fitness in the months leading up to this, it might have been that her body was just able to cope with it the first time. The second and subsequent times might be tougher. She spent a bit of time resting in the afternoon, but by no means spending any great time in bed. The return from school pick-up by Jarrod and Jean-Jacques with the kids reminded Marianne of her duty as a parent. Her conscience overcame any opportunity of feeling sorry for herself, and the afternoon rush started.

Jarrod kept himself to the side of proceedings, perching himself on the corner of the couch in the living room, half-heartedly reading a letter that had come from the FFA in Australia. It felt like he was watching a reality TV show, Aneka being polite but demanding with Mireille, Seb dealing out the cards for a game with Jean-Jacques, and Marianne rushing around the kitchen in a fervour.

Jarrod had read about the possibility of mood swings. They were expecting it; the only problem is that while THEY were expecting it, it was only the partner who would have to cope with it and learn to manage it. Jarrod was used to doing a lot around the house. The lion's share of the cooking and cleaning up, as well as captaining a football team with all the stress and tension that goes with it. Put on top of that the kids and the in-laws and there was a lot of pressure, which Marianne did not see. Now to put mood swings into the mix, well that was enough to take the most patient man to tipping point.

"Get off your arse," snapped Marianne in an unusually English tone, furiously wrestling with a baking tray in the cupboard. "Can't you see I need help?"

This was uncharacteristic of Marianne. Her parents stopped what they were doing and looked at her and then at Jarrod, unsure as to which way this would play out. The kids were oblivious. Jarrod couldn't blame Marianne, she was going through a horrible experience. He rocked back on the couch and sprung to his feet, knowing he would have to just suck it up. Any sort of backchat from him would end in a shouting match, Jarrod felt, and it was an almost comical scene as Jarrod walked slowly over to Marianne, bent over and picked up the oven tray that had been causing Marianne such drama for all of two seconds and put it on the bench with a smile.

Marianne's scowl was a picture. Jarrod was thick-skinned, always had been, perhaps he got it from his parents, but a sample of the lines he was to hear that night before he left to join up with his teammates to watch the second semi-final: "I should have left you...", "I wish it was you that had cancer...", "I hate you...". All that interspersed with heaps of praise, love, and appreciation – mood swings.

Jarrod was relieved to get out of the house, wishing his in-laws a good evening, kissing the kids goodnight and then offering an unrequited kiss to Marianne on the way through the kitchen. The club had organised one of the lunchtime cafés in town to open up for the night and show the game on a big screen, and Jarrod made sure he was there just before the coverage started on TV, ordering a long-black double-shot coffee before doing the rounds and greeting his teammates.

The whole team was there, none of the coaching staff were there, and it felt as though they were off-leash. Jarrod was happy there was no alcohol, although he was sure that Gav Selley had a red wine in his takeaway coffee cup, and there was a roar as the highlights came on of the previous night's game. Jarrod's length-of-the-field decider drew cheers from his teammates, as if they hadn't been there on the field to see it. That was one hell of a run, he remarked to himself. He had been very fortunate not to overrun the ball with his second-last touch.

Mansfield and Chesterfield had served up the most turgid goalless draw at Field Mill. The away team did offer some attacking intent in the first half, but once the second half was underway, they shut up shop and seemed happy to settle for the result. No away goals was always a danger, so the emphasis would be on attack, and this could be an absolute cracker.

A few hangers-on made their way into the café. A couple of guys asked to join the team and brought in a four pack each, which worried Jarrod – he was happy though to see all his teammates refuse the offer of a beer, and they settled in for an absorbing evening in front of the TV. Jarrod felt nervous. He hoped to see a great game, but he hoped to see chinks in the armour of the team that won. He also secretly hoped for injuries, red cards, and for a couple of the players on a yellow, a matching yellow to get them suspended for the final, but he kept that all to himself.

A hush descended in the café as the commentator took over from the show's presenters and the game got underway. Chesterfield would be the absolute favourites for this one. They had been good when they went down to watch them, and Mansfield had not shown anything in the two games against Darlo to suggest they were good enough for promotion. Six minutes in, though, and a corner from the right was nodded down and the lanky central defender pounced to flick the ball home for a priceless away goal. The Darlo players were clearly rooting for Mansfield and the collective yelp as the goal went in confirmed where the allegiances lay for the evening.

This could be quite an upset, and Darlington would fancy themselves against Mansfield. The commentator was absolutely loving it, and he had the café mesmerised, Jarrod completely absorbed in the flow of the game. The inane facts being served up and the quips from the co-commentator made it even more theatrical. He didn't watch enough games live on TV, he thought to himself. How exciting must last night have been for the TV viewers? Chesterfield were predictably on the attack now and were laying siege to a rather flimsy-looking Mansfield rearguard. The goalkeeper was called into action on a number of occasions to smother at feet and punch the ball away from danger. Just as the clock showed on the screen for 40 minutes, Chesterfield conjured up a moment of magic. A break down the right drew in two defenders and left a huge gap on the left. The left back had made a break into the space and the ball was swung over from the right perfectly.

The rampaging defender looked a dead cert to blaze the ball over with a first time swinger, but he took a touch to get the ball under control and smashed the ball with the outside of his left foot, sending the ball swerving away from the keeper and into the top left-hand corner of the goal. Barely a reaction from the Darlington players as the stadium erupted on TV, fans jumping on the field in joy to celebrate with the home team. It was an absolute screamer of a finish, confirmed by the slow-motion replay from behind that showed the young defender catching the ball as sweetly as he could possibly catch it. The trajectory of the ball was even more enhanced as it flew into the net.

Half-time allowed the Darlo players to grab another coffee or tea, and the consensus was they would be playing Chesterfield in the final, despite the game being finely poised at one a-piece. Word had obviously got around the team was at the café and there were a few more in there by the time the second half started. Jarrod cleared away any beer cans just in case the local paparazzi were out – not a good look! The adverts over and done with and coverage switched back to the game, and Mansfield had made a defensive-looking substitution. This could be a long half for them if they were trying to play for the away goals victory.

The second half started very cagey and grew into quite a battle. There were some meaty challenges and a couple of yellow cards. It did look though as if Chesterfield could step it up just a little more, and with fifteen minutes remaining and a sense of panic starting to seep into the home team's game, the inevitable second goal arrived. A free-kick from the left, right in front of the camera position, was floated to the far post and there was the tall defender again to leap highest and meet the in-swinging cross with a thumping header that sailed into the goal.

Definitely one player to watch – two goals already to his name, and Chesterfield were soon back on the offensive, turning the screw, and ending the resistance from the valiant visitors. After two glorious saves had kept them in the game, a moment of madness from the goalkeeper saw him haul down the Chesterfield centre-forward who was going nowhere. A penalty, ten minutes to go.

Memories of Leicester City and Watford's unbelievable play-off semi-final all those years ago came flooding back. A simple penalty kick and Chesterfield were home and hosed. Up stepped the striker who fired the ball high and it smashed off the bar. The ball cannoning off the back off the goalkeeper who could only watch as the ball looped back into the net. Surely no coming back from that. A spirited finish from Mansfield made it exciting for the neutral, knowing that one goal would make it nervy for the hosts, but Chesterfield weathered the storm and came out victorious.

There was apathy at the result in the café, most people conceding that the best team won, whilst having hoped for an upset away win. The Mansfield players lay on the ground in despair as their counterparts celebrated with the home fans. Jarrod knew exactly how that felt; the hopes and dreams of a town in tatters, careers taking a swift change of direction, and the impetus of the club all but lost.

"Lads," said Jarrod as the majority of hangers-on had left. "Look at the Mansfield players. Be scared of ending up like that. We've been on a high all season. Don't be like Mansfield."

His teammates were in agreement and a buzz came over the café. They felt confident, but they were apprehensive after seeing Chesterfield win relatively comfortably.

"See you all in the morning," he chirped, trying to sound enthusiastic and merry, but he didn't feel at all like that. He knew he was feeling a little down. After all, reality would strike the moment he walked back through the front door at home.

"Don't forget, also," he continued as the chairs scraped and the players got up. "Friday golf day. Be there!"

Jarrod sat in his car and made sure he typed up a post on all the social media platforms about the golf day on Friday. He had neglected to do that previously, mainly because he hadn't been sure of Marianne's fitness for purpose. He now had an opportunity to post something when a lot of people would still be up and about and craving some news from their favourite footballers. He didn't wait around for replies though and started the car to head for home.

Part Ten
Emotional

Jarrod could feel the pressure building on all fronts since Wednesday night. Today would be a great distraction, and Jarrod was hoping his efforts with the press, increased social media presence, and openness with the local journalists would help draw a few extras at the golf event. Marianne had been there all day yesterday, despite feeling drained, and Jarrod was surprised at how well she had coped with the after-effects of the chemo. She was even putting together the final pieces of the event last night, and Jarrod was happy to take the reins and entertain the in-laws. His attempts at French caused much hilarity with the kids. It was LE beurre dans LE frigo, Mireille reminded him after getting his genders all wrong again.

Marianne had left early to be there for the event set up, and Jarrod had made sure everyone was ready on time to do the school run for the last day of term. Jean-Jacques and Mireille loved being at school for assembly, Seb was proud to introduce them to his French teacher, and Aneka encouraged Jean-Jacques to act the fool, so her friends could get a laugh.

They rolled into the newly-renamed Northallerton Golf Club, not so aptly named being in the town of Thirsk, but the club was in an absolutely beautiful setting. Driving into the carpark, surrounded by beautiful trees and immaculate, shiny new buildings, he could sense that his in-laws were impressed. He was too − it had been ten years since he had been here, and it had changed dramatically. The amount of cars here too was unbelievable, spilling out of the car park and on to a grassy area where a flustered youngster was doing his best to manage the parking overflow. They were ushered to possibly the furthest car park of them all, Aneka using her Timbuktoo line, and they all got out into the warm spring sunshine and made their way to the club house.

TV cameras were there, and there was a helicopter coming in to land. Jarrod had a quick glance in the side window of a parked car to check out his attire, he hadn't expected this to be such a big event. He had been to many fundraising events, but this was something else. They got their names ticked off at the door and were handed a glass of champagne, the real stuff (that would have been Marianne's insistence) and Jean-Jacques and Mireille were immediately at ease.

They walked together through the golf club and into the gigantic marquee that was just outside. As soon as they walked in, Marianne saw them, and quickly made her way over to the entrance, passing on a few instructions as she passed the many helpers for the day. She had organised a 'chaperone' for Jean-Jacques and Mireille, a delightfully elegant Belgian lady who broke into French as soon as she came over and planted the 'bise' on both cheeks of her guests. Great, thought Jarrod, time to work the room. Marianne held out her hand and Jarrod squeezed it, and he knew she didn't have any time for small talk. Off she went into the throng. A band got up on stage and started to play some gentle jazzy music, there was a buffet-style area overstaffed with servers, making the line go very quickly, and there were coffee carts everywhere. Jarrod was accosted by Dominic from the radio. He was dressed in his golfing gear and had just finished.

"Jarrod, your wife knows how to put on an event, that's for sure!" Dominic said, and tucked in to the pastry he was holding.

"This is way fancier than I was expecting," Jarrod exclaimed.

Jarrod had to speak up as the music was getting louder. He spied one of his old Gateshead teammates in the distance and gave a wave. The music came to a stop and the MC for the day, a local TV presenter, got up on stage with his microphone and started the introduction.

"Breast Cancer Care welcomes you to Northallerton Golf Club for a fundraising event like no other!" he said. "Welcome to all our sponsors, all our esteemed guests, and a big thank you to all the people who have made today possible."

Jarrod and Dominic stood side-by-side watching on expectantly.

"Today you will have or will have had the chance to experience nine holes at this fantastic new facility. We have a fabulous buffet for you all, we have tea, coffee, wine, and beer for everyone. All rounds will be finished by 11.30am and we will start the next round at 12:30pm, after our main presentation here in the marquee."

Jarrod loved it. The MC spoke so eloquently.

"Please, enjoy the hospitality on offer, and I'll catch you back here at 11.30 when we will run through a special auction to raise money for this most fabulous charity."

There was a huge round of applause. It just felt like a proper day off. There were waiters bringing around wine and beer, just like at a wedding, and Jarrod found himself moving into the next conversation with a local referee, who had officiated at a few of the Darlington games during the season. There were faces from all the football clubs in the area, there were some celebrities interspersed with models and pop stars. The further he got into the crowd, the more people he knew, and he started feeling overwhelmed.

Many questions came about Marianne, and the shows of support, pats on the back, arms around the shoulder, all made him feel really loved. Jarrod was the man of the moment and felt he and his wife were the number one topic of conversation. Jarrod loved it, getting the chance to refine his answers with every repeated question, until he had perfected his responses.

"Yes, Marianne is looking radiant today. She is a strong lady."

"Breast Cancer is now part of our lives now, Marianne is battling through it."

"The support we have had from family and friends has been amazing."

The marquee was now very full and very loud as a result, and the MC was ready to start with the main presentation.

"Ladies and gentlemen," said the MC. "I present to you our spokesperson for the Breast Cancer Care charity, Marianne Black."

There was a hearty round of applause and Marianne gingerly walked on to the stage.

"Oh, my goodness," she started. "There are more people here than I could have ever imagined!"

She took a moment to steady herself.

"Only a few short weeks ago," she started. "I found out I had breast cancer." There was a hush.

"This event was already being organised, but I was then thrust into a cancer journey of my own. It was at the hospital in Newcastle that I came into contact with the Breast Cancer Care nurse, the lovely Gharda. She was a wealth of information and guidance and helped me through the early stages, when I knew nothing about the process and the journey ahead."

She went on to tell her story so far, so that she could express her thanks to the Breast Cancer Care nurse. There were tears in the audience as she described when she told her husband, how the kids reacted to it, and how wonderful everyone had been ever since. She had the marquee in the palm of her hand and seized the moment to pass on the microphone at just the right time to the MC. He started the ball rolling by announcing the first auction item, a top of the line Range Rover. The bidding was starting at one thousand pounds, and they would continue until they had a winner. This car was an absolute beauty, and had obviously been donated by the local dealer, who Jarrod knew. The auction leapt into action, bids of five thousand pounds bringing it quickly past its probable reserve price and it just kept on going. An astonished MC finally stopped the auction at just over two hundred and thirty thousand pounds; the winner punching the air and racing on stage to collect the keys. This was amazing.

The next item was up, and it was a holiday, a little more affordable. The sponsor again was someone Jarrod knew dearly from a travel agency in Newcastle. The auction was quick and punchy, and they went through six or seven different items, raising almost half a million pounds. Each time, Jarrod knew the sponsor. He started to feel as though his standing in the community had indeed contributed a great deal to the success of this event, and he was absolutely delighted. Marianne again got up on stage to conclude the auctions, finishing on a poignant note.

"Jarrod, my darling Jarrod," she said, looking around the room until she found him. "This is going to be one hell of a ride, but I'm so glad to be going on it with you. Look at all these people here today, they're here to support this charity, to support us, to support me, and our family. I hope our efforts today make a difference to the lives of many breast cancer patients in the region. Thank you."

The marquee erupted, Jarrod could feel hands on his back and his hair was being ruffled, what a crazy moment. Marianne had stolen the hearts of the entire audience and this day was going to go down as one of the most amazing ever. The marquee started to thin out as golfers went on their way and people took advantage of the huge grounds to bask in the sun. Jarrod remained and took advantage of the hospitality on offer and enjoyed meeting up with a lot of familiar faces.

Jarrod was exhausted by the time they got in the car. It was around seven and the event had concluded, a number of the more refreshed attendees heading off into an after party in town. Marianne would be defying doctors' orders and would be at the venue until late with the post-event process. Jean-Jacques and Mireille were in their element too. Jarrod had to get the kids from Pippa's, where he hoped the welcome wasn't wearing thin. It was the end of school though, so he imagined it would be quite a party there too.

Marianne was absolutely ragged, she didn't get out of bed until well after midday on the Saturday. Jarrod had gone to and returned from training and Mireille had checked up on Marianne – she was sound asleep all morning despite the shrieks and hollers of the kids playing their new favourite game Finska in the back garden with their Grandparents. Jarrod felt as though he had broken the spell when he returned, the kids for once giving their Mama and Papy all of their attention, and he made a point of joining in the ruckus to keep the momentum going and to allow Marianne plenty of space to catch up on her much-needed sleep.

Marianne's appearance with a cup of coffee as the game was just drawing to a close and lunch was being prepared confirmed she was indeed struggling. Her face said it all, sunken eyes, pale complexion, and lines where she had never noticeably had lines before. There was a small patch of slightly whispier hair than normal at the meeting of the parting at the top of her forehead, but Jarrod just put that down to the hours of pillow-to-head action that she had been through. Sebastian raced past Marianne and barely brushed his Mum, but she made an exaggerated move to avoid him, slopping coffee over the side of her cup, and taking a step back, cup held out at arm's length, a look of fury on her face.

"Sebastian," she hollered. "Why did you do that?"

Seb had stopped before he got inside and turned to say sorry to his Mum.

"Show some respect," shouted Marianne, before he could get his words out, "that could have burned me."

Jarrod looked at Seb, keen to race to his defence. They both looked at Mireille, with eyebrows lifted, and Mireille took the cue to get involved and make it all better, moving in with a napkin to wipe Marianne's hands and putting her hand gently on Seb's head to let him know the situation was in hand. Marianne was tutting and swearing in French, her Mum fussing, but only so much that it distracted her daughter. This was a definite sign the chemotherapy was taking hold, and a combination of exhaustion and chemo-brain was starting to change Marianne's outlook on life. Jarrod slipped away, closely followed by a concerned Aneka, and he raced up to Seb's room to find him sitting on his bed looking totally shattered.

"Seb," said Jarrod. "We have to be strong. Mum is in a difficult place right now, and we're just going to have to play the game."

Jarrod sat down next to him and put his arm around his son, Aneka climbing slowly on to the bed and putting her arm on Sebastian's.

"I've got your back, Seb," said Jarrod, and his son reached over and buried his head in to his chest. The slow sobs that eventually came told the story that the kids were, in fact, being affected. Aneka simply looked at Jarrod with sad eyes and held her brother.

By Wednesday, play-off fever had definitely hit Darlington. There were honks from cars as he waited at traffic lights. There were autograph hunters whenever he got out of his car, and the kids around town on their school holidays were keen to get their selfies taken with the players. Jarrod and Ghali had bumped into each other in town that Wednesday after training and decided to get their hair cut on a whim at the funky barbers on the main street. Jarrod immediately felt guilty that he wasn't going back to the hairdressers where he'd last been just the other week, but this was special – it was a week for special things.

They both sat down at the same time. The owner of the barbers sensed that these were two men on a mission and cranked up the music. It was soon a carnival atmosphere in there as the two burly workers set to work on their vastly different subjects. Ghali's hair was thick and wiry, and he wanted it thinned out and short at the sides, whereas Jarrod's non-descript hairstyle was simply in need of a minor trim to take it from slightly dishevelled to stylish.

As soon as the first kid outside noticed the loud music and took a curious glimpse through the window, it didn't take long for a crowd to form, and people started to come in to the shop, some hoping for a haircut, others just hoping to join the party. The Housemartins, or maybe it was the Beautiful South, came on the music system, the Caravan of Love causing the two players to immediately break into acapella, Jarrod doing the boom boom and Ghali doing some really smooth aaaahs, the owner catching on and clicking the music up another notch or two.

There was a pause on all haircuts as Jarrod broke into song and some of the people in the shop who knew the song started to sing along too. It was the sort of moment that made you feel good to be alive and was totally impromptu. Ghali was up off his seat, clicking his fingers to the beat to his audience. A great round of applause greeted the end of the performance, and both players sat back down, and the haircuts resumed as if nothing had happened. There were still twenty or so people in the barbers, and they were all sticking around. The conversation turned to football. Jarrod was loving it. Everyone had an opinion, everyone was positive. Darlington was buzzing.

It was now Friday and Marianne had a 1pm meeting at the clinic in Newcastle for her second chemo session. The anxiety of the first visit was replaced by a feeling of calm. Marianne knew what was coming, she knew that it was a very pleasant place to undergo an unpleasant treatment, and she bounced in to the clinic and saw a lot of the faces she had seen the first time. Jarrod, who had dropped her at the door and quickly gone off into the town centre to get a present for a party that Seb was going to that evening, finally made it back as Marianne was getting hooked up for the second dose of medication. The sun was streaming in, and Jarrod could see that her hair was starting to look dry and damaged. He thought about commenting, but knew it would not be well received, so he simply ran his hand over her head by way of a tender greeting, a few hairs sticking to his hand as he took his hand away.

"You're taking me to Margie's on the way home," said Marianne, grabbing Jarrod's hand and looking at the hairs that had brushed off her head. "I'm booked in at 4pm."

Jarrod smiled and said nothing. He was almost at the point where saying anything would be the wrong thing to do, and he was finding it hard to think of neutral topics of conversation that wouldn't irk or annoy his wife.

Jarrod made himself a cup of tea and brought a couple of tiny sandwiches for Marianne to have with hers. She refused them and sat back in her chair and closed her eyes, Jarrod taking the opportunity to pick up the day's Journal, glancing at the back page to see a piece about Darlington's road to promotion sandwiched between news of Newcastle's potential new owners and Sunderland's own play-off hopes in the Championship decider. They'd even made the back page in Newcastle. The club was making people sit up and take notice!

The welcome was as warm as any welcome he could remember when they got to Margie's hair salon. Jarrod felt a tinge of guilt as he walked in with his fresh cut and could feel Margie checking him out with a shake of the head, but this was all about Marianne, and she walked right in and greeted Margie with a hug.

"Lovely to see you, pet," Margie said with gusto.

"Thanks for fitting me in. Let's talk about what we're going to do," said Marianne. The door opened and in came Pippa Robson, and she raced across to Marianne and they gave each other a big hug, Pippa letting a bottle of Prosecco peek out of her bag and pointing suggestively at it to Margie. Jarrod knew it was time to leave the ladies to it, this was obviously going to be a big natter-fest.

"Hun," said Jarrod, putting his hand on Marianne's arm, "what time am I picking you up?"

"I'll give you a call," she said. Jarrod was dismissed.

Jarrod had driven to the Arena, not sure what to do while he waited. Pauline spotted him as soon as he had walked through the front gate, and she leapt out of her car where she had been camped on the phone since arriving at the stadium herself. She was still on the phone and simply grabbed Jarrod, opened her passenger door and beckoned him in. When Pauline climbed in the other side, she placed her mobile in the cradle and the speakers in the car picked up the conversation. Pauline grabbed a pen and scribbled on a parking meter receipt two things: "Radio 5," and "Live on air in 3 minutes," as she carefully changed the tone of her conversation from an, "I'm sorry," into, "Oh wait a minute."

This was indeed Radio 5 on the phone, and they had been looking for time with Gary, but he was busy with two other interviews already this afternoon. Jarrod had essentially saved the day – Pauline hated missing out on media opportunities, and she asked if they would like to speak with Jarrod. There was a rustle of papers and scraping of chairs at the other end of the phone and some muffled shouts, as they prepared for an unscheduled interview. Pauline took the time to fill in Jarrod.

"They're going to ask you about preparation for the game tomorrow," she said. "You're going to say that preparation has been perfect. Clean bill of health for the squad. Everyone is pumped, that sort of thing."

Jarrod nodded. The usual fodder.

"Then they're going to ask what you expect from Chesterfield. You can give an honest answer there, but make sure you sound confident and make it sound as though we're not going to let the opposition affect us."

Jarrod smiled and nodded. This really was rushed, and he could feel Pauline getting a little frantic. She checked again that she had muted the phone.

"And finally, they're going to ask about your last time at Wembley. And you're going to say that your previous experiences of play-off games are going to be the inspiration you need to win tomorrow. How does that sound?"

Jarrod gave a wink. "All good," he said.

The interviewer came on, a familiar voice of one of the main presenters of the football on Radio 5. Jarrod immediately felt honoured. A producer's voice counted them in and the interview started. Despite the rushed pep talk prior to the interview, Jarrod was perfectly prepared and delivered a near-perfect interview, only a couple of minutes long, and once they had finished and hung up, Pauline gave him a kiss on the cheek and punched the air as if she had scored a goal. Jarrod loved this.

Everyone was excited. They got out of the car and walked into the Arena and the atmosphere was one of nervous excitement. The eerie quiet as they walked in and the fact that the gear for tomorrow was getting prepared next to the foyer made it seem all very real. This was going to be a huge event, and Jarrod could feel a hint of butterflies in his stomach. Gary appeared from the media room.

"Jarrod!" he shouted, pumped up from his interviews. "Time to go off and get some sleep. Early start tomorrow. How's Marianne going?"

"She's doing remarkably well," said Jarrod, choosing not to give anything away.

"That's good to hear," he said. "Now I'll see you here at 6am."

Jarrod clasped Gary's hand and they went their separate ways. Jarrod was off to the lockers to check his boots, and Gary off out into the sunshine to make his way home. He definitely had a spring in his step.

It was starting to get a bit late now, nearly seven, and Jarrod made his way to Margie's even though there was no phone call to pick up Marianne. He got the shock of his life when he walked in. Marianne had her hair cut short, in what she coined as a Pixie cut. What's more, she had it dyed in a silvery colour. Jarrod had never seen her with short hair and had definitely never seen it any other shade than dark. Jarrod was immediately intrigued.

"First, we started with this one," said Margie, proudly showing Jarrod her phone and a photo of a sexy bob hairstyle. "We really liked that one."

"Then we made it wavy," said Marianne, flicking the phone to the next photo. "Then we decided to take it even shorter."

"And the colour?" asked Jarrod.

"Why not?" said Marianne. "I'm just about to lose my hair, and this colour might disguise it for the next day or two. I'm coming back on Monday for the Sinead O'Connor."

"Oh, my goodness!" said Jarrod, but he was secretly thrilled looking at Marianne right now. He could see one sexy lady with one sexy hairstyle. It seemed to accentuate the length of her neck and he was turned on.

"Just wait until I get you home," he laughed, and they all cracked up. Margie was blushing and struggling to breathe between laughs.

Part Eleven
Final Score

The plan was all set. The family were catching the early train down to London – the club had booked the whole of the first class and Marianne, her parents, Seb, and Aneka were whisked away in a taxi just before Jarrod got in his car to drive to the Arena. Despite the early hour, the kids were excited, and Marianne was almost unrecognisable with her striking new look.

The squad were flying down on an 8am flight to London City airport, a gesture that owner Gerry Lincoln had promised, and he was putting them up in one of London's best hotels that night with their families. What better incentive to win? The last of the supporters buses were leaving when he got there, and he seized the opportunity to hop onto each of the three buses yet to leave and wish everyone a great day. The final bus erupted in song. Jarrod joined in with, "Tell me Ma, me Ma, I won't be home for tea..." then quickly jumped down off the bus leaving behind a raucous coach load of fans who were already in full voice. Jarrod jogged over to the players' entrance before stopping and grabbing his hamstring, then turning around and laughing – only joking but tempting fate a little.

The players were all there and were all excited. Jarrod remarked at how relaxed everyone looked, especially Connor Naughton, who had been so meek the first time he had been involved only two months ago. He now had his chest puffed out and looked like a man with purpose. Gary was mingling with the players. He had seen it all as a player and won so much, but this would be something special for him too.

The upbeat mood remained throughout the very smooth journey to London and then through the traffic to Wembley.

This was the only game happening in the country today; only a Scottish Second division play-off final to compete with, but that was an early kick-off. All eyes would be on Wembley for the first in a three game weekend which would decide who would go up and who would stay down for another year in each of the three divisions of the Football League.

Ticket prices had been slashed and the game had been promoted extremely well. The offer of free tickets to the League One play-off final the next day tempted a lot of people to snap up tickets for this one and make a weekend of it. The East Coast train service had added five extra services to London, direct from Darlington, and there was a fleet of coaches carrying almost half the town to the capital to cheer on their team.

Kick-off was 3pm and they were at the stadium at 10.30am, possibly the earliest they had ever arrived at a game, but the Wembley effect would mean that the minutes would flash by. There was a short session on the hallowed turf – they had been allocated a 45 minute slot to get used to the surface, and Gary made sure they did passing drills and a ten minute game to get a feel for the run of the ball, before six of the players practiced penalties while the opponents Chesterfield filed out for their allotted session on the field.

Wes wasn't exactly throwing himself around at the penalties, looking like Peter Shilton at Italia 90 as the penalties rained in, but Jarrod couldn't help feeling that Gary had asked him to let them all in. All the players went over to a section of seats and watched their opponents go through their warm-up. Gary pointed out a few familiar faces in their ranks. Dec Hines was going to do a marking job on their athletic central midfielder, and Des was in his ear, geeing him up. Gary made a point of calling the team back into the tunnel as if to suggest to Chesterfield they had seen enough. Very subtle mind games, but this was coming from a manager who had been there himself, and on many occasions.

Jarrod didn't feel like food, but they were taken to the players' café and offered their choice of anything from the menu. He knew he had to take on something, but the nervous feeling in his stomach was telling his brain otherwise. In the end, a small bowl of rice, some green beans, and some scrambled eggs made his tray look like a Bento box, and as soon as he started eating he realised how hungry he really was. Will had his customary mountain of pasta with butter, Raynor had a steak. This was all very fancy – normally there was one or maybe two choices, today they were dining like royalty.

The moment that game day turns into match time is usually when the players head to the changing rooms and get a feel for their surroundings. When they find their spot next to their shirt and unpack their bag ready for the day. Today was like any other. All the shirts, shorts, and socks were laid out perfectly, and the changing facilities seemed palatial. Plenty of room to put everything and no bums in faces when getting your boots on.

Certain players went through their protracted bandaging routines, while Jarrod took an opportunity to get his hamstrings massaged by Sash, who had set up the physio table in the middle of the room. Gary and Des were pacing the room, checking on every player once and then a second time. They were making sure everyone had everything they could possibly need and were starting to pass on tactics to the individual players who had specific jobs to do.

With most players ready, Gary then opened the door and let the players head out to warm-up on the Wembley field. Walking out from the shadows of the tunnel and into the daylight when a crowd had suddenly appeared was always exciting. The crowd was already filling up, the empty seats disappearing quickly. This was going to be a huge crowd, thought Jarrod. There was a roar as the players fanned out from the tunnel. The Darlo players made sure they went to the end where the majority of their fans were housed. Jarrod was collared for a quick TV interview, answering two similar questions to those he'd answered last night, before joining the rest of the players for their now traditional warm-up routine. There was an edge to everyone's demeanour. Jarrod knew that the other team would be feeling much the same, but somehow there was an extra something to this Darlington team, and Jarrod felt ready to go in to battle alongside these great men.

The teams were read out, although the whole squad being read out didn't give away any starting eleven at this stage. The only question mark was Dean Minto, who had turned his ankle over in training the other day but was warming up confidently. Gav Selley would be the obvious replacement anyway, as they were so used to him coming on as a second half sub. Des gathered the players in for a huddle, and they went through the basic structure – Dec man-marking Steve Robey, Will playing as a lone striker with Ghali in behind, the rest of the team was as usual, Dean able to start.

Gary called the players in to the changing rooms. This was a scene that had been played out all season but playing at Wembley in front of a proper crowd made this seem like such a ceremony. It was also the last game of the season, whatever the scoreline, so they knew this would be the final game for a while, and that simple fact made the desire even more to get the result.

The roar was unbelievable. The national anthem had been played and belted out by the crowd, definite lump in your throat time, even for an Aussie. The roar continued right until kick-off, reaching its peak as the referee blew for the start of the game. Darlo had won the toss and chosen to swap around for the first half, playing in to a stiff breeze. There was a promise of even windier conditions later in the game, so the tactic would be to slow down the game and soak up any pressure in the first half and then come home strongly in the second half. Chesterfield sensed they should be pushing to take advantage of the conditions and took the game to Darlington from the kick-off.

A cross-shot was not dealt with by Wes, but Sam Basaan was there to nick the ball away from the winger who was closing in for the kill. Darlington then broke up the left, Dean weaving his way on to a through ball from Freddie Asquith, clipping in a beautiful cross that Will met on the stretch, the ball just clearing the bar to a chorus of 'oohs' from the crowd.

The first corner of the game from Chesterfield was then swung in to the penalty area, Wes couldn't reach it, and Jarrod found himself with a bouncing ball at his feet, half a yard from goal and facing the wrong way – any touch would send the ball potentially into the goal. He shielded the ball as the Chesterfield players came flying in to apply the final touch. Wes dived and got a finger to it, the ball ricocheted off the post and hit Raynor Gunn on the knee and trickled into the goal for 1-0.

An own goal in the play-off final, how unlucky, but the Chesterfield players celebrated as if it was their goal. It could and perhaps should have been 1-1 straight away, Dec picking up a loose ball and playing Connor in with a superb through ball, but the defender got back quickly and kicked the ball into Connor's shins, the ball rebounding across the empty goal where Dean had just given up his run thinking the chance had gone. Ghali's head was in his hands, what a chance missed.

More pressure from Chesterfield saw a neat through ball down the left-hand side of the area where Mitch cleared up the trouble. The Chesterfield player flung himself theatrically to the floor as if he'd been caught. The Darlington players surrounded the striker, the referee coming across to intervene and producing a yellow card for the dive. The game was finely poised – one goal down at half-time, and a big chance to use the conditions in their favour in the second forty-five.

Gary and Des were still relaxed at half-time. Darlington had enjoyed roughly half the possession in the first half of the game and had created chances. Gary's words at half-time involved a plea for patience and a request to play some of that one-two stylish football they had dished up so often this season.

They would be up against negative tactics from Chesterfield in the second half, and their opponents would be employing all of the time-wasting tactics if the game continued at 1-0. Some dallying in midfield by Dean right at the start saw him cough up possession midway inside the Darlo half and Chesterfield quickly broke, the ball played out to their tall striker, who shaped to shoot but was surprised to see Sam race back and get the block in. A fantastic last-ditch challenge from the Darlington fullback.

There were nerves now, an hour into the game and Darlo still behind. Chesterfield were taking forever with their throw-ins, much to the annoyance of the Darlington fans, and that coveted promotion spot looked to be drifting out of reach. Cue a calamitous moment – a corner from the Darlo right whipped in by Dean Minto. The heads went up in the middle of the penalty area and they all missed, the ball falling at the far post where Ghali stuttered and then made sure he got any part of his body to the ball to force it over the line. Cries of handball went unheard as the ball bounced off his chest and into the goal for a dramatic equaliser. The crowd exploded. That was a very ugly goal, but the Darlington fans didn't care, it was a relief.

If the crowd thought a complete turnaround was on the cards, they were wrong. Chesterfield came straight at Darlington and a cross from the left was deftly headed away from the incoming striker by Freddie. The resulting corner saw a firm header from ten yards out sail just over the corner of post and bar, and the warning signs were there. Jarrod was having trouble getting into this game, Dec was tied up with his man-marking game and wasn't able to provide the attacking option from midfield.

It took a moment of magic to give Darlington the lead they were so desperate for, defender Mitch Short choosing to overrule Connor and take a free kick, dead centre, some thirty metres from goal. The crowd were urging him to shoot, despite his season's conversion rate of zero, and he used that as a decoy to check his run and float a delightful ball towards the penalty spot. Jarrod had broken clear of his marker and met the ball with a glancing header, sending it arcing through the air and over the stranded keeper for 2-1. Jarrod raced off to the Darlington fans at the other end of the stadium, a great goal, and Darlo were in the lead.

This was cue for some cute time-wasting tactics from Darlington, giving the Chesterfield players a taste of what they had been trying to do earlier in the half. Will was bundled to the ground and stayed down, the referee coming across to check if he was okay. Sash was called on to administer some treatment and Will just stayed on the ground on his back, letting the referee know he was winded. Those three minutes wasted were enough to make the Chesterfield players and bench uptight, so when Ghali stayed down a moment later after a crude challenge deep into Chesterfield territory, the players were straight over to him to pull him up off the ground.

Ghali made a point of dropping to the ground again, before the referee intervened and ushered away the angry Chesterfield players. Gary had never been an advocate of time-wasting, but he wasn't saying anything. Perhaps it was an appropriate tactic his players were employing, given what was at stake. Eight minutes remaining and a free-kick in a promising situation.

Could Raynor come up with another pile-driver. Would Connor smash one around the wall and into the top corner? In the end, another two minutes of waiting was ended when Will peeled away from the wall and raced over to the corner flag. Raynor stepped up to drive the free-kick out to him, clearly not going for goal at all. Will took the ball down beautifully and turned his back, shielding the ball with his bulk, and managed to eat up another thirty seconds before turning and drilling the ball off the defender's legs for a corner.

More seconds wasted. Dec, who had marked danger man Steve Robey out of the game, then found himself with the ball deep in his own half, facing his own goal. He felt a hand from behind under the slightest of pressure and crumpled to the ground as if run over by a bus. The referee was right on the scene and had seen enough time-wasting, producing the yellow card for the dive by Dec. Dec's hands went on his head when he realised, and when the referee saw that the first name in the book early in the game had been the same player, he sheepishly pulled out the red card, flashing first the yellow, then the red and almost apologetically sending Dec to the sideline.

There was uproar from the Darlington fans and the stadium was rocking all of a sudden. Three minutes of normal time and surely a good chunk of additional time remaining, this was going to be a grandstand finish. Dec made sure he took as long as possible to get off the field, slowly walking to the sideline, clapping to the Darlo fans as he ambled.

Jarrod called Will back to help out in midfield. Ghali was left up there by himself, but from the free-kick, every Darlington player was back in the penalty area defending. This felt very familiar; a similar scene having played out twelve months ago as Gateshead piled on the pressure to get a late equaliser in the Championship play-off decider. Jarrod was relieved to be on the other side, leading with only moments left.

Surely it would be a matter of time before the goalkeeper made his way up to join the attack. A long throw-in caused havoc in the Darlington penalty area, Mitch hacking the ball away, and Ghali raced across to just keep the ball in. He raced down the right and drew the defender in for the tackle, and made sure he got caught, going over the outstretched leg and hitting the ground with arms and legs sprawled.

A definite free-kick, and one that Darlington could milk. The customary two minutes were spent getting the wall the required distance and Will raced to the corner again, this time Raynor using it as a decoy and lifting the ball into the area where Connor met the ball with a thumping header, but straight at the keeper. The keeper rolled the ball out to himself and set off on a run, but the long blow on the whistle followed by two further blows saw the Darlington players give up the chase and race to the sideline to celebrate with each other. Fantastic scenes for the winners, and total devastation for the losers, the trademark of the play-off lottery. Jarrod kept away from the throng and made his way around the Chesterfield players, shaking hands, and handing out hugs to anyone who needed it. He knew exactly how they felt, and he wasn't going to jump around celebrating in their faces.

Having said that, once he had run out of hands to shake, he broke into a jog and made his way over to the Darlington fans with the rest of the squad, arms raised in triumph, fists clenched, and a look of steely satisfaction on his face. TV cameras and reporters tried to stop him for an interview, but he breezed straight past, hands raised in applause to the fans. All he could feel was relief, there was little joy – it was more about getting the job done and achieving what they should have achieved before the play-offs.

The younger players on the team though were going to town on this one, and Jarrod was more than happy to join in. There was water being thrown around from the water bottles, scarves being picked up from the edge of the pitch and swirled around. Gary was tackled to the ground and picked up by the players and tossed into the air, quite an effort given his big frame. The cameras were lapping this up, and the kids and families came on to the field to join in the love. Seb raced over to his Dad and jumped into his arms. Aneka jumped on to them both with a look of total joy on her face. Marianne came bounding across, looking absolutely thrilled and planted a lengthy kiss on his lips. This was a glorious moment.

The players' lounge was the place to be after the game, the Chesterfield players were quick to leave, giving the Darlington contingent free rein. Marianne was courting a lot of attention from the cameras, and to be fair she looked smoking hot; the slightly sallow complexion and sunken eyes adding to the mystique. This was a lady who was two chemo sessions in to cancer treatment, barely two weeks from being in intensive care after a huge operation. What a woman.

While the Darlington players were still celebrating in the changing rooms, the rest of the entourage was lapping up the atmosphere, and the paparazzi were going to town. When Jarrod arrived, the reporters were straight on the scene, getting Marianne and Jarrod together for interviews. Jarrod pushed the limelight squarely on to Marianne and the endorphins were making him gush. This would be front cover stuff for the trashy mags at the supermarket checkout next week, and Jarrod was more than happy to give them plenty of fuel. All the while Aneka and Seb had found some friends and were playing hide and seek, totally oblivious to their Mum and Dad, and Jean-Jacques and Mireille were back on the champagne again, loving every moment.

That weekend was truly one of the best weekends ever for Jarrod. His wife was at her sparkling best, despite her condition. She was surrounded by family, they were staying in a great hotel, the weather was warm. Jarrod had fulfilled all his duties and they were off sightseeing for the day, taking in the Tower of London and going for a cruise on the Thames. Jarrod didn't even check the score in the League One final until late that night on the way home. The newspapers and news websites had gone to town on Marianne and Jarrod, and Pauline had been on the phone with multiple requests for in-depth interviews. Jarrod wasn't that keen, but if Marianne was happy to do it, he would be a willing participant. They had a lot to talk about after all.

These twelve months had been nothing short of astonishing; the last two months had been testing and had totally altered Jarrod and Marianne's lives. They knew that they were still in the middle of a voyage into the unknown, and Marianne was sure to get sicker as the chemo took hold. On the Monday when they returned to Darlington, Marianne drove herself to Margie's and got her hair cut in a number one all over and walked out of there with a headscarf on and her head held high.

Jarrod himself had some good news when he received a call on the Monday afternoon – Mike Jerszek had called him up to the squad for the two upcoming games. He had made the cut and he was going to represent his country, over ten years since his last foray into international football. That wasn't the end of it either. Dad had phoned up soon after. Jarrod thought he was congratulating him on the Socceroos call up, but no.

"Have you seen the World Game website?" he asked excitedly. Jarrod obviously hadn't. "Let me read the headline. Socceroos renaissance for Jarrod Black alerts Premier League giants."

"EH?" said Jarrod. "Who are they talking about?"

Dad continued reading, having a bit of trouble holding his phone to his ear while holding his iPad at arms' length to read the smaller print.

"...dah dah dah... Black's displays for Darlington this year have demonstrated to Newcastle United scouts..."

Dad paused and swallowed loudly as if he was welling up.

"... that he could be the player to steer the ship in the coming season as the club undergoes a change of ownership."

"Oh my god!" shouted Jarrod. "Oh my god."

"What do you think about that?" asked Dad, absolutely bursting with pride at the thought of his boy turning out for his boyhood team at St James Park.

"Oh my god..."

Darlington had their end of season dinner in town that night, and after a superb evening in one of the restaurants in town, they were driven back to Gerry's house to party on. The players had an idea of just how much of a bon viveur he was after Saturday evening in the players' lounge at Wembley, but there were definitely no paparazzi at Gerry's house. Jarrod thought he had seen everything, but Gerry put on one hell of a party that night.

Marianne had indeed become a lot sicker as the treatment continued, and the interviews were curtailed. Jean-Jacques and Mireille had gone back home, and Jarrod had taken on the role of carer for the final two weeks of chemo. They had time to take stock of everything that had happened and get their family life back to some sort of standard routine.

A second visit to the oncologist brought home some interesting truths about Marianne's cancer journey. Jan Keever had explained the journey they were on was like a roundabout. They would be on that roundabout for the duration of the treatment, and that people would disappear from their lives, but at the same time new people would come into their lives. Once they got off the roundabout, their world would be a very different place. Not only physically for Marianne, but emotionally, and psychologically for the whole family. It was important they work through this together. Those words were taken on by Marianne and Jarrod, and it gave them hope and encouragement that they weren't the first people to go through this.

Marianne walked into the final chemo session as if she owned the clinic. There was not a flinch as the canular was put in, and she gratefully accepted a sandwich with her cup of tea. Jarrod had a scheduled meeting with an agent at a coffee shop near St James Park, which he had insisted on walking to. He was back now, with a smile on his face, in good time to wrap up the chemotherapy sessions for good and say goodbye to the friendly faces they hoped never to see again. Marianne was thrilled to be walking out of the clinic. She was clearly quite sick, but such was the emotion of the moment, she asked Jarrod to take a photo in front of the sign and she leapt in the air when he took it. It took a few goes to get the right shot, but the joy was written all over her face.

Marianne 1 Cancer 0.

Acknowledgements

At this point I must give a massive shout out to Fair Play Publishing for giving Jarrod Black a chance via their imprint, Popcorn Press. An Australian publishing house just for football books. Outrageous.

This book would also not have come about if it wasn't for the kind reviews of the first book in the series, Introducing Jarrod Black. This gave me a reason to keep writing. Jules, you indirectly helped me finish that book. Barry, you were the first to read the book. Ronnie, you gave it the best review, and everyone else who left a review and kept the dream alive, I thank you.

Thanks to everyone associated with West Ryde Rovers Football Club. Some of the football experiences over the last 12 months, plying my trade in a Championship winning Over 35s team, have been reflected in the action of this book. Football is such a rich topic to write about, and there is drama and excitement even in a goalless draw. Hopefully there is another action-packed 12 months to come that inspires the next book in the series. I don't know about anyone else, but I'm excited to find out what happens next.

Finally, it would be remiss of me to pass up such an opportunity to share the sentiments of millions of Geordies around the globe:

"Get out of our club!"

Want some more really good football books from Fair Play Publishing?

Encyclopedia of Socceroos - Every National Team Player
by Andrew Howe

The World Cup Chronicles - 31 Days that Rocked Brazil
by Jorge Knijnik

Playing for Australia The First Socceroos, Asia and World Football
by Trevor Thompson

Support Your Local League - A South East Asian Football Odessy
by Antony Sutton

Jarrod Black - Hospital Pass
Part 2 of the Jarrod Black series by Texi Smith

'If I started to cry, I wouldn't stop'
by Matthew Hall

Coming Soon:

Soccer in Australia to 1949
by Peter Kunz

Encyclopedia of Matildas - Every National Team Player
by Andrew Howe and Greg Werner

From US partners, Powderhouse Press:

Whatever It Takes - the Inside Story of the FIFA Way
by Bonita Mersiades

Find them all at www.fairplaypublishing.com.au